My Song of Gratitude

I extend my continual gratitude to Abraham, the non-physical teacher, on whose words this book is based. I am incredibly appreciative to Esther and Jerry Hicks (www.abraham-hicks.com) for allowing me to use Abraham's words to create not only a beautiful novel, but a book filled with wisdom and truth.

The teachings of Ernest Holmes (1887-1960) have been a source of comfort to me, as well as a confirmation of the eternal truth that abounds. His teaching on the Science of Mind compliments the teaching of Abraham-Hicks and may be even more relevant now than in his own time.

The encouragement of my family and friends has been a precious gift. A heartfelt thank-you to my husband and best friend, Ron—his patience and his belief in me have made this journey possible. I'd like to thank my friend, Judy, for her tireless proofreading and valuable suggestions and insights. As well, I am grateful for the talent of my friend, Paulette Grant. She was able to reach inside my thoughts and so perfectly capture the image that I had for the cover of this book.

Finally, I thank the Universe for effortlessly orchestrating everything as I continually learn to trust the LAW OF ATTRACTION in my life.

Jeane Watier

Prologue

As they sat and listened to Quinn play the piano, Valerie glanced over at her daughter. Dayna's eyes were closed and her head was moving in time to the music.

It was an interesting connection that Dayna had with Quinn. She was helping him with his music, but Valerie sensed it could be more than that. She'd seen the way that Quinn looked at Dayna; he was attracted to her.

As far as Valerie was concerned, Dayna wasn't ready to be in another relationship; it was too soon. And Quinn was a bit of a mystery; Valerie didn't know what his situation was. Nevertheless, there was something happening that she couldn't deny—something in the music that connected the two of them at a deeper level, a level that maybe neither understood.

A recent series of traumatic events had turned Dayna's life upside down, but as difficult as they had been, they'd caused her to look at life differently and Valerie was encouraged by the changes that she could see in her daughter. No longer the hard, cynical person that she had been, Dayna was beginning to ask questions and was open to new ideas. She was learning how to feel again, to trust her emotions, but it would take some time.

As the enjoyable music continued, Valerie began to relax. Taking a deep breath, she reminded herself that everything was unfolding in its own perfect time. Circumstances had shown her that she could trust the powerful Law of Attraction to take care of the details in her own life. It was at work in her daughter's life, as well—Dayna just didn't know it yet.

* * *

Part I

*"Life is just this ongoing, never-ending
vacation adventure.
You can't get it wrong
and you never get it done."*

ABRAHAM-HICKS

Chapter 1

An ocean of stars shimmered in the ebony sky. The full moon was low on the horizon, rising slowly above the houses on the quiet cul-de-sac. Dayna nodded a greeting to her neighbor, who was just arriving home. As she looked around, everything seemed remarkably normal. In that solitary moment, she could almost imagine that she was just out walking Lacey on a peaceful, winter evening. The girls were at home with their dad. Life was as it should be.

Unfortunately, the moment was short-lived. The memories came crashing in and Dayna was quickly brought back to the reality of her situation. Mark had cheated on her and left her for another woman. Their marriage was over. Nothing would ever be the same again.

Her mom had arrived from out of town that afternoon to help with the girls. Dayna appreciated the gesture, but she wasn't close to her mom. Having her there was already proving to be uncomfortable—so much so, that Dayna was looking for ways to avoid her. Taking the dog for a walk allowed her to have some space and think through the problems that were overwhelming her.

"What am I going to do; how can I raise the girls on my own?" she questioned, silently. *"How could I have been so blind? I didn't even see the evidence that was right in front of me. How many times has he cheated on me? How many women have there been—just the one like he claimed?"*

She sighed, *"Does it even matter, now that he's gone?"*

A quote from one of her favorite Jane Austen novels came to mind.

"She felt the loss of Willoughby's character yet more heavily than she had felt the loss of his heart..." [1]

Dayna could relate to the sentiment all too well. She realized, now, that she'd lost Mark's heart a long time ago. If she were honest with herself, she had to admit that their marriage had become a sham; they had only stayed together as long as they did because of the girls.

Nevertheless, it was comfortable having him there. He was a good father to the girls. They had a routine that worked and they never really fought. Each of them had been busy with their own careers, their own interests; they'd simply drifted apart. But never once did she think that he'd cheat on her.

Now she realized that the evidence had been there all along; she'd just chosen not to look.

"How many people have known, but not said anything?" The barrage of questions continued. *"This is so humiliating! How can I face our co-workers and our mutual friends? How can I continue working on the same campus, seeing him, knowing he's with someone else?"*

An assistant English professor at the University, Dayna had met Mark on campus. He was head of the Geology department, single and good-looking. Mark had been married once before, but didn't have any kids. He'd made it clear as soon as they got together that he wanted children.

Dayna had been more hesitant. At twenty-eight, her career was her sole focus, but she knew that she wanted children one day, so they tried right away. She got pregnant within the first year of their marriage and Mark was thrilled.

The girls were the best thing that had ever happened to Dayna; she had no regrets. She just hadn't planned on being a single mother.

She wasn't used to things taking her by surprise. Her life was always well planned out and organized. Lesson plans were ready weeks in advance and she rarely ever missed work, but Mark's unexpected announcement had left her devastated. She needed time to think, so she'd taken a week off.

Her mom was there to help now and her sister, Rachael, lived close by. As she thought about her family, Dayna conceded that having them there did ease her situation a little.

"But what about next week, or next month, or next year?" she argued. *"I have to get myself together. I need to make a plan."*

Dayna was a planner; it's what she did best. She didn't know what it would look like yet, but she took a measure of comfort in knowing that she could find a solution... somehow.

"Let's go home, Lacey," she said to the honey-colored cocker spaniel at her side. Lacey looked up at her with dark, expressive eyes. The name suited the dog; her silky hair curled into lacey ringlets. She was such a happy, loving dog. Dayna had had her for nearly six years and she'd become a loyal friend.

"How was your walk?" Valerie called from the kitchen as Dayna returned. "Would you like some tea? I'm just making some."

"Thanks," Dayna replied, politely, as she hung her coat by the side door. "That would be nice; it's chilly out there."

They sipped their drinks quietly for a few moments before Valerie inquired, "How are you doing with all this, Dayna?"

"I'm fine, Mom," Dayna responded, reluctantly. She wasn't accustomed to sharing her feelings with anyone, especially her mother. "People get divorced all the time; it's just a fact of life. I'll be all right. It's the girls who'll have it the hardest."

She glanced at the woman sitting across from her. Her mother was a stranger in many ways. Dayna's parents had split up when Dayna was nineteen and her mom and sister had moved away. She'd felt abandoned. She could have moved with them, but she was already focused on her career and didn't want to change to another university.

Her dad had tried to stay in contact, but she was angry with him for breaking up their family and had refused to talk to him. Eventually, he stopped calling.

"I know what you're going through," Valerie said. "I've been there. It helps to talk about it."

"What is there to say? It's over." Dayna was starting to feel very uncomfortable with the way the conversation was heading.

"Just don't keep your feelings bottled up inside. It isn't healthy."

"Mom, you don't need to worry about me." Dayna rinsed her cup and put it in the dishwasher. "Are you finished with your cup? I want to turn this on before I go to bed."

Dayna felt guilty for being abrupt with her mother. She knew that she just wanted to help, but Dayna wasn't ready or willing to deal with the painful emotions that came up around the issue and she resented her mom for bringing it up.

They had never really talked about her parents' divorce. She knew from Rachael that their mom had gone through a rough time, but Dayna had been removed from it. Rachael, on the other hand, had been there through it all and had suffered a great deal because of it.

Even though they lived in the same city and saw each other quite often, Dayna had to admit that she and her sister weren't very close, either. They were only three years apart in age, yet they really didn't have much in common, other than the fact that Rachael adored Dayna's girls and loved to spend time with them.

Rachael wasn't married yet, but Dayna got the impression that that may be about to change. She and Brian had been dating for several months now and it sounded like things were getting serious.

Despite their differences, Dayna wished nothing but the best for her little sister. She truly hoped that marriage would work out better for Rachael than it had for her.

* * *

Rachael set down the phone. Her hands were trembling. Her emotions were running rampant. She wasn't even sure what she was feeling, exactly. The news she'd just received was causing all kinds of memories to make their way to the surface.

The call was from her mom. She was in town, staying with Dayna. That, in itself, was a surprise; her mom never came to visit, unannounced. It was what she'd said, however, that shocked Rachael. Dayna's husband had left Dayna for another woman.

Her mom had said something else, too, 'It's happening all over again, just like it did with me.'

"What did she mean by that?" Rachael wondered. *"Dad left, but he didn't cheat on Mom. Why would she compare the two situations?"*

Rachael began to put on her coat, intending to head over to her sister's place, when she stopped and took a deep breath. She realized that she needed to collect her thoughts before she went there. She wanted to get some clarity on how she was feeling. She also wanted to work her way up the emotional scale.[2]

The emotional scale was an important part of a teaching that had changed her life. The Law of Attraction—the concept that what you focus on expands to become your experience—had helped her to move from a place of depression, three years earlier, to a place of consistent joy. Now, amazing things were happening in her life. Dreams and desires were manifesting in so many areas.

Rachael knew exactly what she needed to do in that moment; she needed to identify what she was feeling about Dayna's situation and then find a way to think about it that felt a little better. There was always one dominant thought, or more specifically, one dominant emotion bubbling beneath the surface. If she got still, she could identify it.

With that in mind, she sat back down on the sofa to spend some time meditating. She closed her eyes and tried to quiet her thoughts, but her mother's words continued to echo loudly in her mind, 'It's happening all over again.'

Suddenly, Rachael wondered if there was more to the story than what she had always believed. She began to suspect that her father must have cheated on her mom all those years ago.

"That makes so much sense! That would explain why he left so abruptly and why Mom hated him so intensely. That's what she meant when she said it's happening all over again."

Rachael felt herself being swept up into a whirlwind of emotions again and she wanted to stay focused, so she asked herself, *"How does this revelation make me feel?"*

The new information caused her to remember some of the pain and confusion she'd experienced in the past, but more than anything, she felt the pain that her mother and now her sister, must be feeling.

"Okay," She breathed in deeply and let it out slowly, feeling its comforting cleansing. *"I need to put this in perspective. My father cheated on my*

mother and I wasn't aware of it. Now my sister's marriage is over.

That's what is," she reminded herself. *"I can't change what is. I need to find a way to think about these things that feels a little better."*

She stopped for a moment and tried to recall some of the truths that she'd come to understand on her journey to well-being.

"There is only well-being flowing to me
—I can choose to let it in or not.
Nothing is more important than feeling good.
I'm the creator of my own reality
—no one else creates for me.
My emotions are guiding me
in the way that I want to go.
Good feelings mean that I'm on
the right path."[3]

As much as she wanted to move to a better feeling place, her thoughts kept going back to her mom and her sister and the pain that she knew they must be experiencing.

All of a sudden, the situation became clear. Rachael knew what her angst was about. She was taking on their pain—identifying with them and feeling their emotion. Her rush to want to go there was in an effort to fix things.

She'd spent so many years trying to fix people, especially her mom. She'd shared her mom's pain and always felt that she had to be there for her—to the point where she was an emotional wreck, herself. Consequently, Rachael had spent years battling depression. She'd been on medication and in therapy, but all that was over now.

Having recognized what was at the root of her negative emotion, Rachael felt a renewed power. Taking care of herself was her first priority. The best way to help her sister and her mom was to focus on them in a way that felt good. That was her work.

She decided not to go over to her sister's place. She would in time, but she needed to take care of herself first.

The phone rang, revealing Brian's number on the call display. She smiled as she thought about the man she loved.

"It's so good to hear your voice," she said, breathing a sigh of relief.

"You sound like you haven't heard from me in weeks. Is everything okay?"

Rachael told him about the news from her mom and the emotional roller coaster that she'd just been on. "I'm okay now. It's just that my first response was to rush over there and try to fix things. I thought I was past that."

"Are you sure you're all right? Phil's working tonight and it's not busy. Why don't I come over?"

Brian owned a bar downtown called Trophies. It was where Rachael had first met him. The business was doing really well and Brian loved being his own boss, setting his own hours.

"You're not just coming over to fix me, are you?" she laughed. "I really am okay." Then she added, "But I'd love to see you. Are you sure you can get away?"

"Yeah, I'm sure. I'll be right over."

Rachael was still in awe at the thought of the wonderful relationship that had developed; she was so in love. Brian was everything that she'd always wanted in a man. They'd only been dating for a few months—everything was happening fast, but it felt right. They'd just spent an amazing ten days on a Caribbean cruise. Now it was getting harder and harder to be apart, even for a day or two.

When Brian arrived, Rachael let herself be swept up in his strong arms. She loved the feel of being close to him. They held each other silently for a few moments.

"Sounds like you've had an emotional evening," he said softly into her hair.

"It came as such a shock," she explained. "Not even just the news about Dayna and Mark, but realizing that my father had an affair. I can't believe I never knew about it."

"Are you sure it's true? Did your mom actually say it happened?" Brian poured them each a glass of Rachael's favorite liqueur.

She smiled. Her liquor cabinet was always well stocked now that she was dating a bartender.

They moved to the sofa with their drinks. Brian stretched out his long legs and Rachael curled up beside him.

"Not in so many words," she replied, "but it all adds up. So many other things make sense now, too. I could never understand the reason for my mom's anger toward him. I think that Greg and Dayna knew about it, as well. Dayna didn't want anything to do with him after the divorce and maybe Greg felt he had to choose sides. I don't know. It's all in the past now; I really don't think I want to try to figure it out. What's done is done."

"Do you think if you'd have known about it, that you would have reunited with your dad?" Brian stroked her hair as he asked.

Rachael had to think for a moment. She hadn't seen her dad at all for several years and only contacted him after she'd moved back to the city to live. They'd become quite close before he was killed in a car accident.

"Wow." Rachael took a sip of the rich, creamy drink. "That's a tough one to answer. Who knows what direction my life might have taken? That one piece of information throws a whole different flavor in the pot. I'd like to think that I could have gotten past that, too."

"I'm sure you could have. Maybe it would have caused you to move into anger even sooner, instead of staying in depression for so long."

"Maybe."

Brian knew what Rachael had gone through in the past. He understood about the Law of Attraction now, as well, and was beginning to share some of what he was learning with people at the bar, staff and customers alike. It was exciting to see how passionate he'd become about it, not to mention the influence he was having on others.

"My work, now, is to feel good—to focus on my well-being. I can't let myself get drawn into their pain." Rachael shook her head. "But I realized, tonight, that I'm not as immune to it as I thought I would be.

"When I was helping Jenna, it was so much easier to stay neutral and maintain my own well-being." Rachael thought about her friend. She'd been able to help Jenna overcome her depression by teaching her about the Law of Attraction and showing her how to move up the emotional scale. It was exciting to see how she'd blossomed. Jenna was growing and expanding in exciting, new ways. She'd even changed careers.

"Family is such a different dynamic, though. There's so much more involved, so much history."

"But isn't the process the same?" Brian asked.

"Yeah, you're right. I've said it enough times; I just need to stay focused on what I want and keep reaching for a better feeling thought."

She smiled as she thought about what a wonderfully clear and simple process it was. She'd moved up the emotional scale, herself, more times than she could remember. She was so used to feeling good. She knew what to do and now she didn't want to waste any more time thinking about what she didn't want.

"Dayna is creating her own reality," Rachael began. "She has attracted some circumstances that seem difficult and painful; my mom did the same, years ago. But I know that everything happens for a reason. I love my family and I believe in their well-being. And who knows, maybe this will help Dayna to open up more and let people in. Maybe this will help her to learn to listen to her emotions, instead of shutting them off.

"There's good in everything and our higher self is always in control. Dayna's higher self is guiding her, too." Rachael could feel her vibration lift; she never tired of the process. "It will be exciting to see what comes of this. Well-being is just waiting, ready to swoop in and show itself to her. This may be what it takes for her to let it in." She turned to Brian with a look of satisfaction.

"You know, I never get tired of watching you do that." Brian caressed her cheek and kissed her tenderly. "There's something magical about it. I can actually feel when your vibration changes."

Rachael was tingling with excitement. She loved moving up the emotional scale, but to be able to share the experience with Brian just added to the joy of it. The connection that they had with each other was amazing; she'd never felt so close to anyone before. She loved that Brian was open to learning new things. He was in tune with his emotions and learning to connect with his Inner Being.

"It's because we're connected. We're one." Rachael ran her hand across Brian's chest as she relaxed in his arms.

"All beings are," she added. "But it's when we really connect with our own higher selves that we feel that deeper connection with each other."

"I never knew a relationship could be this incredible." Brian looked into her eyes. "Even the words, 'I love you', don't do justice to what I'm feeling right now."

He lovingly ran his fingers through her hair and then smiled that smile that still took Rachael's breath away. "But I don't know what else to say, I'm so in love with you."

* * *

Chapter 2

Dayna awoke suddenly. Her first thought was that she'd overslept and was late for work. Then, instinctively, she reached her hand across the other side of the bed to see if Mark was up yet.

She reproached herself for the lapse in memory and steeled herself against the avalanche of emotions that threatened to overtake her.

"I have to get through this. I have to keep my head and not let these emotions rule me." Her resolve gave her a slight sense of power, but she couldn't deny that, despite her determination, the pain seemed unbearable at times.

She got up and set her mind to the day ahead as she dressed and tidied her room. Then she went across the hall to the baby's room. Abigail was awake in her crib and reached out to her as she entered the room. If nothing else, Dayna knew that she had to be strong for the girls. It was so unfair to them. They were the innocent ones and yet they were the ones who would suffer the most.

She sat down in the rocking chair and cradled the baby in her arms. Abby was such a contented baby. They had thought long and hard about names, but settled on Abigail because it means, 'father's joy'. It was perfect, because every moment with her had been a joy.

She was turning a year old, soon. She'd been walking for almost two months and was beginning to say quite a few words. Mark had captured each new achievement for both the girls on video.

"How could he do this to us?" Dayna felt a new wave of anger rise up with the thought. *"How could he leave? How could he just walk away from the life we had planned?"*

As quickly as it arose, Dayna put the unsolicited emotion in its place, certain that anger would no better serve her than grief. Then she turned her attention back to Abigail.

"Let's get you your bottle, Abby."

As she walked out of Abigail's room, Dayna saw that her mom was reading with Madison. Madison loved books. She had dozens of favorites, 'reading' most of them from memory. She loved pre-school and was learning new things every day. She'd also begun a ballet class and her tutu had become her outfit of preference most days.

Dayna and Mark had similar views on raising children. They both believed in indulging kids. They'd filled their daughters' world with structure and stimulation and enthusiastically encouraged them to explore and be independent.

Madison was strong-willed and determined, but she was also a delightful child, so grown up for her age. She was only three and a half, but she had the vocabulary of a five year old and sometimes even older. She absolutely adored her father, often preferring him to Dayna.

The break-up would be the hardest on her. She wasn't old enough to understand what was happening. She'd already been bombarding Dayna with 'what', 'when' and especially 'why' questions. Dayna was running out of answers.

It had been barely a week since Mark left. He came by every day after work to spend time with the girls. Dayna left them alone and pretended to be busy with her lesson plans. It was nice to have that break, but having him there in the house, hearing him laugh, play and read with the girls was difficult. It was even harder when he didn't stay for dinner and she had to explain the reason to Madison. One answer was never sufficient; each answer just seemed to evoke a new question.

That afternoon, Mark came into the study, where Dayna was working on grading some papers.

"Dayna, can we talk?" he asked. "Now that your mom's here, can you get away? We really need to make some decisions."

Dayna found it hard to answer him. She knew that they had to talk about it. For the kids' sake, they needed to make plans and set up a routine that would be best for them, but the words wouldn't come. As an English major, she was rarely lost for words, but then she usually had better control over her emotions. Lately, especially when she sat listening to Mark with the girls in the next room, it was all she could do to keep her emotions at bay.

"I know this is tough on you," he continued when she didn't respond. "I'm sorry. But Dayna, it's not easy for me, either. We have to find a way to make this work."

The anger quickly surfaced. She wanted to scream and tell him that the whole mess was his doing, but she couldn't. She refused to give way to it.

She took a deep breath and somehow found her strength. "Let's give it a day or two. The girls are just getting used to having Mom here." She looked at her day planner, more as a way to avoid eye contact with Mark than anything.

"What about Saturday afternoon?" Dayna felt like she was scheduling a business meeting, rather then making time to talk with her soon to be ex-husband about the welfare of their children.

"Sure, Saturday's fine. What if I come by in the morning and pick up the girls. I'll bring them back in time for Abby's nap and then we can talk."

Dayna penciled in the appointment and closed her book. Mark had already gone back into the living room to say good-bye to the girls.

"Here we go again," Dayna winced. Madison was clinging to Mark and this time she was crying. Her behavior was getting more extreme as the days went by. Dayna felt her heart being ripped apart.

"Will this ever get any easier?" She knew she'd get through it somehow, but she wondered if the girls would suffer any emotional damage from the experience. She made a mental note to do some research on the effects of divorce on small children.

* * *

Brian drove Rachael to work in the morning. They'd gone back to Brian's the night before. It was more practical to stay at his place because of the dogs—two beautiful golden retrievers named Duke and Cassie. They were like family to Brian and now Rachael had fallen in love with them, too.

"See you later?"

"Mmm." Rachael nodded, enjoying the moment in Brian's arms. "Gail and I will stop by after work, as usual. Rob's meeting us there."

They were planning to go out with Gail and Rob for dinner and a show. Gail was Rachael's best friend. The four of them got along really well.

Gail and Rachael worked together, as well, and at lunch, Rachael met Gail in the cafeteria. She told her the news about her sister.

"I guess it's not that surprising," Rachael admitted. "I've always wondered what kind of a relationship they had. They were both so into their careers and when they had kids, that became their whole focus. I don't know if they ever developed a real relationship with each other."

"And your mom's here?"

"She flew out as soon as she heard the news. It sounds like she's going to stay a while to help look after the girls."

"Aren't they used to being in daycare?"

"They are, but Dayna and Mark juggled their schedules so that the girls didn't have to spend full days in daycare. I think Mom really wants to be there for Dayna, though. Mom went through the same thing. I just found out that my dad cheated on her; that's why he left us."

"Seriously?" Gail asked. "And you didn't know anything about it until now?"

"I just put all the pieces together. It seems so obvious, now. Back then, nobody told me and I was too young and naïve to figure it out."

"It's surprising that your mom never said anything before now."

"I guess, considering what I was going through, she probably figured I couldn't handle it."

"Maybe it would have been better for you if you'd have known. Things might have made more sense."

"That's what Brian said, too, but it's all good. Going through those years of depression and confusion caused me to ask powerful questions. Those questions brought me the amazing answers that I know now—about myself and about life and particularly about the Law of Attraction."

"Yeah, it's amazing how things work out, especially when you can stand back and look at the big picture," Gail agreed.

They were both quiet for a moment, contemplating what Rachael had just shared. Then Gail asked, "Do you think that Dayna will ever be open to hearing this stuff?"

"I don't know," Rachael shrugged. "I've tried to bring it up before but she didn't want to have anything to do with it."

"Maybe this will cause her to start asking some powerful questions of her own."

"I hope so."

* * *

Valerie watched her daughter. She saw the heartache, so cleverly hidden. Dayna put on a brave front, pretending she was fine, but Valerie knew what she was going through.

The news of Dayna's failed marriage served to bring up so many painful memories. Valerie had finally come to terms with her own difficult past, but it had taken years.

She could still remember what it felt like to be cheated on. It had left her feeling no better than a second-hand shoe, or a once-loved toy—something to be tossed aside. She'd been traded in for something newer, better, prettier. Her self-esteem had been damaged, almost beyond repair.

That was thirteen years ago. She'd made a lot of progress since then—years of counseling, asking questions, seeking answers, reading countless self-help books—she'd really come a long way. Now it felt like history was repeating itself with Dayna.

Valerie had been planning to visit her children. She wanted to make amends for the past and attempt to re-unite her family. She'd finally made peace with herself. Now she wanted, more than anything, to be close to her children and share with them the things she was learning. Her greatest desire was for them to be a real family again.

She had more to tell them, too. She was ready, now, to share her past. She'd lived with a secret for far too long and was determined to finally tell her children what they deserved to know.

That was before she'd received an e-mail from Dayna. It had been simple and to the point—just letting her mom know that Mark had left.

Valerie had booked the first flight that she could get. All she could think about was helping her daughter get through such a difficult time. Now that she was there, however, things were more than a little strained between them. Dayna had so much to deal with. She was hurting and yet she wasn't open to talk about what had happened.

Now, Valerie was beginning to wonder if the time was right to share what she had been hiding all those years.

* * *

Chapter 3

Rachael went with Gail to Trophies after work. They pulled up in the back, beside Brian's car, and walked up to the back door. Rachael punched in the code on the alarm and opened the door. They entered a long hallway that accessed the kitchen on one side, washrooms and a small office on the other. Brian was busy in the office, talking with a middle-aged man, but he smiled when he saw Rachael and Gail.

"I'll be a few minutes. It's busy out there, but I asked Tracy to reserve a table."

Rachael assumed that the man must be the new manager that Brian was training. Things were going really well for him with the business and now having a full-time manager would mean that he was free to come and go as he liked. She was proud of Brian for all that he had accomplished.

As they entered the bar, Tracy came up to them right away, giving Rachael a hug. Rachael had gotten to know Brian's younger sister and they'd become good friends.

Tracy was a year younger than Rachael, had Brian's good looks and a bubbly, outgoing personality. She always wore a smile and the customers loved her. She had a rapport with all the regulars, especially the men. She was single, but not for lack of offers. Brian had said that she'd had at least three serious marriage proposals. He was a typical big brother, always watching out for her; he'd even introduced her to some of his friends, but for now, she seemed to love single life.

Rachael noticed that their favorite corner table was reserved for them. They walked over to it and, as they sat down, Tracy took their drink orders.

"You know, I loved it here before, but this V.I.P. treatment is great," Gail declared.

"That's one of the perks of dating the owner."

"Just one of the many perks," Gail winked.

Rachael had to agree. Dating Brian didn't seem to have a downside. She was happier than she'd ever been in her life. That feeling was magnified even more, because she'd learned to live in the moment. She'd spent many years trying to escape how she was feeling. Even in the good times, she often missed what could have been great, because her focus had been elsewhere. Now, she just wanted to savor every second.

"So when are you seeing your mom?" Gail interrupted her thoughts, causing Rachael to turn her attention to her friend.

"I might go over to Dayna's tomorrow morning," Rachael answered. "I'll see how it feels."

Tracy brought their drinks and Rachael took a sip of her Mai Tai. Brian had introduced her to all kinds of new drinks, but that continued to be one of her favorites.

"I love the way you don't commit to things," Gail commented. "There's such freedom in that."

Gail's words, though meant as a compliment, affected Rachael in a strange way. They reminded her of words she'd heard often as she was growing up. People were always admonishing her to finish what she started. When she was eight, she'd taken baton lessons and dropped out half way through the year. At ten, she'd started piano lessons and quickly realized that she didn't care for them.

Her grandma had paid for the piano lessons and, for years afterward, continued to remind Rachael of the fact. Rachael could still hear the words echo in her mind, 'If only you'd kept up with your piano lessons, then you could play like your sister.' Dayna loved the piano and played beautifully.

"This thing with your sister has really affected you, hasn't it?" Gail asked. "You seem distracted. You're not yourself."

"I'm sorry," Rachael apologized. "I guess it has. It's brought up so much stuff from the past. And what you said just now, about not committing to things—that brought up some more negative emotion." Rachael realized that her thoughts were pulling her in a direction that she didn't want to go.

"Do you want to talk about it?"

"Thanks, but no. The Law of Attraction is just doing its job. I've been thinking about my sister and letting my mind go back to things that happened when my dad left, so I'm attracting more thoughts of the same. But it's not what I want to focus on.

"I don't feel really bad," Rachael clarified. "But those thoughts don't feel good, either. There's no benefit in them. I want to work at moving to a better feeling place."

"Well, I know you'll be fine," Gail assured her. "And if your sister's anything like you, she'll get through this, too, and be all the better for having experienced it."

"You're right." Rachael was thankful for her friend's encouragement. Gail knew her extremely well and so often she had just the right words to say. "I keep reminding myself of that."

"And you know another thing," Gail added. "This may seem like history repeating itself, but it's not the same. And you're not the same helpless, little girl that went through it back then, either."

Rachael felt her vibration climb. She reminded herself of how far she had come and praised herself for how much she'd learned.

All of a sudden, she began to feel optimistic about what lay ahead, not just for her sister and her mom, but for what she would gain from it, as well. She silently thanked her Inner Being for always guiding her perfectly.

Leaning forward, she grinned at her dear friend. "What would I do without you?"

"Well, let's see," Gail joked. "If it hadn't been for me, you wouldn't have your job. And if we weren't working together, we wouldn't have started coming here for drinks after work on Fridays. Then, of course, you wouldn't have met Brian..."

"Okay, okay, I'm eternally indebted to you," Rachael laughed. "But I was referring to your words of encouragement."

"Oh, that," Gail shook her head. "Knowing you, you'd probably attract someone just as wonderful." She smiled as she added, "But probably not as witty or as charming."

"Or as conceited," Rachael laughed.

Brian walked up just then and, as he sat down, noted, "You ladies look like you're having a good time." He winked at Rachael and asked, "How many drinks have you had?"

"You should know by now, Brian, that we don't need alcohol to feel good," Gail chided, jokingly. "We've discovered the secret to happiness."

"Well don't say that too loud in here, or you'll put me out of business," Brian responded in a low voice, pretending to be serious.

They continued laughing and joking and after a few minutes, Gail's partner, Rob, joined them.

"Looks like I've got some catching up to do," he frowned. "How long have you been here?"

They laughed, again, at the presumption that they must be drinking a lot to be having so much fun. They let Rob in on the joke; then Brian added, "But we do serve alcohol here, too. What can I get you?"

Brian got up to get Rob his drink. Rachael watched him walk to the bar, then looked over at her friends and smiled. Having been apart while Rob was away on a business trip, they were now catching up with a lengthy kiss.

Rachael realized that she was already feeling much better. She loved being out with her friends, laughing and having fun. She loved how easy it was to move up the emotional scale. All it took was a desire to feel good and a conviction that nothing was more important. Having such wonderful friends didn't hurt, either.

* * *

Dayna got the girls ready; Mark was picking them up in half an hour. She wasn't looking forward to her meeting with him that afternoon—particularly because she didn't know how they'd be able to agree on a schedule for the kids. She couldn't bear the thought of the girls spending whole weekends away from her, but she knew that they needed to be with their father, too.

They needed to talk about the girls, but she also wanted to talk about what Mark had done. She wanted answers. Nothing would make up for the fact that he'd cheated on her. Nothing he could say would make her feel better, but she still wanted to know the truth.

The situation had left her feeling exposed, like a flower that had been pulled up and left to wilt in the sun. She felt raw, as if someone had torn part of her away and she hated feeling incomplete.

Dayna had always been independent—growing up fast, living on her own when her mom moved away. She'd spent eight years on her own before she met Mark and was used to doing things for herself without depending on others. Since they'd been together, however, she'd come to depend on Mark and, now, he was gone.

"I want to wear my tutu," Madison said, demanding Dayna's attention.

"I'm not sure that's the best thing to wear today, sweetie. Daddy's taking you out somewhere really special."

"Da da," Abigail echoed.

"That's right, baby girl." Dayna kissed Abigail as she finished dressing her. Then she picked her up and went next door to Madison's room. She pulled two of Madison's favorite dresses out of the closet and held them up. "Do you want to wear your pink dress or your green dress?"

"Pink, pink, pink," Madison jumped up and down. "I want to wear my pink dress!" Dayna was thankful she'd forgotten about the tutu. The child could be headstrong when she wanted something.

After a few minutes, Dayna heard the front door open. Assuming it was Mark, she felt a wave of anxiety over the thought of their meeting. She breathed a sigh of relief at hearing Rachael's voice. Dayna barely got Madison's dress zipped up, before the little girl went running to see her favorite aunt.

* * *

Rachael walked into Dayna's house, feeling ready to spend time with her mom and sister. Her mom immediately went over and hugged her daughter, holding her for a long moment. There were tears in her mother's eyes when she finally released Rachael from her embrace.

"It's so good to see you, honey."

Rachael noticed a difference in her mother. Something had changed, but she wasn't sure what.

"It's good to see you, too, Mom," Rachael replied. Looking around, she asked softly, "How is Dayna handling this?"

"Stoic, as usual," Valerie said in a lowered voice. "Putting on a strong front, but hurting inside, no doubt. She's just getting the girls ready. Mark's picking them up right away."

Madison came running down the stairs and squealed as she saw Rachael. Rachael scooped her niece up in her arms and kissed her.

"How's my favorite ballerina?"

Madison immediately jumped down and began to put on a performance for her aunt, walking on her tiptoes and twirling around the room.

Dayna came down carrying Abigail. The baby reached out for Rachael as soon as she saw her. Rachael took her from Dayna and did a twirl around the room alongside Madison. Abby laughed as she spun around in Rachael's arms.

Mark arrived, causing another flurry of excitement as the girls saw their father. After goodbyes to the girls, Rachael followed Dayna and their mother into the kitchen.

Dayna took a deep breath and exhaled, audibly. "I guess Mom told you the news."

"Yeah," Rachael replied. "More or less."

"I'm sorry I didn't tell you, myself."

"It's okay," Rachael said, compassionately. "It must be really difficult." She noticed a look of pain in Dayna's eyes as she turned away.

"Do you want some coffee?" Dayna offered.

"Sure." Rachael could feel Dayna's discomfort and wondered if she'd talk about what happened.

Dayna poured a cup of coffee for Rachael and turned to get some cream out of the refrigerator.

"How did you find out?" Rachael inquired.

"He told me," Dayna replied, quietly. "He said he couldn't handle sneaking around anymore."

"How long had it been going on?"

"A few months, I think."

Rachael wondered how Dayna could be so calm. She wondered what was going on inside her head. Then she looked at her mom and saw that she was crying. Rachael went and put her arm around her.

"I'm sorry," Valerie said. "It just brings up so many memories."

"It's okay," Rachael soothed, handing her mom a tissue. After a moment, Rachael asked softly, "Mom, did Dad cheat on you?"

"Yes, honey, he did," she sniffed. "I'm so sorry I never told you."

Rachael looked at Dayna. "Did you know?"

Dayna nodded. There was such a look of pain in her sister's face that Rachael wanted to reach out to her. Dayna looked down and poured some cream in her coffee. After stirring her drink, she looked up at Rachael again. "I overheard him talking on the phone. You and Mom were out shopping and I guess he assumed that I was with you. But I was home and I heard him telling someone that he loved them. He said he'd find a way that they could be together."

"She told me about it that night," Valerie continued the story. "Our marriage hadn't been good for a lot of years, but it was still a real shock."

They were all quiet for a few minutes. Rachael closed her eyes and felt the comforting presence of her Inner Being as she silently asked for strength and wisdom. Going back and digging up the past wasn't going to benefit any of them. She wanted to find a way to move forward and hoped that she could help them do the same.

"That's all in the past," Valerie said, echoing Rachael's thoughts. "It happened a long time ago and your father's gone, now. This is about Dayna. We need to help her through this."

Dayna glanced at her mother and then at Rachael. "Thank-you," she replied stiffly, looking very uncomfortable.

"Well, if you'll excuse me, I need to go and look over my day-planner." Dayna got up and started to walk away. "I want to have some ideas about how we can arrange the girls' schedule before I meet with Mark."

Rachael watched her sister walk out of the room and then turned to her mom, "You're right. She really is putting on a strong front, but I could see the pain in her eyes. She's hurting."

"I know," Valerie stared into her teacup.

Looking at her mom, Rachael noticed, again, that something was different. She was still an attractive woman at fifty-two, but she'd been sad for a long time and, in the past, it had always shown in her face. Now, even though she was worried about Dayna, something in her mother's countenance had changed. She looked more contented, somehow.

"How long can you stay?" Rachael asked.

"I'll stay as long as she needs me, or wants me to," Valerie answered. "Greg and Amy's baby is due soon, too."

"I know. I just saw them on the weekend; Amy's getting really big." Rachael loved to spend time with her older brother and was thrilled at the idea of a new little niece or nephew.

"How are you doing?" Valerie brightened. "You're looking good," she smiled. "Being in love suits you."

Rachael was pleasantly surprised by her mom's comment. "Is it that obvious?"

"Well, you do look happier than I've ever seen you, but you also talk about him non-stop in your emails. I'm looking forward to meeting Brian."

"He's picking me up." Rachael looked at her watch. "He should be here soon."

Brian had taken the dogs for a run while Rachael visited with her mom and sister. She wanted time alone with them, but she also wanted an excuse to leave, knowing that it might be difficult to be with them, seeing their pain.

At the sound of the doorbell, Rachael went to the front entry. Dayna was already greeting Brian when she walked up. As Valerie joined them, Rachael introduced her mom to Brian.

"It's so nice to finally meet you, Brian," Valerie smiled as she shook his hand. The four of them stood and chatted for a few minutes. Then, after agreeing to get together again soon, Rachael and Brian said their good-byes.

"How did it go?" Brian put his arm around her as they walked to his vehicle.

"It was tough," Rachael answered. "There's so much I want to say to Dayna, but I already know how she feels about the things I believe in. I have to keep telling myself that she's not broken, but when I see the pain in her eyes..." Rachael felt the tears begin to well up.

Brian opened the door for her and, once they were in the vehicle, drew her into his embrace. Everything always seemed better when she was in Brian's arms. It helped to remind her that well-being was always flowing to her and that she was able to choose the details of how it flowed.

The dogs were waiting in the vehicle. With the back seats down to make more room for them, Cassie was able to poke her nose between the front seats and put her paw on Rachael's shoulder. It seemed as if she were trying to offer comfort, as well.

Rachael turned and stroked the dog's head. She'd formed a special bond with Cassie, right from the beginning. Both dogs were playful and friendly and she loved them dearly, but sometimes Cassie looked at her as if she knew what Rachael was thinking or feeling.

Rachael's heart was filled with appreciation for the love that surrounded her in that moment. She knew that she'd created it. She knew that it was just another extension of her own, loving Source.

* * *

Chapter 4

Dayna sat and stared at her day-planner. She'd come up with some ideas about how they could each spend time with the kids and she hoped that Mark would be open to it. The last thing that she wanted was a custody battle. They were mature adults and she knew that they could work things out without having to drag it through court.

She walked back into the kitchen, where Valerie was busy making lunch. Dayna was glad that her mom felt at home in her house and didn't need looking after. She didn't feel up to being a hostess.

"Are you hungry? I made some sandwiches."

"Thanks." Dayna had no appetite, whatsoever, but she put a sandwich on a plate and poured herself some milk. She didn't want her mom worrying about her health, as well.

"Brian seems nice," Valerie commented. "And Rachael sure looks happy."

"Yes, he is nice. I think things are starting to get serious between them."

"I hope it works out for her."

"The women in this family don't exactly have a great track record when it comes to relationships." Dayna didn't even try to hide the sarcasm in her voice.

"I didn't set a very good example for you girls."

Dayna looked at her in surprise. "Mom, you don't blame yourself for Dad cheating, do you?" She was offended by what her mom was implying.

"It takes two to make a relationship work," Valerie sighed.

"What are you saying?" Dayna didn't know if her mom was talking about her own failed marriage, or Dayna's, but she felt herself getting angry. Whether it was her dad or Mark—neither one deserved to be let off the hook for what they had done.

"I've had thirteen years to sort this out. It wasn't until your father passed away, last year, that I really came to understand."

"Understand what?" Dayna was uncomfortable talking about the subject, but she needed to know what her mom was trying to say.

Valerie took a deep breath. "I thought I'd given everything I had to your father. I was a faithful wife. I supported him. I made a home for all of us…"

Her mother looked like she was close to tears and Dayna felt herself begin to panic. She'd learned to let her head guide her. Emotions were to be controlled. But in that moment, for all she had trained herself, Dayna's emotions were dangerously close to controlling her.

As Dayna fought to overcome the turmoil that was going on inside of her, Valerie continued, "What I didn't give him was my heart."

"But you just said you were faithful; you supported him." Dayna was struggling to control her anger. "You were a good wife. I don't understand why you're blaming yourself."

"I'm sorry," Valerie said. "I didn't mean to upset you, but there's something I should have told you, long ago." She waited until Dayna looked over at her before she stated, "I never really loved your father."

"What?"

"I mean… at first, I thought I could learn to love him," she clarified. "He was so in love with me. He was a good man and I was fond of him. He was a good father, too."

"But he cheated on you! He destroyed our family." Dayna turned away, still grasping at some measure of control. "How can you forgive him for that?"

"Maybe, if I had truly loved him, he wouldn't have gone looking for it elsewhere," Valerie replied.

Dayna sat quietly for a moment longer. She didn't want to hear anymore, but at the same time, she wanted to know what had happened to make her father leave. She'd blamed him all those years, even hated him. Now, she sensed there was more that her mom wasn't saying.

She thought about her own marriage. Something in what her mom had said, struck a painful chord somewhere inside her, but it was all too much to deal with at the moment. Mark would be back soon and Dayna needed to get a handle on her emotions.

She stood up, sandwich untouched. "I need to get ready; Mark will be here with the girls any time."

* * *

Valerie couldn't hold back the tears that wanted to emerge. She wondered how she was ever going to share the rest of the news that she had to tell her kids. She thought it would be best to wait until Rachael was there, too, maybe even Greg, but she had no idea how they'd take it. She had to admit that she was afraid of what they'd think of her.

To ease her anxiety, she tried to recall some of the things that a friend had been teaching her.

"Everything that happens in our lives,
we attract by the thoughts we think.
We can control what comes into our lives

> *by deliberately choosing
> what we focus on."*[4]

She'd struggled with the new ideas at first, but once she'd stopped looking at the past and asking 'why' and started looking to the future and thinking about what could be, everything had changed. She made the decision that she wasn't going to waste any more time with regrets. She had life left to live and was determined to live it.

Valerie knew what she wanted. More than anything, she wanted to tell her kids the truth she'd been hiding for thirty-five years. She couldn't control how they'd respond, but she truly hoped that with the secret out in the open, they could begin to heal the broken relationships and maybe even become a close family.

She wanted to share with her kids what she was learning and be able to help them in their lives, but that decision was up to them. She'd learned that everyone was responsible for their own happiness. She had finally found hers and she truly hoped that her kids would find theirs, as well.

* * *

Rachael made herself a cup of tea and sat down on her sofa, curling up with a blanket. She was glad to be alone with her thoughts. Brian seemed to know that she needed some time to herself and had gone to help his dad with a project that he was working on.

So much had happened in the past couple of days that she wanted to take time to get in touch with how she was feeling. Something Gail mentioned had brought up a lot of emotion and Rachael wanted to get clarity on why she was feeling that way.

All Gail had said was that she liked the way Rachael didn't commit to things. She'd meant it in a positive way and yet it felt negative.

She silently asked her Inner Being, *"What is this feeling all about?"* Then she quieted her thoughts and focused on her breathing. After a few moments, an idea presented itself. She wondered if the feelings had to do with her parent's and her sister's failed marriages. That, in turn, caused her to think about her own relationship with Brian.

"Is part of me afraid that if I marry Brian one day, it could end in failure, too? Am I comparing myself with Mom and Dayna? Am I associating past failures, like not completing music or baton lessons with this, as well?"

She remembered something her counselor had told her once, when the issue of lack of commitment had come up.

*"Don't think of quitting as failure.
Think of it as graduating,
or moving on to the next experience.*

*Only you can know when
the time is right for you."*

Rachael quieted her thoughts, again. Nothing was more important to her than feeling good. She was determined to find a way to do just that.

As she examined her thoughts, she began to realize that she was borrowing regrets from the past and worries from the future—and both of them were affecting her now. She stopped and focused her attention on the current moment, looking for all that she could find to appreciate in it.

"Right now, I'm enjoying this quiet moment. It feels good to be in my home, enjoying this cup of tea. All is well. I'm happy and contented and I have everything I need."

She realized that she'd been letting her inner critic go unchecked, as well. A few years back, she'd created a character for the inner chatter that used to plague her constantly. She'd named him Larry, for no particular reason, except that she didn't happen to know of anyone by that name. In her mind, he looked something like the character from the MAD comics that her brother used to collect. He had pimples all over his face and talked with a stutter. She laughed to herself as the image came to mind.

"Okay Larry, you've had your say. Now I'm in control. I don't listen to you, anymore, and I don't give unnecessary thought to the past or the future. I live in the now!"

A feeling of power returned. She took a deep breath, closed her eyes and smiled as she exhaled. Going to her computer, she clicked on a file where she kept some of her favorite quotes. As she scrolled down through them, one caught her attention.

"Life is just this ongoing, never-ending vacation adventure, you see.
You can't get it wrong and you never get it done
—and we recommend that you have
as much fun as you can along the way."[5]

"I can't get it wrong," Rachael laughed as she began to dance around the room. "If that's true, then there really is no such thing as failure, not for myself, or my sister, or my mom. Wow!"

Suddenly, she felt light and free. She hadn't even realized how far down the emotional scale that her thoughts from the last few days had taken her. A wave of appreciation washed over her and she thanked her Inner Being—that all knowing, loving, broader part of her—for guiding her to the wonderful, new understanding.

As her family came to mind, Rachael realized that the worrisome thoughts were now replaced with love and anticipation of great things to come. She'd said the words before and knew the benefit that they held, but now the improved feelings were pulsing through her entire being in a powerful way. It felt amazing! She was eager to share it with Brian and picked up the phone to call him.

"I feel so much better," she said, after she shared the insights she'd received. "It's like a weight has been lifted off my shoulders. I can really feel that my family's not broken. Before, I was just saying the words. But now I've truly come to the feeling place of it. It's awesome!"

"That's great," Brian said. "I knew you'd get clarity on this. It was just a matter of time."

"I feel like doing something really fun tonight."

"How would you like to go downtown and play some slot machines?" Brian asked. "The new casino just opened this weekend. I know one of the owners; he invited me to stop by anytime. We'd get the royal treatment."

"That sounds perfect."

"Dad and I are almost done here. I'll see you in about half an hour."

Rachael smiled to herself. It was good to feel good, again—to feel the incredible power that coming back into alignment offered. Not only that, but she was looking forward to a fun evening with Brian.

* * *

Dayna got into her car. She had to sit for a moment, before she was able to drive. The meeting with Mark hadn't gone smoothly at all. She'd tried to handle the meeting with diplomacy and remain composed as they discussed the things that needed to be addressed, but she'd lost her cool a couple of times. She found Mark so infuriating.

When she'd asked him why he'd done it and if he'd given any thought as to how it would affect the girls, his response implied that their marriage breakdown had been her fault.

Nevertheless, they'd settled on an arrangement for the girls. Mark had reluctantly agreed that they were too young to be moved back and forth and that they should live with Dayna. She agreed to continue to let him see them after work, three days a week and take them out for a day on the weekends. Once a month, Madison would be spending the full weekend with her father.

They'd parted on a more positive note. Dayna could tell that Mark was trying to keep things civil between them, as well. He'd even apologized for the comment he made and then tried to smooth things over by saying that she was a good mother, but his words weren't much consolation.

Dayna couldn't stop her own mother's words from echoing in her head, 'Maybe if I had really loved him, he wouldn't have gone looking for it elsewhere.' She quickly banished the tears that threatened to overwhelm her.

"No!" she said, aloud. "I'm not the guilty one here; he cheated on me."

She tried to dismiss them, but her mom's words just wouldn't go away. It made Dayna realize that she wanted answers. She wanted to know what had happened between her parents to cause their marriage breakdown. She couldn't shake the idea that she might have repeated the same thing as her mother.

"Did Mark go looking for love because I didn't love him? Did I ever really love him?"

She wasn't consciously aware of her feelings for him having changed while they were together.

"What is love, anyway?" she argued, suddenly feeling defensive. *"It's just another emotion and emotions are fickle; they come and go. What I had with Mark was commitment and respect; we had common goals...*

"At least, I thought that's what we had. I thought that was enough," she sighed. *"Obviously, for him, it wasn't."*

* * *

Chapter 5

As they walked into the casino, they were greeted by Brian's friend and were given the royal treatment, just as Brian had predicted. Following a tour of the establishment, he took them up to the Prestige Lounge, which was reserved for high rollers and VIPs, and invited them to enjoy the abundance of food, drinks and entertainment.

Rachael was glad that she had dressed up for the occasion. Many of the women were in formal gowns with jewels glittering. She loved the energy of the place; the atmosphere was electric and she had fun just watching people interact.

After a drink and time spent mingling, they went down to the casino floor and played the slot machines. Rachael liked the nickel slots the best and won several times. At one point, it seemed like the nickels wouldn't stop pouring out.

"Oh, my God!" Rachael laughed, putting a container under the spout to catch all the coins that were spewing out. It filled up quickly and Brian grabbed another one for her. Suddenly, the nickels stopped, a siren went off and a big, red light began flashing on top of her machine.

"Your machine's out of money," Brian remarked.

An attendant came over, opened up the side of the machine and filled it up. As soon as he finished, the avalanche of coins started again.

"This is abundance!" Rachael couldn't stop laughing as she held her hands under the flow of money. "I like the feel of this."

When it finally stopped, she had three and a half containers full of nickels. When they cashed in, she'd made a hundred and ten dollars.

"That was so much fun!" Rachael cried. "I can see how people get hooked on this."

"Do you want to play some more?"

"Yeah, but there's so much to do here; let's try something else."

The evening flew by; it was well after midnight when they finally decided to leave. Rachael couldn't remember the last time she'd had so much fun. It had been a great evening, not to mention a prosperous one. Brian had won four hundred dollars at the roulette table, as well.

They were still laughing as they walked to the car. As Brian slipped his arm around her, Rachael leaned into him, matching the rhythm of his stride.

The sky was clear and the moon, full. The air smelled fresh. The weather had turned warm, indicating that spring was not far away.

Rachael was reminded of their first date. They'd walked along the boardwalk by the river. She hadn't wanted the evening to end. She could still remember the excitement of their first embrace, the thrill of their first kiss.

"It's so nice out. Do you feel like walking a bit longer?" Brian asked.

"Let's go down by the river," Rachael suggested.

They were only a few blocks away, so they left the car parked and headed to the boardwalk. The moon was sparkling on the water, as they stood looking out over the railing. In the quiet of the early morning hour, they could hear the sound of the water lapping against the rocks.

Rachael closed her eyes and let the energy of the river waft over her. She savored the warmth of Brian's arms around her and the feel of his hand stroking her hair. As she leaned against his chest, feeling the rhythm of his heart, Rachael's mind drifted back to the insights that she'd received earlier that day.

"You know," she said, "what I learned today reminded me, again, how important it is to live in the moment."

"It's all about focus, isn't it?"

"It really is," Rachael replied. "Right now, I could be focusing on what happened to my sister last week or what happened between my parents all those years ago—or I could be wondering how everything will turn out, but I'd be missing this incredible moment, here with you."

Brian kissed her forehead and tightened his embrace. "Mmm..." she breathed. "And I wouldn't want to be anywhere else, right now."

As they held each other, listening to the sounds of the river, Rachael added, "If you think about it, now is really all there is, anyway. The past is just an illusion; it exists only in our minds and the future hasn't happened yet; it's just a window of infinite possibilities."

"That's true. And we get to look through that window and decide what we want to create," Brian said. "That's the part I like."

"Appreciating the moment and being excited about what the future holds," Rachael nodded. "That's the perfect combination."

"I'm excited about what our future holds," Brian whispered softly into her hair.

Rachael looked up at Brian's face. In his smoky, blue eyes, she could see the depth of love that he was feeling for her. She was feeling the same for him—a love so deep that words could barely express it.

She noticed that he'd used the words 'our future'. Although she liked the sound of it, she didn't know exactly what the words implied. It was early in their relationship to be talking about marriage and she didn't know how he felt about it. She wasn't even sure how she was feeling, given the recent circumstances with her family.

However, she didn't want to focus on that. She's just spent a wonderful evening with the man that she loved and now she was enjoying the warmth of his embrace. In the moment, it was all that she desired.

* * *

When Dayna arrived home, the house was quiet. She went upstairs and checked on the baby. Abigail was still asleep. Dayna peeked in her mom's room. Valerie's eyes were closed and Madison was asleep beside her. Dayna was relieved to have a few moments to herself. She didn't feel like answering questions about how the meeting went.

She tiptoed quietly down the stairs, Lacey at her heels. She took a minute to pet the dog, trying to distract herself, but she couldn't stop the thoughts that were buzzing around in her head. What she wanted, desperately, was to be able to turn them off.

She kept thinking about her father. It was almost a year since he'd passed away. So many emotions had come up after he died. She'd worked hard at managing them and thinking logically through it and she'd finally been able to put it behind her, but now, those emotions were surfacing again, on top of all she was feeling about Mark leaving.

Her mother's words were still haunting her, as well, but she refused to let herself go there. She needed to keep busy. The problem, she determined, was that she had too much time to think. Taking the past week off, now seemed like a mistake; it had done her more harm than good.

Distraction was what she needed now. She was glad to be going back to work on Monday. Dayna decided to look over her lesson plans again.

Her dog followed her into the study and sat watching her, head tilted to the side and one paw raised, as if she knew that simply being adorable would raise Dayna's spirits. Dayna couldn't help but smile as she reached down to pet the dog's soft, silky coat, once more.

Lacey was such an affectionate dog, always happy and eager to please. She was gentle with the girls, loyal and loving—smart, too, because her presence and her irresistible personality did serve to make Dayna feel a little bit better.

After a few minutes, Dayna turned back to her desk and opened her notes. She was teaching a course on Hamlet. She loved Shakespeare, and Hamlet was her favorite play. They were studying the play from historical, cultural and social contexts. The class had written papers on their interpretation of the famous soliloquy, 'To be, or not to be.'[6]

She picked up one of her student's papers that had particularly intrigued her. The common interpretation of the speech was that it was a debate on suicide. But the student had suggested that the death he spoke of was not physical death, but rather, failure to really live life.

The girl submitted that the words, 'to be' referred to one's Being, or soul—that part that is not confined by the human body, but is eternal. She suggested that people get caught up in the 'doing', as Hamlet did, and proposed that the reason for his seeming 'madness' was because of that dilemma.

It was a stretch and it didn't necessarily fit with the context of Hamlet avenging his father's death, but she encouraged her students to think for themselves, rather than just side with views that were already out there. Therefore, she had graded the student accordingly.

Dayna set down the paper. It was the idea of being eternal—the concept that there could be more to life than just the mortal body—that captured Dayna's thoughts.

She knew that Rachael was spiritual, but Dayna had always disregarded the things that her sister talked about; some of her ideas sounded so strange.

Now, for some reason, the idea of a power greater than herself being in control of things brought a sense of comfort to Dayna.

She didn't really believe in God—at least, not in a personal sense. The only time that she ever felt a connection to something larger than her was when she played the piano.

Looking out of the study at the piano in the front room, she felt it calling her. She walked over to the piano, an old upright that had been her parents, and her grandparents before that, and ran her hand over the surface. It welcomed her like an old friend.

It had been a while since she'd played—too long, in fact. She sat down and opened the cover, letting her fingers slide gently over the smooth ivory. The keys were so familiar to her; she couldn't help but put her hands in a well-known pose and play a chord. She played softly at first, not wanting to wake anyone. As her hands began to glide over the keys, she was soon playing a song from memory. It was one that she particularly loved and, before long, she was lost in the beautiful melody.

* * *

Valerie listened to the music as she walked down the stairs. She hadn't heard her daughter play in quite a while; she'd forgotten how much she loved the sound. Dayna was very good. She'd even toured with the local symphony orchestra for a few summers before she got married.

The song Dayna was playing had a beautiful, almost haunting melody. She played with a great deal of emotion. It seemed such a contradiction to the way she presented herself to people.

Valerie stood and watched. She didn't want to interrupt. It seemed to be healing for Dayna. She poured herself into it with such passion and intensity. When the song ended, she saw Dayna put her hand up to her eye as if she'd been crying.

Not wanting Dayna to know she'd been watching her, Valerie slipped quietly into the kitchen. After a few minutes of silence, she walked into the front room.

"That was beautiful," she said.

"Thanks. It's been a while since I've played. It really feels good."

"I'd forgotten how well you play. I've missed hearing that." Valerie noticed that Dayna's face was lit up, almost radiant. "You have a real gift."

"I guess," Dayna said. "But I prefer to think it's all those hours of practice that it took to get this good."

"That's part of it, but I think it's more than that. You play with such passion. It's as if you're connected to something bigger than yourself—as if God is flowing through you."

Dayna looked up at her mother with an odd expression on her face. She hesitated for a moment and then said, "Mom, can I ask you something?"

"Sure, honey. What is it?"

"What do you believe about God?"

Valerie was taken aback at her daughter's question. It seemed so out of character for her to ask, but Valerie was excited at the thought of sharing what she'd come to learn.

"I've always believed in a higher Power," Valerie started to explain. "And when I was going through the worst, I cried out to what I perceived as God. But lately, I've come to see things differently.

"I believe we're all a part of something larger. I feel a connection, now, that I've never felt before. Something inside me has come alive and I finally feel like I'm starting to live—really live. Before, I merely existed."

* * *

'*To be or not to be.*' The words seemed to ricochet in Dayna's mind. It sounded like her mom was saying the same thing as the student who had written the paper.

"I'm not sure I understand."

"It's hard to explain. It's a feeling... no," Valerie corrected herself. "It's more than that; it's a knowing. I searched for answers for many years. But it wasn't until I looked inside myself, that I found what I was looking for. I discovered God to be a power that each of us has within us.

"After your father passed away, something changed inside me," Valerie continued. "I'd been holding on to anger and resentment all those years. I'd filed it away. It wasn't something that I gave a lot of conscious thought to, but when he passed away so suddenly, it brought up all those old memories and I knew I couldn't go back there again—I needed to move forward.

"I had been learning how to feel better deliberately, by choosing which thoughts I give my attention to. A friend of mine helped me to walk through it—to deal with the powerful thoughts as they came up and deliberately choose ones that felt a little better.

"I discovered that I could control how I felt. It gave me an amazing sense of power. It's a power that I believe we all have access to. Anyway, that's when I really began to feel better, but I also began to see things from a different perspective. With the negative emotion gone, I was able to see clearly. It was then, that I realized I had never truly loved your father."

"I've wanted to ask you about that." Dayna still felt uncomfortable talking about the subject, but something inside of her was compelling her. She needed to know the truth.

"You mean...why I didn't love him."

"Do you know why?" Dayna knew that love was a complicated thing. In her case, if she truly hadn't loved Mark, she didn't know the reason for it.

"I do," Valerie nodded, slowly. She took a deep breath and looked away. When she looked back, there were tears in her eyes. Dayna felt the panic begin to swell again. She didn't know why talking like that caused her so much anguish. She wondered why she was so afraid of her own emotions.

"There's something I haven't told you," Valerie continued with difficulty. "I loved...someone else...before I married your father."

Madison walked into the room as they were speaking and they both turned to her.

"Abby's awake; she smells stinky," Madison informed her mother and then turned to Valerie, "Grammy, we didn't read the end of my book."

Dayna went to attend to Abigail, relieved that the conversation with her mom was interrupted, but at the same time, frustrated. She wanted an explanation. She needed to know what else her mom had to say.

* * *

The sun was shining and Rachael could hear birds outside the window. Brian walked into the room carrying a tray.

"I made us some breakfast," he smiled. "You looked so peaceful; I wanted to let you sleep."

"You're so sweet," she replied. "I guess I was pretty tired."

They had stayed out late, walking along the river and talking. It had been such a fun and romantic time. Rachael smiled as she remembered the details of the previous evening.

Her mind then drifted to the events of the past few days. As she thought about her family, she realized that those thoughts felt good, too. She'd raised her vibration and now that the negative emotion was gone, Rachael felt excited about what lay ahead for all of them. It was easy to imagine them talking and laughing together. She could even imagine Dayna being open to learning new things.

She remembered how different her mom had seemed. Something had changed and Rachael sensed that it was a good thing. She was curious to know just what it was that had caused the change.

"I think I'm going to call my mom and see if she wants to get together this afternoon. What time are your parents expecting us?"

"Around five," Brian replied.

They'd been invited for dinner at Brian's parents. They went there often, now, and Rachael always looked forward to it.

"You're sure you're up to seeing her?"

"Yeah," Rachael nodded. "I really feel like I am. I'm curious to see what's caused the change in her. I could see a difference when I first walked in the door, yesterday. The sadness is gone. Even though I know she's upset over Dayna's situation, I think something's changed, something deeper."

"When you 'see' something different," Brian asked. "Do you actually see it with your eyes, or do you just sense it?"

"I'm not sure." Rachael was surprised at his question. "I think it's both. She looked different to me, but I was probably sensing her energy, as well. Why do you ask?"

"I heard this couple talking at the bar the other night. I could tell right away that they understood this stuff and you know me," he shrugged. "I couldn't help but join in the conversation."

Rachael smiled. That was how they'd met. Brian had overheard Rachael and Gail talking about the Law of Attraction. He loved to get to know his customers. Many of them came back regularly, just because of him. He was constantly attracting people that were on a similar spiritual journey and he loved sharing what he had learned.

"So what did they say?"

"They were talking about auras. This woman could read people's energy by seeing the aura that surrounds them. Apparently, it can be different colors depending on how that person feels; it can be really bright or hardly visible at all."

"I've read a little about that; it's intriguing. What else did they say?" Rachael loved learning new things, especially with Brian.

"I asked her if she actually saw it with her eyes and she told me it was more like sensing it, than seeing it. She could tell all kinds of things about people by what she read in their aura."

"That's fascinating." Rachael sipped her coffee. "And it makes so much sense. We're made up of energy. Our body seems like it's solid." She held out her hand and studied it. "But it's really just a swirling mass of energy.

"We're not even real, in a sense," she continued. "The 'real' me is an eternal stream of consciousness. This physical version is just an illusion, a temporary manifestation." Rachael could feel her thoughts heading in a new direction. She loved to think and analyze and speculate. She loved to learn. Desiring to find out more, she made a mental note to do some research on the topic.

"What if nothing's real?" Brian joined her in speculating.

"What if everything is just an illusion? We've trained ourselves to see things in a certain way." He picked up a spoon. "My eyes tell me this is silver and shiny. My fingers tell me that it's hard and cold. My ears tell me it makes this sound." He banged it on the side of the tray.

"But where does that information come from if this is just energy, vibrating? Maybe we've trained ourselves to believe that certain things have certain attributes?"

"That would explain why people can bend spoons with just their minds!" Rachael exclaimed. "They just focus on them and they melt like butter."

Rachael was having fun. "They must have to change the way they've learned to think about the spoon. They'd have to convince their mind that the spoon is actually soft and pliable."

"And once they believed that, the spoon could bend easily," Brian added.

"Wow!" Rachael stopped to think about the possibilities. "That would explain how we can create our reality. Our minds are powerful; we create whatever we think about, but if what we're creating isn't 'real'—if it's not the solid stuff that we think it is—then everything around us is just a really incredible illusion."

"Like a giant cosmic hologram."

"This is almost too much to wrap my mind around," Rachael laughed.

"I know," Brian agreed. "It just goes to show that there's so much more for us to learn and understand. We've just scratched the surface."

Rachael looked at the clock. They'd talked for over an hour. She loved Sunday mornings in bed with Brian. Sometimes they talked, sometimes they didn't. It was all so wonderfully delicious.

"Let's take the dogs for a walk." She looked out the window. "It's such a gorgeous morning."

"Sure. What time do you want to get together with your mom?"

"I'll give her a call." She got up and went out to the kitchen, giving the dogs some attention on the way. She spent a few minutes with each of them, acknowledging how special they'd become to her.

She marveled at the idea that dogs could be just illusions, as she stroked their silky coats. Yet, there was something to the concept that intrigued her. She definitely wanted to learn more about it

* * *

Chapter 6

Valerie was thrilled that Rachael had called. She wanted to spend time alone with her youngest daughter, but she wanted Rachael to make the first move. Rachael had distanced herself for a reason and it had proven to be a good thing for both of them. Valerie had come to depend on her daughter too much. It wasn't healthy.

Rachael offered to pick Valerie up, but Dayna insisted that Valerie take her car. The girls napped after lunch and Dayna said she had some work that she needed to do.

As she drove, Valerie reflected on the conversation that she'd had with Dayna the day before. It was so unlike her to ask such a personal question. It showed that she was doing some thinking. Valerie knew that it was just a start, but she hoped that it would lead to more of the same.

As she neared Rachael's house, Valerie could feel her excitement build, but it was coupled with nervousness. She hoped to be able to share with Rachael what she'd come to tell her children. It had been weighing on her and now she was anxious to get it over with. She'd come to the conclusion that it would be easier to tell them individually and Rachael would be more open to hear it. Valerie would just have to wait until the time was right to tell Dayna.

Valerie looked around as she walked into Rachael's house. "Rachael, this looks so nice! You've painted and decorated. It looks beautiful now that you've added your personal touches."

"I guess the last time you saw it, I didn't have much. I've been slowly adding pieces of furniture. I have a girlfriend who's been helping me decorate," Rachael commented as she gave her mom a tour.

"Yes, you mentioned her in an email. Her name is Jenna, right?"

"Yeah. We used to work together. Now she's decorating full time."

Valerie recognized the antique Victorian sofa that had once belonged to her husband's parents. It was still in good shape and she was pleased that Rachael had inherited it. She was pleased, too, that Rachael had reconnected with her father while he was alive; she wanted to tell her daughter so.

"Can I get you a cup of tea?"

"Sure, that would be nice," Valerie replied. There was an uneasy formality between them and she wanted to get past it. She wanted to feel comfortable with her youngest daughter and wanted Rachael to feel the same.

"It may take some time," Valerie told herself. *"We've never really communicated. I didn't know how to talk to Rachael after the divorce. I wasn't able to help her sort out her feelings; I sent her to a professional, instead. Maybe if we could have talked about what we were going through..."*

Rachael brought in a tray with tea and cookies.

"Homemade?" Valerie asked.

"Actually, they are. My friend, Gail, is teaching me how to cook. I've made this recipe several times now. It turns out better each time."

Valerie felt the guilt that she'd so often experienced in the past. She shook her head. "Rachael, I'm sorry I wasn't there for you after the divorce. I should have taught you those things."

"I forgive you, Mom," Rachael smiled. "I know you would have if you could. You did your best."

Valerie closed her eyes in an effort to deal with the emotions that were erupting within. Rachael was such an amazing daughter. Now, she'd turned into a lovely young woman. Valerie was proud of her, but she couldn't help feeling regret for how much of

Rachael's life that she'd missed, just because she'd been so lost in her own.

"Rachael." Valerie took a deep breath, deciding to dive right into the subject that she wanted to discuss. "There's something that I need to tell you. I've wasted too many years of my life; it's time for me to take control of it now. I've changed. I've been learning all kinds of things about myself and about life. And…" she paused, her heart pounding. "I've been living a lie."

Rachael looked at her without saying anything, but Valerie saw love and acceptance in her eyes. It gave her the courage to continue.

"I never had a strong relationship with your father. I told you that he cheated on me, but the truth is, I was the one who cheated him."

* * *

Rachael heard the words, but the meaning didn't sink in. She was silently encouraging her mom to share what she was feeling, glad that she finally wanted to open up. They'd never had that kind of conversation before.

Suddenly, the words hit her. She opened her mouth to speak, to question, but the words wouldn't come. When she finally found her voice, she asked, softly, "You cheated on Dad?"

"No... Well, yes... in a manner of speaking," Valerie replied, swallowing hard. She was struggling and it took her a minute before she could continue.

"I was in love with someone else before I married your father," she said, staring into her teacup. Then she looked at her daughter through tear-filled eyes. "Rachael... I had a baby."

Rachael wasn't sure what to think. She wanted to know more, but she really didn't know what to ask first. She stared at her mother in disbelief.

"Wow," she laughed, suddenly finding the situation humorous. "I didn't see that one coming. Is there anything else I should know? You may as well lay it all on me now and get it over with."

Valerie was crying, but she managed a laugh. "I'm sorry; I know this is a lot for you to take in. First, you find out about your sister's marriage ending and then your father's affair and now this. I should have told you this, years ago," she said, regretfully. "Can you ever forgive me?"

"Of course I can forgive you." Rachael reached over and gave her mom a hug. Valerie was still crying and Rachael held her for a long moment. It felt good, like something lost had been found.

After a time, Rachael said gently, "Tell me what happened."

* * *

With the girls down for their naps, the house was quiet. Madison had been sleeping more, lately, and Dayna attributed it to a growth spurt, or possibly the stress that she was feeling. Whatever the reason, Dayna appreciated the time alone.

She was glad, too, that Rachael had invited their mom over to her place. It was becoming increasingly difficult having her mother around all the time. Dayna always had to guard her emotions; she found it draining.

Dayna was tempted to have a nap, herself, but she wouldn't give in to the temptation, wanting instead, to sort some things out in her mind. She had some regrets about the conversation she'd had with her mom the previous day. In a weak moment, she'd asked a question that had opened the door to issues that Dayna wasn't sure she was ready to discuss with her mom or anyone, for that matter.

"That whole thing about God—why on earth did I bring that up?"

She was usually more than a little critical of people who used God as their excuse for everything. It seemed like a crutch. As far as she was concerned, religion was for people who were weak and couldn't think for themselves. She didn't want to be drawn into that kind of fanaticism. She resolved not to let it happen again.

Then, there was the other issue they'd talked about. That one, she wasn't willing to let rest. Her mom had said that she'd loved someone else before marrying her father.

"What's that all about?" she wondered. *"Is that the reason she could never love Dad? Is that why he cheated on her?"*

So many questions were screaming at her that she put her hands over her ears in an unconscious effort to try to stop them. She paced back and forth, longing for some kind of a distraction. Her piano came to mind; it was calling to her again.

Closing the doors to the front sitting room, she sat down at the piano. As she began to play, she felt the anxiety start to diminish. Once again, she let herself be captivated by the melody and swept away by the music, playing with a fervor that she hadn't known in a long, long time.

She didn't know exactly what it was about playing that she loved so much. She didn't understand why it affected her the way that it did. All she knew was that, in those moments, she was transported to a place far away—a place where the pain, anger and confusion didn't exist, a place where she could feel at peace.

* * *

Valerie felt relief at having shared her secret. It felt good to finally say the words, 'I had a baby.'

At seventeen, she had discovered that she was pregnant. When she told her boyfriend, Danny, they were both scared, but neither of them doubted that they would get married and raise the baby.

As soon as their parents got involved, however, there was yelling and crying, along with hurtful accusations. After that, there was a lot of discussion behind closed doors. Valerie remembered waiting, listening, while her life hung in the balance.

Valerie willingly shared the story with her daughter. Rachael listened quietly until Valerie paused, then questioned, "They made you give up the baby—against your will?"

"That's what people did in those days. Danny's parents were adamant about it. They were well off and had big plans for him. My parents were just afraid of what people would say."

"And you didn't have any say in it at all?"

"We were just kids. We talked about running away, but we'd grown up in a small town and lived a sheltered life. We didn't even know where we'd go or how we'd make it on our own."

"Wow," Rachael sighed. "That's so unfair."

"Danny's parents took charge. They had money and influence; they made all the decisions. It was near the end of our senior year, anyway, so they just let everyone think that we went off to college."

The painful memories flooded back into Valerie's mind. Fighting to keep her composure, she continued, determined to tell the whole story.

"Danny did go away to college," she stated. "And I was sent here to stay in a home for unwed mothers, run by Catholic nuns. His parents made sure we were as far apart as possible."

"So you had the baby here?"

"Yes, I had a baby girl. The nuns took care of everything. I didn't even get to hold her. They told me they had adoptive parents waiting to take her."

Valerie wasn't sure how Rachael was feeling about all that she'd just shared. She didn't merely want to give her a bunch of information. As much as she wanted to tell her children the details of her past that they deserved to know, she also wanted to use it as a way to share how she was feeling and what she had been learning recently.

"How are you feeling about all this, Rachael? I know it must come as a real shock."

"It does," Rachael admitted. "But I'm glad you're finally able to talk about it. You must have suffered all these years with the burden of such a secret."

Valerie wasn't satisfied with Rachael's answer. She didn't just want it to be about herself. She wanted to know how Rachael was feeling, so she tried a different approach.

"That's all in the past." Valerie reached to take Rachael's hand. "Now, I've come to understand that feeling good is the most valuable thing that anyone can possess. I finally found out how to get to that place for myself and, more than anything, I want to share it with you kids. I love you all so much."

* * *

The words sounded absolutely beautiful to Rachael's ears. It wasn't even just the words, themselves; it was the passion and sincerity in her mother's voice. It was clear, now, that her mom had truly changed and Rachael was eager to know how it had happened.

"Mom, I've learned that, too! It's taken me a long time, but I finally reached a place of feeling good, consistently. It's a deliberate choice, now, not just something that happens once in a while."

Rachael knew that her mother had always loved her, but had never been able to show it. Now, she felt the love and connection with her mom that she had always longed for.

"Have you heard about the Law of Attraction?"

"Yes, I have!" Valerie said, excitedly, through her tears. "A friend of mine has been teaching me about creating my own reality, learning to have deliberate control over how I feel and that my thoughts are actually attracting the things that come into my life. It's all so wonderful."

"I know. I came across this a few years ago. My life has completely turned around since I started applying these principles." Rachael sent a loving smile toward her mom. "I'm so glad you know about this, too."

Rachael was elated. She had wanted her family to come to know the wonderful teaching that had brought her so much peace and happiness and now her mother understood it. She reached over and hugged her mom, once more. "I love you so much. I've always wanted to be able to talk like this with you."

"I have too, honey," Valerie admitted. "I'm sorry it took this long."

"That's one of the things I love about this teaching; we get to leave regrets behind. It's all about right now, this moment. What's in the past doesn't have to affect us. Once I learned that I didn't have to go back and sort through all that painful emotion, that's when I really began to feel better."

"Yes, that makes so much sense," Valerie agreed. "I don't want to focus on the past anymore, either, but I do want to tell you kids what happened. You have a right to know. Then I want to let it go and move forward with my life. I want us all to be able to do that."

Her words brought Rachael back to the news that her mom had just shared. Suddenly, a myriad of questions began to form in her mind.

"What happened with Danny? And Dad—did he know any of this?" she asked. "Did you ever try to contact her?" Rachael did the math in her head. "She'd be thirty-four now; I wonder what her life has been like."

Valerie took a deep breath. "She contacted me about a month ago. Her name is Stephanie Morgan. An older couple adopted her; she was their only child. They loved her and provided for her. She's had a good life and doesn't harbor any resentment toward me—that was my biggest fear. I was afraid she'd hate me for giving her up."

Rachael was trying to take everything in. "So I have a sister named Stephanie," she said, slowly, listening to her own words. As her mind absorbed the reality of what she'd just said, a new thought interrupted. "I'd like to meet her."

"She'd like that," Valerie assured her. "I've told her all about you and Dayna and Greg."

"Have you met her?"

"Yes, we spent a weekend together. We've talked on the phone several times and written long letters, telling each other about our lives. I brought hers for you to read."

"Did you ever see Danny again?"

"We kept in touch for a while. He wanted me to move closer to where he was going to college, after the baby was born, but an agreement had been made with the nuns. I was obliged to stay there and help for six months. I think it was part of his parent's plan to keep us apart. A lot of the other girls left soon after their babies were born."

"I got to know another girl that stayed on; we became close friends. Her parents disowned her and she had nowhere else to go. It was through her, that I met your father."

"Aunt Lil?"

The pieces of the puzzle were falling into place. She wasn't really Rachael's aunt. She was a close friend of her parents when they were growing up, so they'd always called her 'aunt'. She'd passed away when Rachael was in her early twenties.

"Yes," Valerie replied. She was always sneaking out to meet boys. Eventually, she talked me into going with her. My time there was almost up and I hadn't heard from Danny in months. I had no money to move anywhere, so Lil and I got an apartment together. I got a job as a waitress and I began dating your father."

"But you were still in love with Danny?"

"Yes," Valerie replied, "but I didn't hear from him until it was too late. Apparently, the nuns had started keeping his letters from me. He'd been writing the whole time. He got my new address, somehow, and wrote to tell me that he still loved me. But there was nothing I could do; I'd just found out that I was pregnant with Greg."

Rachael was quiet for a minute, before another question surfaced. "Did Dad know any of this?"

"He knew I'd had a baby; Lil told him. But we never really talked about it." Valerie looked down.

Rachael reached over and squeezed her mom's hand. Everything she'd just heard had come as such a shock; she couldn't help but look at her mom differently now. It explained so much. It was all in the past, however. She was glad that her mom could finally find peace about it. Not only that, but Rachael was excited at the idea of meeting Stephanie.

The phone rang and Rachael smiled as she heard Brian's voice. Looking at the time, she saw that it was almost four o'clock and they were going to his parents for dinner. She hadn't realized that so much time had passed.

"I should go ..." Valerie stood up to leave.

"Stay for a bit," Rachael encouraged. "Brian's on his way over. You two can get to know each other while I get ready."

"I'd like that," Valerie smiled.

* * *

Chapter 7

Dayna noticed it immediately when her mother walked in the room; she was positively glowing. She'd often noticed that about Rachael, too. Dayna wondered what it was about, but she didn't dare ask. Instead, she tried to focus on the dinner that she was preparing.

The girls were excited that Grandma was back. Valerie went to give them her full attention, leaving Dayna alone with her thoughts. The words that both her student and her mom had said about living life came back to her.

"What does it mean to really live life? And if I'm not truly living," she asked, silently, *"then what am I doing? What does it take to feel happy and fulfilled?"*

She reflected, once more, on the conversation she'd had with her mom regarding God. Her mom wasn't religious; she didn't go to church—nor did Rachael. Neither of them were what Dayna would consider weak—rather, the opposite; they had overcome a lot in their lives.

"What do they have that I don't?"

Once again, the thought occurred to her that she would like the comfort of knowing that something greater than her was in control of things.

"Would that make me weak? Or would it just help to ease some of the pressures of living?"

She pondered a quote from Hamlet,

> *"There are more things in heaven and earth, Horatio, than are dreamt of in your philosophy."*[7]

"Maybe there is more to life than I've allowed myself to believe," Dayna admitted, reluctantly.

Her mom came into the kitchen carrying Abigail and holding Madison's hand. They were singing one of Madison's favorite songs.

It was good to see them happy. Dayna wanted that for her girls. She wanted them to grow up happy and fulfilled and never know pain or heartache, yet she didn't know how she could protect them from all that life would bring their way.

"How can they learn to be happy and fulfilled, when I don't even know how?" she asked, inwardly, as she watched her little ones. *"How can I teach them something I don't know myself?"*

"It's ironic, though," she realized. *"Children seem to be born knowing happiness. Pain and sorrow are things that we pick up later in life."*

As they sat down to dinner, Madison was still singing and Abigail was trying to sing along, too. It was precious and they all laughed together. Dayna treasured moments like that. Those kinds of moments made her life worthwhile. She only wished that there were more of them.

* * *

After Valerie left, Rachael threw her arms around Brian's neck. She kissed him and looked into his eyes, smiling exuberantly.

"You must have had a good visit with your mom," he responded. "I haven't seen you quite this happy in a while. Not since before you got the news about your sister, anyway."

"Oh my God!" Rachael beamed as they walked to his car. "It was amazing! She's changed so much. Someone has been telling her about the Law of Attraction. She's so open to talk now. She told me all about her past." Rachael turned to look at Brian, gripping his arm as she laughed, "I have a sister that I didn't know about!"

"What?"

"Mom was in love with a guy named Danny in high school," Rachael explained. "She got pregnant when she was seventeen. His parents arranged to send her here to have the baby and kept her from getting Danny's letters.

"She met a friend here—you remember me telling you about my aunt Lil? Well, she introduced Mom to my dad and the rest is history.

"...except that Mom still loved Danny," Rachael added. "She didn't hear from him until after she was pregnant with my brother Greg, but Danny had been trying to contact her the whole time."

"Wow! That sounds like a soap opera."

"I know. It is pretty amazing, but it explains so much. Not only did Mom lose the man that she loved, she lost her child. It explains a lot about her relationship with Dad, too. No wonder things didn't work out."

Rachael proceeded to tell Brian about Stephanie, then added, "I think it would be really interesting to meet her."

"I have no doubt that you will some day," Brian replied, giving her shoulder a squeeze. They arrived at his parent's house and started up the front walk. "And you said someone's been telling your mom about the Law of Attraction?"

"Yeah. She thinks it's great. I can't wait to talk to her some more," Rachael exclaimed.

She looked up at Brian, her vibration soaring. Despite how wonderful her life was, she was feeling more incredible than ever. "This is turning out better than I could have imagined."

* * *

Valerie got up from the table and started clearing the dishes. She turned to Dayna. "Why don't you go and spend some time with the girls. I'll clean up here."

"Sure. Thanks, Mom."

With her head still swirling from her visit with Rachael, Valerie appreciated some moments alone to contemplate the amazing turn of events. She'd finally shared her secret. Not only was it a huge relief, but Rachael had been so wonderful about it, even happy for her.

"Rachael knows about this amazing teaching, too!" Valerie cheered, silently. *"She's been studying it for a couple of years already and applying it in her life. That would explain why things are working out so well for her lately."*

She was eager to talk some more with her daughter. Valerie had only recently learned about it and, although she could already see a difference in her life, that kind of thinking was new to her; she still had a lot to learn.

How Dayna would react to the news about Stephanie, Valerie wasn't sure, but she hoped that Dayna would receive it in a positive manner as Rachael had. She questioned if Dayna would ever be open to a teaching like the Law of Attraction. Valerie tried to imagine it as she thought back to some of the wonderful things she'd learned.

> *"When you ask it is given,*
> *every single time, no exceptions.*
> *You are beloved, blessed Beings*
> *who deserve good things."*[8]

And another one she'd memorized,

> *"The Universe is not punishing you or blessing you.*
> *The Universe is responding to the vibrational*
> *attitude that you are emitting. The more joyful*
> *you are, the more well-being flows to you*
> *and you get to choose the details of how it flows."*[9]

She'd learned, too, that she couldn't let herself get caught up in Dayna's pain or negativity. It was difficult, but she knew that she had to think about her daughter in a way that felt good in order to maintain her own well-being. She was so glad that she could talk to Rachael about it now.

It was thrilling to see how the Universe was working things out. Valerie had recently begun to envision her family being open and receptive to the teaching. Now Rachael had told her that she'd been imagining the same.

Valerie breathed a very contented sigh. *"Yes, everything is going to be all right."*

* * *

Dayna enjoyed taking the time to play with her girls. They loved the attention, but it was more than that; it was refreshing to interact with them in that way. She let herself get lost, for a moment, in the simple pleasures of a child's world.

Madison helped Dayna get Abigail ready for bed. After their bath, she picked out a sleeper for her sister to wear and told her a bedtime story as Dayna gave Abby her nighttime bottle. Abigail was still awake, but contented in her crib, as Dayna went to help Madison get ready for bed.

Madison insisted on reading several books with Dayna. She was full of questions, too. "Where does Daddy sleep now? Why doesn't he want to live with us? Why does that lady smell like flowers?"

Dayna was confused by Madison's last question. "What lady, sweetheart?"

"Daddy's friend."

Dayna hadn't even thought about the possibility of Mark's girlfriend being with him when he took the girls out.

Suddenly, her resentment toward him intensified and angry thoughts flared. *"How dare he confuse the girls by introducing them to this woman? Not yet; it's too soon!"*

Battling the rising emotion, Dayna turned her attention back to her daughter. She wanted to ask Madison questions about the woman. She wanted to know more, but she knew that it wouldn't be fair to her three-year-old to use her to get information about Mark's new girlfriend.

"Why does she smell like flowers, Mommy?" Madison asked again.

"Women wear perfume…to smell pretty," Dayna explained, feeling as if she was going to choke on the words.

"Can I wear purrfoome?" Madison asked, innocently. "I want to smell pretty."

Dayna desperately needed to distract her daughter and stop the barrage of questions, so thinking quickly, she lifted Madison in her arms, buried her nose in her hair and took a deep breath.

"You smell so pretty already." She twirled Madison around the room. "You smell like a bouquet of roses."

"No…wait." Dayna pretended to sniff again. "You smell like a field of daffodils in springtime."

She held her daughter close and danced as she quoted Wordsworth,

*"I wandered lonely as a cloud
That floats on high o'er vales and hills,
When all at once I saw a crowd,
A host, of golden daffodils;
Beside the lake, beneath the trees,
Fluttering and dancing in the breeze*

*Continuous as the stars that shine
And twinkle on the Milky Way,
They stretched in never-ending line
Along the margin of a bay:
Ten thousand saw I at a glance,
Tossing their heads in sprightly dance."* 10

Madison laughed at her mom's antics. Dayna hoped that she'd succeeded in changing the subject; she didn't want to answer any more questions about Mark or his new girlfriend.

"William Wordsworth, right?" Valerie asked, entering the room just as Dayna was reciting the poem. "I remember learning that one in school."

"That's right," Dayna replied. Then she set Madison back on her bed. "But enough stories and poems for tonight; it's bedtime."

"Can Grammy read me just one more?" she pleaded, in a voice that was hard to resist.

Dayna looked at her mom.

"I don't mind," Valerie said.

Dayna kissed Madison goodnight and retreated to her own room to try to deal with the powerful emotions that she was experiencing. Madison's question had disturbed her and now images of Mark's 'friend' with her girls were swirling in her mind. She felt the anger surface again.

"What if Mark marries this woman? She'd be a step-mother to my girls."

The thought made Dayna want to scream. The idea of anyone else, besides her, being a mother to Madison and Abigail was upsetting. Nevertheless, it was a very real possibility.

"I hate Mark! I hate him for doing this to us. It's so unfair!" Dayna wanted to break something at that moment. Instead, she sat down on her bed and clenched the comforter in her fists in a deliberate attempt to calm herself.

Silently, she questioned if all men were the same and had to conclude that it was so. The men in her life had let her down and Dayna knew that she could never trust another man. She vowed, there and then, never to let herself be hurt that way again.

* * *

Chapter 8

Valerie tucked Madison in after, not one, but three stories. She was such a precious child; it was hard to say no to her. Valerie treasured the time with her granddaughters. She wanted to have a relationship with them and she regretted living so far away, seeing them so seldom.

She went downstairs to make some tea. When Dayna came down a few minutes later, Valerie noticed a troubled look on her face. She wanted to comfort her daughter and tell her that it would all be okay, but as soon as she saw it, the look was gone, replaced by one that she saw so often now.

Dayna concealed her emotions well. She was a pro at putting on a front for people. Valerie wondered what was really going on beneath the façade. She wondered if Dayna would ever be able to be honest with herself and admit that she was hurting—admit that it was okay to hurt.

When Dayna accepted the offer of tea, Valerie sensed that her daughter wanted to talk. She hoped that they might continue the conversation they'd started the previous day.

"Dayna, I'd like to explain what I said, yesterday," she began, "about being in love with someone else before I married your father."

"I was going to ask you about that."

Valerie started to tell Dayna about her relationship with Danny, but she stopped short of telling her about the baby. Suddenly, she was afraid of what Dayna's reaction might be.

"I don't understand. You never got over this guy, Danny?" Dayna looked frustrated. "So why did you marry Dad?"

Valerie stared down at the counter. She didn't feel the same compassion and encouragement that she'd felt from Rachael. What she was sensing from Dayna made her feel like she had to justify her actions; she wasn't sure she could do that.

Her palms were sweaty. She felt a slight wave of nausea as she silently questioned her decision. *"What if this makes things worse? What if Dayna resents me for it? Maybe now isn't the right time to be telling her this."*

She'd already gone that far and she knew that she couldn't stop there; Dayna was waiting, now, for her to finish. Taking a deep breath, she proceeded to tell her daughter the truth.

"Dayna, there's something else—something I've never told you kids."

"What is it?"

"I got pregnant when I was seventeen." Valerie looked at her daughter. "I had a baby."

She searched Dayna's face for a response and saw a mix of emotions—surprise, disbelief, she wasn't sure what else.

Dayna shook her head, frowning. Valerie wished that she would say something. The moment seemed like an eternity.

Finally, Dayna spoke. "How could you keep this a secret all these years?" Her tone was harsh and her words more an accusation than a question.

"I'm sorry, honey."

Valerie was about to tell her more, when Dayna continued her tirade, "So I have another sister or brother out there somewhere?"

"A sister," Valerie said, weakly.

"And Dad knew?"

Valerie nodded.

Dayna was quiet for a moment longer. "What a messed up family this is," she said, shaking her head.

Valerie heard the bitterness in her daughter's voice and tried to explain, "I don't want things to be messed up any more, Dayna. I want to set things straight. I'm tired of living a lie. I was wrong, keeping this from you all these years and maybe I shouldn't have told you this now, with all you're going through, but you have a right to know."

"Well, congratulations." Dayna set her cup down, angrily, spilling her tea as she did so. "Your conscience is clear. I hope you feel better."

"Dayna, please…" Valerie begged her to listen.

Dayna stood up. "What do you expect me to do with this information?" Her voice was shaking. "As if my husband cheating on me wasn't enough, now I find out that I have a sister I've never met and the father that I've hated all these years was not the contemptible bastard that I believed him to be. Thank-you very much!" She turned and stormed angrily out of the room.

Valerie wanted to stop her. She wanted to explain. More than anything, she wanted to go back in time and take back what she had just shared. The timing was wrong; it was too much for Dayna.

"How could I have been so selfish? I was only thinking of myself and not Dayna. What have I done?" Valerie buried her face in her hands and wept.

* * *

Rachael heard the phone ring. It was late and Brian had just left. She wondered if he was calling from his cell phone. She smiled at the thought of him telling her, once again, how much he loved her, or that he missed her already.

"Rachael, it's Mom."

"Is everything okay?" Rachael could tell by her voice that it wasn't.

"I've made a mess of things here. I told Dayna what I told you—about Stephanie."

"Was she upset?"

"She wouldn't even let me finish. She got really angry and then went upstairs."

"Wow." Rachael let out a breath.

"I was so focused on myself and getting this off my chest. I wasn't thinking. It's too soon for her. She's got too much on her plate already." Rachael could hear her mom crying.

Rachael closed her eyes and took a deep breath, making a quick petition to her Inner Being for wisdom. She could sense her mom's pain, but she felt supported, knowing that she could find a way to look at the situation that felt better. She truly hoped that she could help her mom find that place, too.

"Mom, let's look at this from the broader perspective. Everything is unfolding perfectly, both for you and for Dayna. The Universe is answering both your desires in ways that you may not be able to see right now."

Rachael thought for a moment and then asked, "What do you want when you think of Dayna?"

"I want her to be happy."

"That's understandable, but what I've learned is that the Law of Attraction won't bring you feelings of happiness from a place of anger and resentment. Those emotions are too far apart.

"What Dayna has access to right now," Rachael continued, confident in her knowing, "is a feeling like blame. Blame is higher on the emotional scale; it actually feels better than anger."

Her mom was still crying, softly, so Rachael added, "Don't take this personally, Mom. Dayna is angry with a lot of people, right now. This is an issue that she has to work out for herself. I know you feel her pain, but you can't help her from a place of sadness. It's an inside job. She has to find her own way and, as odd as it sounds, blame is a step in the right direction."

"Thank-you, sweetheart," Valerie sniffed. "I know you're right. I've been learning that, too. I guess I just needed to be reminded."

"You have to take care of yourself. If you don't, you'll have nothing to offer Dayna or anyone else. Nothing is more important than feeling good, but everyone has to find that place for themselves.

"You and I have found happiness," Rachael added. "Dayna will find it, too."

"I was beating myself up for what I said to Dayna, but you're right, a higher power is at work here. Maybe those were the words that Dayna needed to hear."

Valerie laughed, softly, and added, "This kind of thinking is so different than the way I used to think. Sometimes, I have a hard time getting my mind around it."

"I know," Rachael agreed. "My whole belief system has changed radically, too. But it's our belief system that is the basis for what we attract into our lives, so unless it changes, our circumstances can't change, either."

"I never thought of it like that." Valerie's vibration had shifted; Rachael could hear it in her voice. "Then Dayna's belief system is being challenged right now, also."

"Yes!" Rachael felt exhilarated, just knowing that her mom understood.

"And our job is to think about her in ways that feel good to us and trust that no matter what she seems to be going through, she's being guided and supported by her own Inner Being," Valerie summed up what Rachael was thinking.

Rachael was close to tears at hearing her mom's words, but they were tears of joy.

For so long, she'd wanted her mother to experience happiness. At first, Rachael had focused on the lack of it, but as she gently turned her attention to what she did want, she was able to come to a place of letting go—knowing that all was well with her mom and knowing that she would find her own place of well-being. And now she had.

As she hung up the phone, Rachael breathed a contented sigh. She knew that Dayna would be all right, too. The anger and blame that she had expressed that evening toward their mom was an important step in getting in touch with feelings that she'd been suppressing for a long time. Her sister was on the path to well-being.

* * *

Dayna ran up the stairs and into her bedroom, her heart pounding wildly. She knew that she had to get control of herself, but the emotional wave was just too big, too powerful. The startling information that her mom had just shared pushed Dayna beyond what she was capable of handling. Something snapped and the anger that she'd been trying so hard to control took over.

"How dare she?" Dayna raged. *"How dare she tell me that just to clear her own conscience?"*

The anger that Dayna was feeling was intense; she actually hated her mom in that moment. She despised her for all her weaknesses. It seemed, now, that her mother was to blame for the break-up of their family, not her father.

That just served to bring up another torrent of emotion. Dayna hated her father all those years, believing that she had sufficient reason. Even so, when he passed away the year before, she'd suffered tremendous guilt over the feelings that she had toward him. Now it seemed that he was justified in leaving. He'd tried to keep in contact, too, but Dayna had wanted nothing to do with him.

All of a sudden, she began to feel dizzy, then nauseous. The situation was getting out of hand and she knew that she needed to calm down. She began to have difficulty breathing.

"Oh God! What's happening to me?"

All at once, a blinding pain ripped through her chest. She grabbed at the corner of her dresser in a desperate attempt to steady herself, but she felt herself falling. Suddenly, everything went black.

* * *

Chapter 9

The large waiting room was nearly empty. An older man paced the corridor and a middle-aged couple sat in the corner, hands tightly clasped, staring out from fear-filled eyes.

Rachael sat with her arm around her mom, trying to console her, but when Greg arrived, Valerie broke down, once again, as she tried to explain what had happened.

Rachael still wasn't sure what did happen to Dayna, but she was trying to make sense of it. According to her mom, Dayna had stormed out of the kitchen, leaving Valerie extremely upset. That's when her mom had called and they'd talked for fifteen minutes or so.

Following their conversation, Valerie had gone to get ready for bed. Walking past Dayna's bedroom, she'd heard the dog make a whimpering noise. Dayna's door was slightly ajar, so Valerie had peeked in, hoping to find Dayna asleep. Instead she'd found her sprawled on the floor. She then called 9-1-1 before calling Rachael.

Valerie had found a number for Mark, as well. He was at Dayna's, now, with the girls. They were still asleep, completely unaware that their mother's life hung in the balance.

Rachael met them at the hospital and then called her brother. Now, they sat waiting. She hadn't called Brian yet. It was four in the morning and as much as she would love to be comforted, she felt she needed to be the comforter.

Her mom was inconsolable. Nothing Rachael said would convince her that it wasn't totally her fault. Now that Greg had arrived, she gave up talking and just held her mother.

Rachael was trying to maintain her own well-being, but she was struggling. It had been hours and they still hadn't heard any news. She was relieved when the doctor finally came and asked to speak to Dayna's family. The three of them searched his face for the answer to their biggest question.

"She's stable. She's come through the worst of it; the next few hours will tell us more."

"What happened?" Greg asked, taking on the role as head of the family.

"Dayna has had a coronary embolism, triggered by a congenital abnormality of the aortic valve," the doctor began. Then seeing their faces, he explained, "In layman's terms, that means that she had a faulty heart valve. A normal aortic valve has three flaps that allow the blood flow from the heart. Hers had only two.

"It's a common abnormality. People with this condition can live normal, healthy lives and never have a problem, or as in Dayna's case, it can trigger a heart attack. It's not proven, but studies show that over time, stress may further weaken the valve. Do you know if she was under a lot of stress?"

"She was," Rachael answered. "Her husband just left her. It was quite sudden."

"That could have had some impact, but like I said, it appears to be a build-up of stress over time and not an isolated trauma that triggers this.

"We've replaced the valve with an artificial one. It's a common procedure, usually done before it causes any heart problems, but in Dayna's case, there may not have been any prior symptoms. There doesn't appear to be any permanent damage to her heart. She's very lucky."

With that, he left them, promising to keep them updated on her condition. Rachael went to call Mark and let him know what the doctor had just told them. Then, she called Brian.

Just hearing his voice was almost enough to cause Rachael to break down. She managed to tell him what happened and he was out the door, talking to her on his cell phone before she could finish. She had hoped he'd come. She needed his support.

Looking back toward the waiting room, she saw Greg talking to their mom and decided to take a moment for herself. As she walked down the hallway, she noticed a stairwell. Opening the door, she sat down on the stairs, closed her eyes and rested her forehead in her hands.

Rachael needed the comfort that her Inner Being offered. After several deep breaths, she began to feel a tingling warmth radiate through her. She let all thoughts go and concentrated on the soothing oneness with her Higher Self.

After a few minutes, an image of Dayna came to her mind. She was wrapped in the same comforting warmth that Rachael was. It caused Rachael to sense a powerful connection—a connection, not only to her Higher Self, but also to Dayna. In that moment, they were one.

Then, with her eyes still closed, Rachael saw herself lying on the hospital bed, tubes everywhere. She felt the warmth, again, as it began to pulse through her in a rhythmic flow. She was in the hospital room, yet instead of the normal sounds, she heard beautiful music. Looking up, she saw Dayna's smiling face.

Rachael opened her eyes and looked around the small space. She didn't know how long she'd been sitting in the stairwell, but it was long enough to have fallen asleep. She was still tingling from the dream she'd had. She assumed it was a dream, but it felt different, almost like some kind of out-of-body experience. Rather than try to figure it out, she got up and hurried back to the waiting room.

Brian was already there with Greg and her mom. He met her halfway across the room, embraced her and then led her back to where the others were sitting.

"Where did you go?" Valerie asked. "I saw you walk off. I assumed it was to call Mark, or Brian. But when Brian showed up here, none of us knew where you where."

"I'm sorry." Rachael touched her mother's arm. "I didn't mean to worry anyone. I needed a minute to myself, so I sat down in the stairwell. I must have dozed off."

* * *

Valerie felt helpless; there was nothing to be done for the time being and sitting around, waiting, was unbearable. Rachael had her eyes closed and was resting against Brian. Greg was immersed in the paper. Suddenly, Valerie longed for fresh air.

"I think I'll go for a walk. I need some air," she informed Greg as she got up. "There's a terrace off this level somewhere. I remember it from when

Grandpa Adams had his heart attack." As she uttered the words, the weight of the situation hit her. "Oh, God; I can't believe this happened to Dayna."

Greg stood up and took her arm. "Mom, you should sit down."

She sat for a moment and then shook her head, adamantly. "No, I need to walk. The fresh air will do me good."

After asking one of the nurses how to get to the terrace, she then described to Greg where it was in case they needed to find her.

Once outside, she took in a refreshing, deep breath. So many thoughts were coursing through her mind. She tried to sum up what the doctor had told them. Dayna had a faulty heart valve. Stress may have aggravated the problem, but it was primarily due to a condition she was born with.

Recalling her conversation with Rachael the night before, she reminded herself, *"The Universe is in control. I need to hold on to that belief. What happened to Dayna is all part of a perfect unfolding of events."*

The rising sun began to paint the morning sky and Valerie watched, mesmerized, as the colors emerged—a hint of yellow, mixed with fiery orange; pink, tinged with purple, fading to dark blue. It was magnificent and she felt comforted, knowing that such beauty could never exist in a chaotic Universe.

The morning air was cool; she was glad she'd brought her jacket. Wrapping it tightly around her, she stared at the rising sun, continuing to seek comfort and finding it in the truths that she had learned in the past few months.

> *"The Universe responds to the vibration*
> *we're emitting. The more joyful we are,*
> *the more well-being flows to us."* [11]

Dayna definitely wasn't joyful. Even before Mark left, Valerie wouldn't have described Dayna as a happy person. She took life very seriously. She worked hard and it seemed as if she always had a chip on her shoulder. It made sense then, that well-being couldn't flow freely to her. She had pinched it off in her life and now it had manifested in a heart attack.

> *"Nothing can occur in your life*
> *experience without your invitation of it*
> *through your thought."* [12]

Valerie used to believe that bad things could happen to good people—that unwanted things could just come 'out of the blue.' That kind of thinking had left her feeling vulnerable to whatever fate might throw her way. She'd always hoped that there was something else at work, something bigger. Now, she understood that it was the Law of Attraction.

* * *

Rachael felt peaceful as she relaxed in Brian's arms. She knew that she should be tired, yet her mind was full with the dream that she'd just had in the stairwell. It had seemed so real.

After a moment, she lifted her head and smiled at him. It was so good to have him there with her.

"Pretty rough night?" He smoothed her hair.

"Yeah," she replied. "I was scared and Mom was so upset." She told Brian about the conversation she'd had with her mom the night before. Then she told him about her dream.

"At least I think it was a dream. Either that, or I was in some kind of altered state."

"When you walked up to us, your face was glowing," Brian remarked. "I don't know if anyone else noticed. Your mom was worried when we couldn't find you."

"How long was it from the time I called you, until you saw me?" Rachael asked.

"Twenty, maybe twenty-five minutes."

"I called you from the pay phone down the hall and then I walked a bit and saw the stairwell. I couldn't have been in there more than twenty minutes then. Given how tired I was, I guess I might have fallen asleep in that time." She shook her head, still somewhat confused. "Weird."

Looking around the room, Rachael noticed that her mom wasn't there. Greg was reading the newspaper a few chairs down and she asked him where she'd gone.

"She's out on the terrace. It's down at the end of that corridor," he pointed.

"I think I'll go and see how she's doing." Rachael turned to Brian, "I won't be long."

"Take your time."

As she walked away, he asked, "Can I get you some coffee or something to eat?"

"I don't think I could eat, but coffee sounds good."

Rachael walked out onto the terrace. She was struck by the beauty of the sunrise that filled the sky with color. As she looked around, she saw her mom sitting on a bench. Valerie appeared to be enjoying the sunrise, too.

"It's breathtaking," Rachael said, softly, as she sat down beside her mom."

"Yes, it is." Valerie reached over and squeezed Rachael's hand. "How are you doing?"

"I was going to ask you the same thing."

"Better," Valerie smiled. "I always feel better in nature. Beauty like this is so reassuring. It helps me to remember that everything's under control."

"Mmm," Rachael nodded in agreement. Words didn't seem necessary, so they sat together quietly for a moment.

After a bit, Rachael said, "I was meditating before." She paused to explain. "...when I was sitting in the stairwell. I had this dream or vision. I was lying in the hospital bed with tubes coming out of me. I could feel a pressure in my chest, but it didn't hurt. I heard beautiful music and I felt this amazing sense of warmth and peace. Then I saw Dayna there, smiling down at me."

Valerie looked at Rachael, "That's lovely. I wonder what it means."

"I'm not sure. It could just be my Inner Being comforting me. It felt wonderful."

"You have such a strong connection to your Inner Being. I'm learning about that. It's something I want to experience more of." Valerie smiled at Rachael, "I'm so proud of you for how far you've come."

"You've come through a lot, yourself."

They enjoyed silence, once more. Then Rachael stated, "She's going to be all right; I know she is."

"I do, too."

The sky was getting brighter. The sun peeked above the horizon, its brilliance diminishing the colors that had preceded it.

"I'm ready to go back in now," Valerie said.

They walked in together. When they got to the waiting room, Brian was just arriving with a tray of drinks in one hand and a paper bag in the other.

"Starbucks?" Rachael walked over to Brian. He set the bag down, took one of the lattés and handed it to her. He handed another to Greg and then turned to Valerie. "Greg said you prefer tea, so I got you a chai tea latté. I hope you like it."

"You're amazing. This is just what we needed," Rachael kissed him. "I love you so much."

"This is delicious. Thank you, Brian. But did you have to drive to get these?" Valerie asked.

"No. Actually, there's a Starbucks here on the main floor by the front entrance. I noticed it when I came in earlier. They were just opening when I got down there. I got an assortment of muffins, too, in case you feel hungry."

Rachael looked at the food and realized that she was hungry after all. The fresh air may have had something to do with it. The others took a muffin, as well, and they all sat silently enjoying their breakfast.

The doctor returned just then and their food and drinks were forgotten, momentarily.

"How is she?" Again, Greg asked the question.

"She's doing well. She's being moved to the Critical Care Unit, where she'll be monitored closely for a day or two. Then she'll be moved to a private room. She'll be here for at least a week altogether, depending on her recovery.

"It could be a while before she wakes up," he continued. "I'll have the nurse come and let you know when she's ready for visitors. I should warn you, though, she won't be able to talk while she's on the respirator and her arms have to be restrained to keep her from any movement."

Valerie shook the doctor's hand and thanked him. Then they all sat down again to wait—this time with lighter hearts, knowing that the worst was over.

* * *

Chapter 10

Dayna heard someone calling her name, but she resisted; she didn't want to go there. She'd just experienced the most wonderful place imaginable. It was serene and beautiful; she didn't want to leave.

"Just a little bit longer…"

The voice wouldn't stop. It was gentle, but persistent. She felt herself being drawn out of the serene place. She didn't know where she was going, but someone was holding her hand, leading her.

She heard another voice and, recognizing it as Rachael's, her apprehension diminished. Dayna knew, suddenly, that she was going to be all right. She opened her eyes.

When her eyes adjusted to the light, she saw her family. Rachael was beside her, holding her hand. Her brother, Greg, was behind Rachael. Her mother was on the other side of her bed. A nurse was there, too.

"Where am I? Why is everyone standing around my bed?" She wanted to say the words, but she was unable to speak.

In an instant, the memories flooded in. She remembered the pain and not being able to breathe. She remembered falling.

"What happened to me?"

The nurse responded to her look. "Dayna, you're in the hospital. You've had a heart attack, but it's okay, now. You're going to be just fine."

A slight movement of her arm told her that she was hooked up to monitors and an IV, but her arms were restrained by her side. She surveyed the people around her again and a feeling of panic gripped her. Her eyes searched the room.

This time, Rachael responded. She was still holding Dayna's hand, gently caressing it. "Mark's at your place with the girls. They don't know anything happened. They're still asleep."

The events started to become clearer in Dayna's mind. *"A heart attack—how is that possible?"*

As she thought back to the previous evening, she remembered the conversation she'd had with her mother. She remembered storming out of the kitchen, feeling extremely angry. Suddenly, she felt a pressure in her chest.

"Just relax," she heard the nurse say. The woman was holding Dayna's hand now and rubbing her arm. "Everything's okay. Just relax."

She closed her eyes and felt herself going back to the safe, tranquil place. This time, her mom was there with her, stroking her hair and comforting her with soothing words.

When Dayna opened her eyes again, the lights were dim. There was no one standing by her bed. She turned her head slightly and saw her mom sitting on a chair. Valerie got up immediately and went to her side.

Emotion engulfed Dayna and tears began streaming down her face.

"I'm here, Dayna." Valerie stroked her daughter's hair. "Everything's okay. You're going to be all right."

* * *

Rachael walked along the corridor with Brian. She'd just called her work to let them know that she wouldn't be in. She decided to take the entire week off so that she could be there for Dayna and be a support to her mom, as well.

Greg had gone home to be with Amy; the baby was due soon and he didn't want her to be under any unnecessary stress. Valerie was with Dayna; she wanted to be there in case Dayna woke up again.

With Brian's arm around her as they walked, Rachael gladly relaxed against his sturdy frame. It had been a long night, an emotional one, too. Nevertheless, she felt good.

When she thought of Dayna, she still held on to the image from the stairwell. She knew that Dayna was safe and protected; her smiling face assured Rachael of that. Even so, it was baffling, because her sister rarely smiled.

"I wonder what happens when a person is unconscious," she said, thinking aloud.

"You mean Dayna?"

"Yeah. When she was unconscious, she wasn't focused in the physical, right? So where did she go; what kinds of things did she experience?"

"I read this book once," Brian said. "It was about people who've had near death experiences. The other worlds that they described were surreal and peaceful—so beautiful, in fact, that in most cases, they didn't want to come back.

"When they did, though, they were never the same again. They had all changed in some way. They all looked at life differently. Some even had clarity and wisdom on subjects they'd never known anything about before."

"I wonder if Dayna experienced anything like that?" Rachael asked, pensively.

They walked along quietly for a few minutes, Rachael still deep in her own thoughts.

"Why don't we see if your mom would like to go and get a few hours sleep? I could take her back to Dayna's," Brian offered. "If you want to stay here for a while, I can come by and pick you up later. You'll need to get some sleep soon, too."

"I feel okay, right now, but if you don't mind taking my mom back, that would be great. Mark was planning to drop the girls off at daycare this morning, so the house will be quiet. At least she'll be able to get some rest."

Rachael appreciated the fact that Brian was concerned about her. She stopped and put her arms around him, just to let him know how much she loved him. He'd become such an important part of her life—so much so, that she could scarcely imagine her life without him, now.

She closed her eyes and let herself be swept away by the flood of emotion that she felt for him. Holding him tight, she breathed in his wonderful smell, savoring his warmth and his strength. She marveled at the incredible well-being that had come to her in the form of a man. Brian was an integral part of a truly wonderful reality that she had created for herself.

After a few minutes, they went to Dayna's room. Dayna was asleep and Valerie was sitting beside the bed with her eyes closed. Rachael went over to her mother and gently touched her shoulder. Valerie opened her eyes.

"Mom, why don't you let Brian drive you back to Dayna's? I'll stay here for a while."

The nurse looked over as they were talking. "She's heavily sedated, now. She'll sleep for a while. Might be a good time for all of you to go home and get some shut-eye."

Suddenly, the idea of sleep sounded very appealing to Rachael. She nodded in agreement. Taking care of herself was important, as well. She turned to Brian. "I have my car here. Do you want to meet me back at my place?"

"Are you okay to drive?" Brian asked.

"Yeah," she smiled. "I'm fine."

As she headed to Dayna's place to drop Valerie off, she and her mom discussed the events that had just taken place.

"Dayna's different," Valerie commented. "This has changed her."

"What do you mean?"

"I'm not sure, but I could see something different in her eyes. I don't know how to describe it."

Rachael thought about the conversation she'd had with Brian about near death experiences. She was glad that she'd arranged to take the week off. She wanted, more than ever now, to spend time with Dayna. She hoped that they could finally connect in the way she'd been dreaming.

She hugged her mom before dropping her off, then headed back to her place. Brian was waiting there as she pulled up. He came over to her car, opened the door and took her hand. She was getting used to that kind of treatment, but she appreciated it just the same. Those small gestures added such quality to their relationship.

Brian walked her up to her door and, when she opened it, followed her inside. She looked up at him, smiling suggestively, "I'd love it if you could stay, but I understand if you have things you need to do. The dogs are probably wondering where you ran off to so early."

"Actually, I called my dad. He said he'd stop by and feed them. I'm sure he'll probably take them for a walk, too. I've got enough staff scheduled today and I already let them know I won't be in."

He tenderly stroked her face. "I wanted to be available if you needed me."

"I do need you," she winked.

With that, Rachael took Brian by the hand and led him to her bedroom. She slowly removed her clothes, as he watched with a smile.

Then, she pulled back the covers and slipped between the cool, soft sheets, reaching out to Brian with an inviting look. He shed his clothes, as well, and immediately joined her beneath the blankets. It was heavenly to feel the warmth of his naked body next to hers.

With one hand, he caressed the length of her back—slowly, ever so lightly—down and back up again. Then he wove his fingers through her hair. She loved the way it tingled on her scalp and sent a shiver down her spine.

Rachael closed her cyes, just for a moment, to enjoy the exquisite sensations and was soon mesmerized by the relaxing pleasure of it. She could feel herself beginning to drift and even the thought of making love to Brian couldn't bring her back. She fell into a deep, peaceful sleep in the arms of the man she adored.

* * *

Chapter 11

Dayna's eyes scanned the room; it was empty, now. She had no idea how long she'd been there or what time of day it was. She did remember why she was there, however; the nurse's words were clearly etched in her mind. Still, she was having a hard time believing it.

"A heart attack? I'm only thirty-two. I eat healthy and exercise regularly. How could this have happened to me?"

As much as she wanted answers, she didn't want to focus on that now. Something else was on her mind. She'd had some amazing dreams—not even dreams, really; it actually felt as if she'd gone to another place, a peaceful, warm, inviting place.

It had felt safe there. She remembered being called, but not wanting to come back. She remembered her mom there, as well, comforting her. When she awoke, her mom was standing by her, stroking her hair.

"Is it just the medication I'm on? Am I so drugged up, that I'm hallucinating?"

That was the most likely answer. She didn't want to let her mind start thinking that she'd had some sort of spiritual experience.

Then, she remembered a conversation she'd had with her mom, but she could recall only bits and pieces of it.

"Was that here in the hospital or at home?"

The memory was foggy; she struggled to piece it all together. She didn't like the feeling of not remembering, not thinking clearly. She recalled having said something to her mom about wanting to really live, not just exist anymore. Now, she wasn't sure if she'd actually said it, or merely dreamt it. She felt a tear run down her cheek.

"God, what's the matter with me? Why am I getting so emotional about this?" Her practiced response of quickly getting unchecked emotions under control seemed to fail her.

Dayna reached for the memory of that peaceful place that she'd experienced. Something inside her wanted to hold on to the memory, even try to recreate it, but there seemed to be a battle going on between her logical mind and something bigger, more powerful within her.

As she thought about it some more, she realized that she wanted that power, whatever it was, to win.

She wanted to believe in that part of her that had kept her safe and protected through the ordeal that she'd just experienced.

She wondered, again, about the heart attack. *"How serious was it? Could I have died?"* An odd mix of feelings was percolating inside of her. Where her logical mind told her that she should feel fear, she felt strangely calm.

Then, she remembered the music.

* * *

Rachael walked into the hospital room. Dayna's eyes were closed. She was off the respirator and there was more color in her cheeks than there had been the day before.

As Rachael approached the bed, Dayna opened her eyes. Rachael noticed something different about her sister, just as Valerie had said. She could see it in her eyes.

Rachael smiled, "Hi."

Dayna reached out her hand to Rachael, without saying anything. Rachael took it with both of hers and stood there as they looked at each other for a few seconds.

Dayna wiped a tear from her eye. "I'm an emotional mess," she apologized, shaking her head.

"You have every right to be. You've been through a lot."

"The doctor said I had a faulty heart valve— something I was born with."

"I know." Rachael was still holding Dayna's hand, gently caressing it. "It was pretty serious."

"I was scared," Dayna admitted. "But at the same time, I felt calm. Somehow, I knew I'd be all right."

After hearing her sister's words, Rachael knew she wanted to share her dream with Dayna, but she wasn't sure what her reaction would be.

"I thought about you," Dayna admitted, looking up at her sister. "I felt you there with me, somehow. I felt Mom there, too."

Rachael couldn't resist, she knew she had to tell her. "While we were waiting," she began. "I took a moment to myself and closed my eyes. I was imagining you safe and protected and, suddenly, I felt myself lying in your place. I saw the tubes coming out of me and felt a pressure in my chest."

She searched Dayna's eyes to gauge her reaction before she continued, "Then I saw you smiling at me and I knew you'd be okay."

"Maybe that's what I was feeling, too."

"Oh yeah," Rachael remembered. "And I heard beautiful music playing."

"You heard music?" Dayna sounded surprised.

The nurse had come in while they were talking; she began to change Dayna's intravenous.

"Speaking of beautiful music," she interjected. "A couple of us went down to the chapel on our break to hear this man play the piano. He was brought in several weeks ago. Car accident. Pretty serious. He almost didn't make it.

"Anyway, he kept asking if there was a piano anywhere in the hospital. Seems he'd taken some lessons as a kid, but after he nearly died, he had this incredible desire to play again. There's no rhyme or reason to it, but now he can play like a pro. It brought tears to my eyes." The nurse finished with Dayna and turned to leave.

"Could I have heard the music from where I was, during my surgery?" Dayna inquired.

"Oh no, honey," the nurse shook her head. "The chapel's down on the second floor."

After she left, Dayna remained silent with a puzzled look on her face.

"What's wrong?" Rachael asked.

"I heard music, too," she frowned. "It was a piano sonata. Beautiful, but one I've never heard before."

"When you were unconscious?" Rachael asked.

"Yes."

* * *

Valerie sat in the waiting room. Rachael had gone in to see Dayna, but Valerie wanted to take a moment to herself before she visited with her daughter. They hadn't talked since their explosive conversation, just before Dayna's heart attack. Valerie was still feeling guilty about telling her the things that she did and for not being more sensitive to her needs. She wanted, needed really, to ask Dayna's forgiveness and hoped she would receive it.

Forgiving herself was important, as well. What had happened to Dayna wasn't her fault. She wanted to love and accept, rather than beat herself up over what had happened.

Focusing on her breathing, she tried to feel a connection to her Inner Being. Valerie was inspired by the close connection that Rachael seemed to have. As she closed her eyes, breathing slowly and deliberately, she was able to find thoughts of appreciation for her loving Source. She knew her Source to be pure love and acceptance and she welcomed those feelings. She also knew that her Source, that broader part of her, was the same Source that was loving and guiding Dayna.

Thoughts of Dayna caused immense love to well up in her heart. Valerie was proud of her daughter's accomplishments. Dayna worked hard and she was a good mother to her two little girls. Valerie admired how strong Dayna was, especially considering all she'd been through.

She tried to envision Dayna seeking her own connection to Source and finding it. She imagined the joy that Dayna would feel when she finally came to know who she truly was.

Soon, Valerie realized that she was feeling much better. She congratulated herself for finding a more positive way to think about Dayna and all that had happened.

As she opened her eyes and saw Rachael walking toward her, she smiled.

"Do you want to go in and see Dayna now? Rachael asked. "I'll wait out here, so you can have some time alone with her."

"Thanks."

"And Mom," Rachael said, as Valerie began to walk away, "you were right, she has changed."

As Valerie walked into the hospital room, she looked into Dayna's face. Her usual strong look of self-reliance and determination had been replaced by something softer. Her face was pale, her eyes bright with tears. There was tenderness there, mixed with vulnerability. As she looked up at her mother, Dayna smiled slightly.

"Mom, I'm sorry I got so angry at you."

"Dayna, you had every right to be upset. I should have told you years ago that you have another sister. Can you forgive me?"

Dayna nodded. She squeezed her mom's hand. Valerie treasured the moment of closeness that she and her daughter had never shared before.

"When you're up to it, I'll tell you all the details," Valerie said. "For now, I want you to rest and get your strength back. The doctor says you're going to be just fine. You'll be able to get back to a normal, healthy life."

"Did I ask you...?" Dayna started. Then she shook her head. "I remember a conversation that I had with you. I must have dreamt it, though. It's just that it seems so real."

"What was it about?"

"You said something the other day about really living, not just existing." Dayna looked away as the tears ran down her cheeks. "I want that."

"Oh, Dayna," Valerie exclaimed. "I want that for you, too. I want you to be happy. Rachael has learned the secret and I'm just beginning to understand it. It has to do with who we really are. We're the very essence of God and, therefore, we're powerful creative beings."

"I gave up believing in God a long time ago." Dayna shook her head. "But when I was unconscious, I felt like...like something bigger than me...was in control." She was struggling to find the right words.

"There's a Power, a Source, God—call it whatever you like. I believe we're all connected to it and we have access to that power to change our lives for the better."

Just then, Dayna yawned. "I'm sorry." She touched her mother's arm. "I really want to hear what you have to say, but I'm so drowsy."

Valerie decided that she shouldn't overwhelm Dayna with too much to think about. There would be plenty of time in the coming days to discuss the topic further.

"You need rest, more than anything, right now. We'll talk about this another time." Valerie remained by her daughter's side, gently stroking her arm. Dayna quickly drifted off to sleep.

Valerie was glad that Dayna could sleep. She'd have a lot to deal with in the days and weeks ahead, but she was strong and Valerie knew that she'd get through it. Now that Dayna truly wanted to feel better and was open to new ideas, she was definitely headed in the right direction.

* * *

Chapter 12

The first few days following her surgery seemed to drift by as if Dayna were in a dream. Rachael and Valerie took turns visiting her during the day and Greg stopped by one evening. Dayna vaguely remembered talking with them, but she was in and out of sleep, dreaming and having conversations in her dreams. She wasn't even clear on what really took place and what she had dreamed.

When she was alert, however, she thought about her girls. She wanted to see them so badly. Having never been away from them that long, she missed them terribly.

Mark was staying at her place and taking the girls to daycare in the mornings. He stopped by the hospital after work one day to see Dayna. Their visit was short and somewhat awkward. At first, he acted overly polite and kept saying how sorry he was for what had happened to her.

Dayna tried to ignore it; she just wanted to know how the girls were doing. He said they were fine, considering, but that Madison kept asking endless questions about where Mommy was.

"How do you explain to a three-year-old that her mother's had a heart attack?" he asked. "She remembers this hospital from when Abby was born. I've had to tell her more than once that you're not here to have another baby." He shook his head. "And now, she keeps talking about this man that plays the piano."

"What?" Dayna's thoughts came screeching to a halt. She looked at Mark, incredulously.

"Yeah, there was something on the news about it the other night. Some guy was in a car accident. Almost died. Now he's started playing the piano, even composing music. They said he's in this hospital. Anyway, Madison keeps talking about him. She calls him the 'pinano man'. It's strange."

Mark left then, in search of the doctor, to inquire how soon the girls would be allowed to come and visit Dayna.

Dayna reflected on the strange coincidences that were happening. *"Both Rachael and I dreamt that we heard music playing. Then the nurse told us about the man playing in the chapel and now Mark just mentioned it."* There seemed to be a connection, but Dayna couldn't quite piece it together. *"And why would Madison be interested in him? It's all so bizarre."*

So many things were going through her mind. She kept thinking about where she'd been while she was unconscious; the memories still felt warm and comforting. In addition, there was a kind of battle going on in her mind—something powerful was making its presence known and it kept challenging her practiced ways of thinking.

"Is there a greater force out there?" she wondered. *"Is it even 'out there'? It almost seems like it's something within me, something new; I just don't know how that's possible."*

She'd decided not to bring the subject up again, after talking with her mom and sister that first day. She was feeling a little foolish for being so emotional about it all. The thing was, she still had so many questions.

Rachael had brought her a book when she was in, earlier that day. She claimed that it had answered many of her questions. Dayna appreciated the gesture, but had set it on the stand beside the bed, not sure that it would be of interest to her. Now, she reached for it. She was still skeptical, but something was compelling her.

As she picked it up, the book fell open to a page. It was dog-eared and underlined. The words jumped out at her,

*"It is possible that you have been using
the power of your mind to produce
the very limitation from which
you wish to extricate yourself."* [13]

Dayna re-read the words, 'power of your mind.' It didn't sound like the weak-minded spiritual dogma that she was expecting.

"How could the power of my mind have been limiting me?" she asked herself.

She flipped to another page and found more underlined words,

*"Have the will to be well,
to be happy and to live in joy.
Recognize that there is nothing
in your past that can deny
you the privilege of living happily."* [14]

For thirteen years, Dayna had been letting the events of the past cast a shadow over her. She realized now, that the anger she'd felt toward her father had been based on assumptions.

A sharp pang of guilt arose as she thought of the way things had turned out. She'd never meant to cut him totally out of her life—merely punish him for breaking up their family. Wanting her father to make the first move, to admit his wrongdoing, she'd waited, believing that they would mend things eventually. But as time passed, reconciliation seemed more and more unlikely.

When Rachael moved back to the city and talked about seeing their father again, Dayna had been tempted to try to make amends, but her pride kept her from calling.

As she read the quote from Rachael's book again, she silently questioned how she could keep the past from affecting her present.

"Is it possible, by sheer will, or by some kind of power in our minds, to be happy and live in joy? Is that what Rachael and Mom have discovered?"

She turned to another page. There, she found an answer to her question,

> *"It is impossible for you to*
> *experience the full joy of living*
> *while you identify yourself*
> *with anything less than that.*
> *The images of your thought attract to you.*
> *Once you fully realize this,*
> *you will understand that to change*
> *undesirable conditions,*
> *you must of necessity change the*
> *basic pattern of your thought."*[15]

Dayna's mind was brimming with the new ideas. Something about the words made sense to her, resonated with her at some deeper level, but her logical mind still wanted to argue.

When Mark came back into her room, Dayna closed the book and set it aside. The doctor had told him that Dayna was recovering well; the girls could come for a short visit the following day.

When he left, Dayna could think of nothing but her precious daughters. She couldn't wait to see them again. She wanted to hold them in her arms and kiss them. They were her whole world—her joy and they made her life worth living.

She held the wonderful images in her mind as she closed her eyes, feeling the pull of sleep. While she drifted off, the beautiful piano sonata came, unbidden, to play in her mind once again.

* * *

Rachael and Valerie brought the children to visit Dayna the next morning. Arriving at the hospital, they went directly to her room. When they looked in, however, the nurse was making up the bed; Dayna wasn't there.

Before they could ask, the nurse responded, "They've just taken Dayna for her bath. Are these her girls?" She fawned over Madison and Abigail for a minute, then addressed the women, "She might be close to half an hour. There's a children's playroom down on the main floor. That would keep the girls occupied until they can see their mom.

I'll call down when Dayna gets back," the nurse smiled. "I know how anxious she is to see them."

After thanking the nurse, they went down in search of the playroom. Madison liked the elevator ride and wanted to push all the buttons, so they stopped on every floor.

On the second floor, the elevator opened for a woman pushing an elderly man in a wheelchair. It took a moment for the woman to align it and back it into the elevator. As they waited, they could hear someone playing the piano. Rachael thought the piece sounded familiar, but she wasn't sure where she'd heard it before.

Madison looked up at Rachael and said, excitedly, "That's the pinano man!"

Rachael had been holding Madison's hand, but let go of it to hold the door for the couple entering. The child immediately darted out of the elevator in the direction of the music. The door started to close, but the man in the wheelchair stuck his foot in the opening.

"Thank-you," Rachael said to the man as she slipped past him to run after Madison. To her mom, she added, "I'll meet you down at the playroom."

Rachael looked in both directions, but Madison was nowhere in sight. She felt a moment of panic, until she heard the music again. Going in the direction it came from, she found double doors leading into a small chapel. At the front, a man was sitting at a baby grand piano. He'd stopped playing and had turned to look at the small child who was standing beside him.

* * *

Dayna couldn't contain her excitement. The nurse told her as soon as she returned to the room that her mother and sister had arrived with her girls.

Madison hesitated a moment as she saw her mother lying in the hospital bed. Then she squealed with delight and ran toward her. Rachael lifted her up to sit beside Dayna. Abigail reached out for her mother's arms. With Valerie and Rachael holding them carefully, Dayna was able to embrace them. She drank in their scent and the sound of their voices. She couldn't stop the tears of joy that flowed down her cheeks.

"Don't cry, Mommy," Madison soothed, wrapping her arms around Dayna's neck.

"I'm just so happy to see you." Dayna looked into their precious faces. "I missed you both so much!"

"We missed you, too." Madison sounded so grown up. She stroked her mother's hair as she spoke. "Daddy's taking good care of us, though."

"I'm glad," she smiled, hugging them tightly.

"What have you been up to?" Dayna wanted to know everything she'd missed in the days she'd been apart from her children. "Have you learned anything new at preschool?"

"I made a picture for you." Madison handed her a folded piece of paper.

Opening it, Dayna saw two stick figures captured with child-like simplicity in bright, colorful brushstrokes. One was lying down; the other one was sitting beside a box.

"That's you in the hospital," Madison pointed at the figure lying down. "And that's the pinano man."

Dayna looked at her daughter and then at Valerie. She knew of Madison's fascination with the man she'd seen on the news, but Dayna couldn't understand the reason behind it.

"Sweetie, that's beautiful!" Dayna turned back to her daughter. "Thank you. That's a lovely painting." Curious to know more, she asked, "Did you see the piano man on TV?"

"He talked to me," Madison informed her mother. "He told me not to be sad."

"What?"

"Dayna, we heard someone playing the piano when we took the girls down to the playroom." Rachael explained. "The elevator door was open and Madison ran out before I could stop her. I followed her and found her in the chapel, standing beside the man the nurse told us about."

"And the man talked to you?" Dayna wasn't comfortable with the idea of a strange man talking to her three-year-old.

"No, Mommy. He talked to me in my bedroom, when I was crying."

* * *

Later, Dayna reflected back over the events of the day. It had been a strange one to say the least. Having been upset earlier, she was still very confused. She couldn't help but wonder about the 'piano man.'

"What is it about this man? Why is everyone talking about him? Madison claimed that he spoke to her in her room. Impossible, of course, but why would she make it up? And why is she so enthralled with him in the first place?

"Children have vivid imaginations," she reasoned. *"We've always encouraged Madison's pretending, but this is just too weird. Maybe it's because I'm a part of it, too—I heard piano music—or maybe it's because it has to do with a real person that none of us know anything about."*

Dayna was curious about the man. The nurse had told them that he'd nearly died. Since then, he could play the piano, supposedly very well, having only taken a few lessons as a child. Now Dayna wanted to see him play; she was having a hard time believing the incredible story.

"Maybe he's just looking for publicity. Maybe he's a pianist, out of work, down on his luck and after the accident, saw the opportunity to capitalize on it. But someone would surely know the truth or recognize him; he was on TV."

She played it all around in her head, but nothing seemed to make any sense. Dayna wasn't even sure she wanted to figure it out. It was more reasonable to simply let the incident pass, in the hope that Madison would forget about it, as well.

Starting to feel sleepy, Dayna closed her eyes and let her thoughts drift. Soon, she was walking in a valley—a familiar one; she'd dreamt of it a lot lately. Rolling hills, lush with green grass and wild flowers along a meandering stream, the pristine setting enveloped her. She could hear the water cascading over the rocks as it followed its course, yet rising above it, was the distinct sound of piano music in the distance.

* * *

Chapter 13

Rachael's mind was full with all that had taken place at the hospital earlier that day. She was confused by it, but she had a sense that something bigger was unfolding. There were too many coincidences to dismiss it as anything else.

"What is it about that man and his music?" Rachael questioned, silently. *"And why the connection to Dayna?"*

Valerie seemed to be lost in her own thoughts, as well. "I'd forgotten how well Dayna plays the piano," she said. "I came downstairs one day last week and she was pouring herself into the music with such passion. When she stopped, her face looked radiant. I remember thinking how odd it is that she puts such emotion into her music and yet withholds it from every other part of her life."

"I know what you mean; I love listening to her play," Rachael agreed.

"I hope this didn't upset her too much today." Valerie took a sip of her tea. "She doesn't need any more to worry about. Madison does have a very active imagination. She probably saw the man on TV and then, for whatever reason, pretended that he came to visit her. Maybe she found his music comforting, just like when her mother plays."

"I guess."

"You don't think it's more than that, do you?"

"I don't know." Rachael looked in the bottom of her cup and swirled what was left of her tea. "It's a subject I don't know a lot about, but I don't like to dismiss things as impossible.

"Brian and I were talking the other day and I got an even clearer understanding of how the universe works. If everything is made up of pure energy vibration, then it's possible for things to take on many different forms. The reason that we see things the way we do is that we've trained our minds to interpret the vibration in a certain way. I know that if we believe strongly enough in the possibility of something, we can alter the way we see and experience it.

"I think, too, that children see things differently than we do. Maybe they can even see things that we can't. It's possible they just haven't learned yet that it isn't 'supposed' to be that way?"

Rachael stopped talking as she looked at her mother. Valerie had a smile on her face and she was shaking her head.

"I never realized just how much like your father you are," Valerie said. "I'm sorry. I didn't mean to interrupt you; what you said was interesting, but the way you said it and the way you question everything—your father was just like that."

"I don't really remember it from when I was young, but we used to talk about things like this..." Rachael hesitated a moment, searching her mother's face. "When we got together... before he died."

"I'm glad that you re-connected with him," Valerie smiled at her youngest daughter. "I've wanted to tell you that."

"Thanks, Mom. I didn't know how you felt about it. I'm glad you understand."

"I saw how the Universe worked things out for you—allowing you to get this house, completely paid for. I was so happy about that. I was sorry that you didn't have longer to really get to know your father, though; he was a good man." Valerie looked away.

"No regrets." Rachael reached out and took her mother's hand. "Remember, it's all about right now and how we feel in the moment."

"Yes." Valerie smiled at Rachael. "You're right. And right now, I'm so proud of you. I'm excited to see what's unfolding for Dayna, too. Whatever this all means, I know that the Universe is in control of things."

Rachael finished her tea and sat back with a feeling of satisfaction. Things were working out. She could see it; she could feel it. Her mom was sitting there with her and they were sharing things together in a way that Rachael had only dreamed of in the past. And Dayna, as much as she had just been through, was all right, too.

Rachael's life was very good. It was a life she had created for herself—co-created with those she loved and she was looking forward to what the future held for each of them.

* * *

Dayna was feeling anxious. It was already proving to be the longest week of her life. Her mom and Rachael came by every day and they'd brought her girls to visit twice, already. She appreciated her family's support, but Dayna couldn't wait to go home. Her doctor was coming in that morning to examine her and let her know how much longer she would have to stay in the hospital. She hoped that his news would be good.

She was thankful, at least, that she could get up and move around now. She decided to go and check at the nurses' station to see if they knew when the doctor would be in to see her.

"He's been delayed this morning, but he'll be in this afternoon for sure," the nurse informed her.

Dayna couldn't hide her disappointment.

The nurse was sympathetic. "Time gets kind of long in here, doesn't it?"

Dayna nodded.

"If you like music, I could have an orderly take you down to the chapel. Mr. Radford plays down there every morning. He's getting to be quite famous. They've aired the interview he did for the local TV station, on national TV. There's even a rumor that Oprah wants to have him on her show."

Dayna had all but forgotten about the man. She'd been determined to make it a non-issue and was relieved that Madison didn't bring it up the last time they were in. She was still convinced that it was some kind of hoax, though, and rather liked the idea of checking it out for herself. She gladly accepted the offer.

An orderly came with a wheelchair and they headed to the elevator. He was talkative, prattling on about Mr. Radford, or the 'piano man', as he was commonly referred to. Dayna concluded that there must be a lot of gullible people around, but she decided to question the young man, anyway, as they rode down in the elevator.

"Have you heard him play?"

"Yes Ma'am, I have. I was particularly interested because when I heard the name, I realized that I'd met him before. He's actually related to my aunt through marriage."

"You know him?" Dayna was perplexed, but even more curious.

"Not very well. I've only met him once at a family gathering."

"What did he do?" Dayna asked. "Before the accident, I mean."

"He owns a construction company. My cousin worked for him for a while. I guess he can still run it now, but he won't be able to do much of the physical work himself."

"So he was hurt pretty badly?"

"Yes, Ma'am. It was a close call, but he's doing much better. There's still a lot of nerve damage in his legs, though. He's able to walk, but with difficulty."

"And he'd never played the piano before?" Dayna still didn't want to believe that it was a miracle. There had to be a logical explanation.

"I know it's hard to believe, but I even asked my aunt. She said that she was talking to his mother, who would be her sister-in-law, and she confirmed it. He took lessons for one year when he was eight or nine. That's it."

When they reached the second floor, the orderly wheeled her down the hall toward the chapel.

"I don't hear him playing yet," he noted.

As they entered the doors leading into the chapel, Dayna noticed a housekeeper dusting and an elderly man sitting in one of the pews, but no one was at the piano.

"If you don't mind waiting here, I'll go and see if he's coming down this morning." He pushed her halfway up the wide center aisle and put on the brake. He left before Dayna could answer him.

She looked around the small chapel. There were six pews on either side of her. At the front was a table, a pulpit and a couple of ornate chairs.

It was the baby grand piano just off to the right, however, that captured her attention. She looked at it longingly. It was shiny and black and the keys stood out in bright contrast. Dayna realized how much she missed playing; it was just one more reason that she longed to be going home. It would feel good to put her hands on the keys again.

The light was streaming in through the stained glass windows at the front of the chapel. The colors splashed playfully over the pews and gave the room a cheerful quality.

Dayna felt peaceful as she waited. She was reminded, again, of the peaceful place that she'd first visited when she was unconscious.

"What is it anyway? Is it a random feeling that comes and goes? Is it from some source outside me, or is it something within me, trying to get my attention?"

She hadn't read any more of the book that Rachael had left for her. She was tempted, but she kept resisting. It was as if it threatened to take her to a place she wasn't ready to go—a place that she was curious about, but terrified of at the same time.

A noise from behind jarred her from her thoughts and as she turned, she saw a man in a wheelchair entering the chapel. He looked to be in his late thirties, maybe early forties. A big man, with reddish brown hair and a ruddy complexion, he fit the orderly's description of a construction worker; he was muscular and looked like he spent a lot of time in the sun.

A beard and moustache concealed much of his face, but as he wheeled past Dayna, smiling, she noticed something in his eyes. There was a softness there that didn't quite match the rest of him.

Her eyes followed him to the piano. She watched as he struggled to get himself up out of the wheelchair and then take a moment to get comfortable on the piano bench.

Holding her breath as she waited, Dayna expected to hear child-like playing, to hear him pick out a simple melody with one hand. She was astonished when he put both hands on the keys and began to play enchanting music. It was a peculiar sight—the big, rugged-looking man creating such lovely sounds.

The performance left Dayna completely enthralled. She didn't even know how long she'd been there listening to him, when the same orderly that had wheeled her down, tapped her on the shoulder. She'd been so caught up in the music that she failed to notice anything else around her. The chapel was more than half-full. Patients, staff and visitors had come to hear the man play.

"Ma'am, it's time to take you back to your room," the orderly informed her. "They'll be bringing your lunch by any time now."

Dayna didn't want to leave. She still didn't know how it was possible, but the music he was playing was truly amazing. She would have expected to hear that caliber of music from a concert pianist, not a construction worker. The pieces sounded original, too. Dayna hadn't heard any of them before—except one—the same one that she'd been hearing all week in her dreams.

* * *

Chapter 14

Rachael was looking forward to spending a quiet evening with Brian. She'd spent so much time at the hospital and with her mom during the past week, that she and Brian had hardly seen each other. She missed Gail, too, missed seeing her every day at work. They had talked on the phone, however, and decided to meet Friday, as usual.

As she drove to meet her, Rachael thought back over the events of the week. Besides her sister having a heart attack, she'd learned that Dayna's marriage had ended and that their father had had an affair. Rachael also learned that she had a sister she'd never met. In addition, she spent the better part of a week with her mom, talking about the Law of Attraction.

When she summed it up like that, Rachael had to laugh at the way the Universe was orchestrating it all. Even Dayna's heart attack seemed to be part of a perfect plan. She was recovering well; the doctor had said that she'd be able to lead a perfectly normal life. But now, other strange things were happening that made Rachael think that something bigger yet, was unfolding.

As Rachael walked into Trophies, she smiled to herself. She loved Brian's bar. It almost felt like home; she had so many good memories there. Even before she'd met Brian, she and Gail had gone there regularly. They'd spent many happy hours laughing, contemplating life and discussing the things they were learning. Gail had been open to learning about the Law of Attraction right from the start. She wasn't into studying as Rachael was; she just liked to hear new things and could apply them in her life with very little effort.

Brian's sister, Tracy, intercepted Rachael before she got very far. They hugged and Tracy asked about Dayna. They talked for a moment before Rachael looked toward the bar. Brian was standing there with a smile on his face, watching their interaction. Rachael felt love radiate through her, as she looked at the man she adored.

As Rachael began to make her way toward him, Brian came around the side of the bar and took her by the hand. She looked up at him and smiled questioningly. He smiled back, but didn't say anything as he led her toward the back. He opened the door to his office and, once they were inside, he pulled her into his arms and held her for a long moment.

"Mmmm," Rachael moaned pleasurably as she relaxed into his embrace. "I've missed this."

"I've missed you," Brian said.

Rachael took a deep breath, savoring the deliciousness of the moment.

"How's Dayna today?" Brian asked. They'd spoken every day, so he was up to date on most of the things that had taken place during the week.

"She's doing really well," Rachael replied. "The doctor came to check on her while we were there, this afternoon, and told her that he's very happy with the progress she's making. She should be able to go home, Sunday."

"I'll bet she was glad to hear that."

"Oh yeah," Rachael replied. "She's been going crazy. Every day, she's talked about getting out of there and being at home with the girls.

"She seemed different today, though, telling us about that man that's been playing the piano. She went down to hear him play this morning and was impressed by his music. She seemed really affected by it, talking about the quality and beauty of his songs with such emotion. It's unusual to hear her talk about her feelings like that."

"I've been hearing about him here, too. He seems to be getting a lot of publicity." Brian frowned. "So is he really as good as they say?"

"He'd have to be to impress Dayna. She has high standards and, in the past, she tended to be a bit of a critic." Rachael didn't want to focus on her sister's negative qualities, but Dayna could be very outspoken when it came to people's shortcomings.

Rachael noticed the time and realized that Gail would be arriving any minute. She leaned into Brian, drawing him closer. "I'm going to catch up with Gail for a bit, but after that, I'm all yours. What do you want to do tonight?"

Brian smiled and his silence spoke volumes.

"Okay," Rachael laughed, reading him clearly. "What else do you want to do tonight?"

"I have a little surprise planned."

* * *

Dayna was looking forward to home-cooked meals again. The hospital food wasn't terrible, but it definitely lacked flavor. She had a good appetite, however, so she finished her meatloaf and potatoes, but as she took the cover off the small fruit bowl, she grimaced. It was tapioca for the third time that week. She pushed it aside.

Remembering the banana bread that her mom had brought in earlier, she opened the drawer of her bedside table to take out one of the nice, thick slices. As she did, she noticed Rachael's book. Dayna could still feel some apprehension, but this time, the curiosity was stronger. She picked it up.

More questions were erupting all the time, it seemed, about God and finding happiness in life. As she ate her treat, she turned to a page and read,

> *"Nothing can be nearer to you than*
> *the very essence of your being.*
> *Your outward search for God culminates*
> *in the greatest of all possible discoveries*
> *—finding God at the center of your own being.*
> *Life flows up from within you."*[16]

"Is it true, then," Dayna stopped eating and stared at the words, *"that what I felt was missing all my life is actually within me? Is this what Rachael and Mom have found?"*

She continued to read,

> *"A basic harmony exists*
> *at the center of everything.*
> *There is peace at the center of your being,*
> *a peace that can be felt through the day*
> *and in the cool of the evening*
> *when you have turned from your labor*
> *and the first star shines*
> *in the soft light of the sky."*[17]

Dayna liked the descriptive prose. Again, she experienced that warm, comforting feeling that she'd felt earlier in the chapel and during her surgery.

The feeling evoked a sudden desire to go back to the chapel. She wondered if Mr. Radford played the piano in the evenings, too. Dayna didn't mind the idea of hearing him again, but more than anything, she wanted to be in that serene place. In fact, she longed to be able to play the piano herself.

When a woman came in to take her dinner tray, Dayna decided to ask about it.

"Do you know if Mr. Radford plays the piano in the chapel during the evenings?"

"No, the hospital likes to keep the chapel as a quiet place for people to go and pray or meditate. Mr. Radford draws such a crowd now; they had to limit him to a couple hours each morning."

"I'd like to go down there."

"I'll let them know at the desk. They'll send someone to take you down."

"Thank-you." Dayna put the book away and got up to put on her slippers. After a few minutes, a young woman came with a wheelchair to take her down to the chapel. They chatted about the weather and the girl asked when Dayna would be going home.

"Sunday afternoon, if all goes well," Dayna smiled. She got excited just thinking about it. One more day and she could go home to be with her girls. She was glad, now, that her mom was staying at her place. The doctor said that Dayna was going to have to take it easy for a few weeks yet and her mom had already assured her that she would stay as long as Dayna needed her.

As she entered the chapel, Dayna looked around. She was pleased to see that no one was there. The main lights were off and the lighting on the walls bathed the room in a soft, amber glow. It gave the sanctuary a warm, inviting feel.

The girl pushed Dayna's wheelchair up to the back pew and then helped her up.

"Most people prefer to sit in a pew if they're able," she smiled at Dayna. "I'll leave you to yourself, now. Just pick up the phone by the door there," she pointed, "when you're ready to go back to your room. Someone will come and help you."

"Thanks." Dayna returned a smile to the friendly, young woman. People had been so helpful and courteous to her during her stay. She was unaccustomed to so much kindness. Sometimes, she wasn't sure how to respond.

Her family had been wonderful the past week, also; she owed them so much. They'd helped her through her ordeal. It made Dayna realize just how much she loved them and how rarely she'd shown it in the past. She truly wanted that to change. She wanted to be more open with them and really get to know them. Rachael had something about her, a strength that Dayna admired. She'd seen something new in her mom, too. Dayna wanted to find out more.

She walked up to one of the pews near the front, sat down and closed her eyes. The serene stillness seemed to embrace her. She felt the peace that she'd read about in Rachael's book. It felt like it was coming from within.

"Is this the God within?" she asked the silence. *"This peaceful feeling—is it coming from the part of me that's connected to God?"*

As she heard the words in her head, she realized that she wasn't afraid anymore. Whatever the feeling was, it was part of her and she wanted to get to know it. She wanted to experience more of it.

* * *

Valerie got Lacey's leash down to take her for a walk. The dog was obviously missing Dayna. She'd run to the door every time it opened and, when she discovered anyone other than Dayna, she would immediately go back to her bed in the kitchen and lie down. Then she would look up with big, sad eyes. She had lost her best friend and there was no way of explaining to her that it was any other way.

They both enjoyed the pleasant walk. A temperate breeze was signaling the change of seasons; spring was approaching. Valerie loved springtime. She loved the newness that it represented. Everything was re-born, or revived after a restful sleep.

It reminded her of all the changes that were taking place in her life and the lives of those she loved. Her's had been completely altered since she'd reunited with Stephanie. Rachael was happily in love, now. Greg and Amy were expecting their first baby, soon, and Dayna had just gone through a life-changing experience.

Valerie knew that Dayna would never be the same again; she'd seen the change in her right away. And when they were visiting, earlier that day, Valerie noticed something different again. Dayna seemed taken with the piano music that she'd heard in the chapel and had described it to them with passion and enthusiasm.

Expressing emotion was new for Dayna; so, too, was asking questions. Valerie knew that Dayna had more questions; she could see them in her daughter's eyes. She looked forward to Dayna coming home on Sunday, so they could have time to sit and talk.

Sunday was significant for another reason, also. It marked one year since Valerie's ex-husband had passed away. She wondered about commemorating his life in some way, for the kids' sake. She decided to talk to Rachael about it.

His sudden passing had caused Valerie to look at life differently. Learning about the Law of Attraction helped to put it all into perspective. Valerie had gained so much clarity in the past year. Letting go of the resentment she'd held so long toward her husband allowed her to see things in a new way. It allowed her to feel other emotions, too. It was good to feel again—it was good to feel good, again.

She hadn't dated much since the divorce. Friends had tried to set her up a few times over the years, but none of the men she'd met really appealed to her. She liked the idea of being in a relationship again, but was beginning to doubt that it would ever happen.

Valerie didn't know if she could find someone who could make her heart sing again. She didn't know if it was even possible, but she longed to have the kind of love that she saw between Rachael and Brian—the kind of love that she'd shared with Danny once, so long ago.

In many ways, she still felt young. Her body had begun to age, but in her mind, she was a young woman with dreams and desires. Now, more than ever, she felt like she had a lot of living left to do.

Before she'd come to stay with Dayna, Valerie had received an email from Stephanie saying that she'd contacted her father. Valerie hadn't heard any more since, but she was curious to learn what had come of it. She wondered what road Danny had taken and what his life was like. His parents had moved away from their hometown before Valerie moved back there. His father had since passed away; she'd seen the obituary in the local paper.

She knew, from hometown gossip, that Danny had married and she wondered if he'd found happiness. She truly hoped that he had.

* * *

Dayna was enjoying the peaceful sanctuary. It was a new experience for her, just being alone with her thoughts and feeling good about it. She knew that she'd changed somehow. She didn't understand it, but she no longer had any desire to resist it.

In the solitude, she looked around and her eyes were drawn to the beautiful piano. She didn't think anyone would mind if she played it. Walking to the piano, she sat down at the bench, lifted the cover and lovingly caressed the keys. Her eyes scanned the dimly lit room, once more, to assure herself that she was alone. Then she began to play.

It was an exquisite piano in many respects. It was tuned perfectly and the sounds that it made were richer than her upright at home. As she played one of her favorite songs from memory, Dayna felt the familiar pull. She allowed the emotion that she'd been feeling all week to flow into the music, producing a connection beyond anything she'd previously felt. It was like a drug to her. Music was so much more than pleasure or entertainment; it was healing. It opened up a part of her that nothing else could.

The music evoked so much emotion that a tear escaped and ran down her cheek. She stopped to get a tissue from the pocket of her robe. As she did, she noticed that someone had entered the chapel. A man was making his way down the aisle toward her. In the dim light, she saw that he was walking slowly with the help of a walker. His head was down, his body leaning forward, as he concentrated on the difficult task.

Dayna closed the cover of the piano and prepared to leave so the man could have solitude, but he paused and motioned to her. "Please don't stop, that was beautiful."

She looked at his face as he said the words and Dayna realized that it was the man she'd seen playing the piano that morning.

"You're the piano man." As she said it, she realized how child-like it sounded.

He laughed. He had a deep, rich laugh that made Dayna feel immediately comfortable in his presence. He reached the front pew closest to the piano and sat down heavily, nearly out of breath.

"It's strange," he said. "Having to teach your body to do the basic things that you took for granted before. A couple of months ago, I could scramble up a rooftop, or walk a length of scaffolding, without giving it a thought."

"You couldn't play the piano, though."

"No, but I enjoyed listening to it. I always wished I could have taken more lessons when I was a kid, but money was tight."

"How did this happen?" Dayna's curiosity wouldn't let her pass up the opportunity. "You being able to play so well, now. I heard you this morning. I was really impressed."

"Thank-you." He looked into her eyes and Dayna noticed the same softness that she'd seen earlier.

"I don't know," he tried to explain. "I just kept hearing music in my head after the accident. I think it was some sort of survival mechanism. I almost didn't make it."

"What was that like?" Dayna felt strangely comfortable talking to the man. She was curious to find out if he had experienced any of the same things that she had.

"To nearly die?"

"Yes."

"Not what you'd think. It was peaceful. I felt like a power greater than me was in control. I'm not sure that I even wanted to come back, but it was the music; it kept drawing me. When I came to, I just knew I had to play. The nurses must have thought I'd lost it. I kept asking if there was a piano in the building. I couldn't even get out of bed for the first few weeks, but the music just kept playing in my head. I assumed it was music that I'd heard somewhere before, but people keep telling me that it's original."

"I believe it is. I've never heard it before." Dayna was tempted to tell him about the piece she'd heard when she was unconscious, but she decided not to. It was strange, to say the least. Instead, she asked. "Have you written any of it down?"

"I don't even know how. It's all just up here." He tapped his head.

"You really should have someone put it on paper. It's so beautiful. You could share it with the world."

"The job's available, if you're interested."

Dayna didn't know what to say. She hadn't given any thought to doing it herself, although she knew it was something that she could do.

"I... I don't know. I could... I guess," she hesitated, but as the thought began to settle in her mind, she felt a strange compulsion. Something was drawing her. All at once, she realized that it was something she actually wanted to do.

"Yes," she replied, confidently. "I'd be honored to do that for you."

* * *

Chapter 15

Rachael came out of the office with Brian following behind her. As she looked around the room, she saw Gail talking to Tracy by the bar. She went over to her and the two friends embraced.

"Sweetie." Gail gave Rachael a knowing look. "If you and Brian want to be alone…"

"Thanks," Rachael smiled back. "But he has something special planned for later. Let's have a drink. We have some catching up to do."

They moved to a table and both ordered drinks.

"Tough week?"

"Yes, and no," Rachael replied. "I'm sorry that Dayna had to go through that. It was scary for all of us. But you know, I believe something big is going to come out of this experience for her."

"What do you mean?"

Rachael told Gail about the music that both she and Dayna had heard. She told her about Madison's fascination with the piano man and about Dayna going to hear him play, earlier.

"Yes!" Gail exclaimed. "I saw him on the news. What an incredible story."

"Madison was adamant that he talked to her in her room one night," Rachael continued. "And Dayna says that the music she heard when she was unconscious was one of the original pieces he played in the chapel this morning. It's all so bizarre."

"Do you think that something supernatural is going on here?"

"What does 'supernatural' mean, anyway? Is it beyond the realm of possibility? I don't think so," Rachael responded. "I'm not sure what this is about yet, but I've been giving it a lot of thought."

"That doesn't surprise me," Gail laughed.

Rachael smiled, ignoring her friend's good-natured teasing. "There seems to be a connection."

"What do you think it is?"

"Well, music is the most obvious. Dayna's love and knowledge of music is a given. Madison may have made a connection between her mother's playing and the man she saw on TV. Who knows what compelled this man to begin composing and playing music?" Rachael shook her head, perplexed. "Whatever's going on, it seems to be powerful."

"That doesn't surprise me, either," Gail replied. "With Law of Attraction at work, anything's possible."

"I know. I've been thinking about that a lot, too. Given Dayna's emotional state, it's not surprising that she attracted a heart attack. The near-death experience seems to have caused a rendezvous with her Higher Self. And that makes sense because Mom said that Dayna was asking about God before the heart attack."

"Really? So then she has been asking some powerful questions."

"Yes. And I'm sure she has a lot more that she hasn't even voiced. But the music and the connection with that man," Rachael shrugged. "I haven't quite worked that one out yet."

Gail laughed and shook her head. "Stop the presses! 'Rachael Adams Stumped by Musical Mystery.' " She held up her hands as if framing the headline on the front page of the newspaper.

"Yes, it's true; I admit defeat," Rachael laughed with her, aware that she was probably questioning things too much. She reminded herself that whatever was happening, it was unfolding in its own perfect time. She sat back and sipped her drink.

"Mom says that Dad was like this, too. Questioning everything." Rachael looked into her drink. Suddenly, a thought occurred to her, "What's the date today?"

"The sixteenth. Why?"

"It'll be a year ago, Sunday, that Dad died."

"Are you going to do anything?"

"I don't know; I'd like to. I found a picture of him and had copies made and framed. I'd hoped to be able to give them to Greg and Dayna one day. I'm just not sure that Dayna's ready. Maybe I'll talk to Mom and see what she thinks."

* * *

"I can have my mom bring me some lined music paper. When would you like to begin?" Dayna felt excited about the project. The pieces that Mr. Radford had composed were really good. She even thought about contacting the head of the symphony in town to talk about incorporating some of his work—if he was open to that, of course.

"I've got all the time in the world right now," he laughed his deep laugh again.

"How long will you have to be in the hospital?"

"Unfortunately, I'll be here several more weeks yet. How about you?"

"I'm hoping to be able to go home the day after tomorrow," Dayna replied.

"Do you have family waiting for you?"

"Yes," Dayna replied. "I miss my kids, terribly. I have two girls. Madison's three and a half and Abigail will be turning one next week."

"Those are nice names," he said. "I have a daughter, too." Dayna could hear the pride in his voice. "Brianna. She's almost seventeen."

Dayna was enjoying the interaction. She'd lost track of time and wasn't even sure how long they'd been talking. As she looked around, she noticed that a couple of others had entered the sanctuary. She realized, too, that she was beginning to feel tired.

"Well, Mr. Radford, I should go back to my room. I assume that you'll be here as usual, tomorrow morning. Let's talk again and plan when we can start getting your music down on paper."

"That sounds fine, but please, call me Quinn." He held out his hand.

"Thanks," she smiled. "I'm Dayna."

* * *

Soft, classical music rose above the hum of voices as people enjoyed their meals. Subdued lighting created a pleasing ambiance. Rachael smiled as she followed the hostess to the little table by the window. It was the same table they'd sat at on their first date.

Brian pulled the chair out for her and, as Rachael sat down, her eyes were drawn, once again, to the spectacular view overlooking the river. The setting sun, the sparkling water—she took a moment to drink in the beauty.

"This is perfect." Rachael looked across the table at the wonderful man who was now her lover and her friend. She thought back to their first date, how nervous and excited she'd been. Brian had told her about a dream he'd had and then shared how he was feeling toward her. She'd been feeling the same—the same inexplicable knowing that he was the 'one.'

"I fell in love with you that first evening," Brian said, reading her thoughts.

She looked into his eyes and saw there a love so deep and so true; it was the same love that was reflected in her own heart.

"I knew it, too. My heart kept telling me that you were the one I'd been waiting for. My head wanted to argue that it was too soon, but my heart knew."

"I'm glad you listened to your heart," he smiled.

That smile could still make her heart skip a beat. Reaching across the table, she stroked his hand. She gazed at his handsome face, his smoky blue eyes, his dark hair and broad shoulders.

When the server came by to take their order, they laughed as they realized that, just like last time, they'd become so involved in each other, that they hadn't even looked at the menu.

Brian winked at Rachael as he asked the girl, "What's your special?"

She described a baked seafood fettuccini with creamed herb tomato sauce.

Rachael smiled at Brian and closed her menu. "I'm sold," she laughed. It was fun re-creating the details of their first date.

They each ordered the special and, when their server left, Brian picked up his glass and made a toast. "To always listening to our hearts."

Rachael lifted her glass and added, "And to always living in the moment."

She thought she noticed something in Brian's eyes as she said the words, but just as quickly, it was gone. They each took a sip of their wine.

The meal was delicious; the atmosphere, romantic; and their conversation, rich. Rachael's thoughts were on Brian and the wonderful time they were having together. Everything else was forgotten.

She absolutely loved living in the moment. Her motto had become,

> *"Content with where I am*
> *and eager for more."*[18]

It was the perfect vibrational stance. She'd lived so many years hating what her life was like and longing for change. Now, she'd found such freedom in knowing that the present moment was all there was, acknowledging that she had created it and realizing that whatever it held, it was perfect.

Their meal was finished and the girl cleared their plates. They both declined dessert and Rachael sat back to enjoy her wine. She noticed, again, a look in Brian's eyes. He sat forward, hands clasped. He didn't seem as relaxed as usual and she wondered what was on his mind. She was reminded of their second date and how shy he'd been in asking her back to his place. That seemed so long ago.

"Do you remember our date at that Lebanese restaurant?" she asked.

"Yeah," he nodded. "You taught me how to eat in a new way. Ever since then, I can't take a bite without noticing the smell first and then savoring the taste. Now I appreciate food more. I think it's a much healthier way to eat."

"How so?"

"I used to be able to eat a huge meal and then, when it was done, have no memory of what it tasted like. Now I've noticed that I consume less because I eat slower and enjoy the food more."

"That can apply to everything in life." Rachael thought about how much fuller her life was since she'd begun to be in the moment and appreciate things. " 'More' isn't always better and 'faster' can cause us to miss out on things. There's so much to enjoy in every moment."

"But how do you balance that with planning for the future? You must give some thought to the future." Brian sat back and ran his hand through his hair. It was an endearing habit that Rachael loved, but one he did when he was nervous or in a new situation.

"I guess I just believe that the future will unfold in line with my vibrational offering. I can't help but have desires, but if I get too caught up in the process or too attached to the results, I tend to offer resistance to the very thing I desire."

"I'm not sure I know what you mean."

"Well, for example, when I first started learning about this, I knew in my heart that it was what I'd been waiting my whole life to hear. It resonated with every fiber of my being. But I wasn't content with my life at that point. In fact, I still hated my life. At the same time, I was eager for more—for better, different experiences. I was out of balance.

"When you hate where you're at and you're so desperate for change, you become dependent on the outcome for your happiness. When you're waiting for something to change before you can be happy, that's a recipe for disaster.

"When I learned to be content with where I was at," Rachael continued, feeling the power of her words, "then things started to change. I have to admit, though, I spent a lot of time resisting the very things I wanted, by noticing they weren't there."

"That almost seems like a catch twenty-two," Brian frowned. "If you focus on your desires, you can't help but notice they're not there. And if you notice they're not there, they can't come to you, because you're focusing on the lack of them."

"Yup," Rachael laughed. "That pretty much sums it up."

"I know the solution, though. You've said it over and over." Brian's look softened. "You just have to find a way to think about it that feels better."

"Thinking about what I wanted, but didn't have, felt awful. I had to find a way to think about those things differently, or not at all. Learning to be content in the moment was a big part of that. So was learning to trust in my Higher Self—knowing that at some broader, cosmic level, I was the one in control of what was happening in my life. Understanding those things helped me to get into vibrational balance."

Brian smiled and caressed Rachael's hand. "You know, I never get tired of hearing you talk. You have so much wisdom. You continue to amaze me."

They sat for a moment, enjoying the silence and appreciating one another. Then Brian, with a hint of mischief in his eyes, leaned forward, taking both of Rachael's hands in his own. With his most alluring smile and one raised eyebrow, he asked, "How would you like to come back to my place?"

"Why, Mister DeWaltt," Rachael said, batting her eyelashes and mimicking Scarlett O'Hara. "I hope that means what I think it means."

They both laughed. The evening had been wonderful, a replica of their first date. Only this time, it wouldn't end with just a kiss.

* * *

"What's come over me? I've just agreed to work with a perfect stranger." As odd as it sounded to Dayna, it was how she felt about it that really surprised her. She felt excited. She felt inspired. She couldn't wait to begin.

There was something about his music that intrigued her, maybe even something about the man, himself.

"What is it about him?" she wondered. *"Is it his eyes? What do I know about him, anyway? He's a construction worker, a family man, a composer of exceptional music...*

"No, not a composer exactly." Dayna's thoughts drifted as she lay in her bed. *"A composer is a rare breed; he begins with an idea and carries it to completion. A composer understands notation and transposition. He uses melody, harmony and rhythm to create chords and series of chords, which together create a score...*

"No, Mr. Radford is unique... Quinn—what an interesting name. I've heard it as a last name, but never as a given name..."

Her mind was beginning to ramble. She wanted to sleep, but a new thought would come in and snap her into focus again.

"What would be the most practical way to get his music on paper?"

Dayna had a well-trained ear. She'd taken years of music theory and ear training. Listening to a scale, she could tell whether it was major or minor. She could distinguish intervals between notes as well as listen to a chord and identify the type—but all that would take hours of time.

"Time, Mr. Radford has, but I'm going home, Sunday. In order to accurately notate his music, we'll need more than just a couple of hours."

All at once, Dayna had an idea. *"If I could record him playing, I could work on it at home. I could listen to a section, put the notes down on paper and then confirm them on my own piano. Yes, that's the solution!"*

Pleased with herself, she closed her eyes. As Quinn's music began to play in her head, she determined the key, singled out the notes and began to write them down on the pages of her mind.

* * *

Chapter 16

Rachael smiled at the offer of breakfast in bed. Brian loved to make it for her. She had done the same for him a couple of times when they'd stayed at her place, but she was still fairly new in the cooking department, so she hadn't ventured to be very creative.

Laying back on her pillow and gazing out the window, she noticed that it was shaping up to be a beautiful day. The only thing visible in the crystalline sky was a jet, leaving a trail that slowly dissipated as Rachael watched. She closed her eyes, imagining the exciting destinations to which the airplane's occupants might be heading.

She'd already decided not to go to the hospital; her mom was planning to go, but could get there herself with Dayna's car. Sunday, she and Brian had offered to bring Dayna home. Rachael was looking forward to taking the girls with them, knowing how excited they would be to pick their mom up.

As for the day ahead, it felt good to have no definite plans.

"I don't care what I do today, as long as it's with Brian. Maybe we'll just stay in bed all day. Actually..." she smiled, *"that sounds rather appealing."*

As she contemplated the idea, she heard Brian coming down the hall. The door opened in front of him and the dogs entered the room. Duke had an envelope in his mouth and Cassie had a pink bow around her neck. Brian was standing behind them holding a tray. On it was an extremely large bouquet of red roses.

"What's all this?" Rachael laughed, trying to think of the possible reasons for the surprise. Brian often surprised her with flowers on their monthly anniversaries, but it wasn't that. It wasn't her birthday or any other special day that she knew of.

The dogs both looked toward Brian and waited. At his command, Duke went to the bed and placed the envelope on Rachael's lap. She gave Brian a questioning glance as she began to open it. He was smiling, but had a look in his eyes that she couldn't quite read.

The envelope contained a travel brochure for a resort in Tahiti. On the front, was a glossy picture of a long, white, sandy beach. It was lined with palm trees and there were grassy huts on stilts out in the water. Rachael looked up at Brian in astonishment.

He just smiled and set the tray down on the bed. Then he signaled Cassie. She went to Rachael and put her front paws up on the bed.

Rachael laughed and shook her head. "I don't know what you three are up to." She rubbed Cassie's ears, admiring the pink bow around her neck. "Don't you look pretty this morning."

Rachael's curiosity was getting the best of her. She was just about to ask Brian what was going on, when something caught her eye. Hanging from the bow around Cassie's neck was a diamond ring.

"Oh, my God!" Rachael's hands went to her mouth as she looked up at Brian.

"I thought Tahiti would be a nice place to go on our honeymoon." Brian went down on one knee beside the bed and took Rachael's hand. "If you'll marry me, that is."

* * *

Valerie drove to the hospital on her own, as Rachael was spending the day with Brian. She smiled at the wonderful relationship that was unfolding for her youngest daughter.

Valerie's excitement increased as she contemplated Dayna coming home the following day. She had been baking and cleaning, wanting everything to be perfect.

Mark was taking the girls to visit Dayna that morning also and was already there when Valerie arrived at the hospital.

"Grammy, we're going to see the pinano man!" Madison informed her as soon as she walked in the room.

"He plays every morning in the chapel," Dayna explained. "I thought it might be nice to go down and hear him."

"I'd love to." Valerie couldn't wait to hear the man play; Dayna spoke so highly of his music.

She was surprised at how many people were in the chapel when they arrived. It was nearly full. There weren't many seats together, so Mark pushed Dayna's wheelchair up to a pew with a couple of empty seats and then went to stand at the back. Dayna held Abigail on her lap and Valerie sat down with Madison in the pew.

Mr. Radford was already playing by the time they were seated and Valerie had to agree that he was very good. She was taken aback as she looked at him, though. For some reason, she had envisioned a smaller, more studious-looking man.

Madison was straining to see, so Valerie lifted her up on her lap. Valerie wasn't sure how long Madison would sit still. Her attention span was typical for a three-year-old. For the time being, she seemed riveted to the man playing the piano. Valerie wondered, again, why her granddaughter was so taken with him.

Looking over at Dayna, Valerie noticed that her eyes were closed and her head was moving, slightly, to the music. When the piece ended, she opened her eyes and looked at Valerie. Her countenance had changed; her eyes were sparkling and she was smiling.

"Isn't he amazing?" she whispered to her mother. Valerie couldn't disagree; she was enjoying the music. She didn't know much about the pieces he was playing, except that Dayna had said they were all original.

After a while, Abigail started to get restless. Valerie turned to signal Mark and he came to take the baby from Dayna.

"If you want to take Abby home, I'll keep Madison here with me," she whispered to Mark.

Mark left with the baby and Valerie sat back to enjoy the music. Madison remained focused on the big man at the piano. Several times during the performance, he turned and looked in their direction. At one point, he smiled at them.

Valerie had to admit that she liked the man; he seemed genuine. Whatever had happened, whatever sort of miracle it was, he was truly into the music that he was playing.

The concert ended and the audience applauded, enthusiastically. As people began to leave, Dayna leaned over, "I didn't tell you, but I talked to Mr. Radford last night. I came down here hoping to play the piano, myself, and he came in while I was playing. We started talking about his music and he asked if I would help him put it on paper."

"What did you say?" Valerie was surprised that he would ask her to do that.

"I said 'yes'."

"But how? When?"

Mr. Radford was still sitting at the piano. Several people were standing around him, asking him questions. He glanced their way again.

"Let me introduce you to him," Dayna said.

Madison jumped off Valerie's lap and darted to the front where the man was sitting. Valerie got up to push Dayna's wheelchair, but Dayna insisted, "I can walk."

At the front, they waited a moment for a couple who were congratulating him. After the couple left, he turned to them and smiled.

"Mr. Radford... Quinn," Dayna corrected herself. "This is my mother, Valerie Adams and my daughter, Madison."

He shook Valerie's hand and then turned to the child beside him, "Well, Madison, we meet again. Do you like music?"

Madison giggled and nodded.

"Can you play the piano?" He lifted her up on the bench beside him and she proceeded to play a scale with one finger.

"Very good, Madison," he praised. "Did your mommy teach you that? I've heard her play; I know she's very good." He smiled at Dayna as he said the words.

"My mommy plays the pinano for me at home and she sings to me. My daddy sings, too, but he sounds funny." Madison seemed totally at ease as she continued to talk to Quinn. "Daddy had to take my baby sister home. She was fussy.

"I drew a picture," she announced, pulling a folded drawing out of her pink, flowered purse. "It's for my mommy; she's coming home tomorrow."

Valerie watched the interaction between her granddaughter and Mr. Radford. Madison acted as if she'd known the man all her life. She wasn't exactly shy around strangers, but Valerie had never seen her that outgoing, either.

They all looked at Madison's picture and praised her work. Then Dayna turned to Quinn, "I've been thinking about how to notate your music. The most practical way would be to record it. Then I could listen to it at home and put the notes down on paper."

"Yeah, that would work," he replied.

"I have a voice recorder at home. I use it when I'm making my lesson plans." She looked at Valerie, "Maybe you could bring it tomorrow morning, early enough so that we could set it up before Quinn starts to play. Mark will know where it is."

"Sure, I can do that." Valerie marveled, again, at Dayna's interest in helping the man. It wasn't like her daughter to simply do a favor for a stranger; she wasn't one who had a hard time saying no to people.

There was something else going on. Obviously, Dayna's love for music played a big part in it. It was her claim to have heard him playing while she was unconscious, however, that puzzled Valerie. She still couldn't understand how that was possible.

"So you're a teacher," Quinn said to Dayna. "May I assume you teach music?"

"No, actually I teach courses on Shakespeare at the University. I'm an assistant professor in the English department."

"Sounds like you have your hands full with work and your family," he said, looking down at Madison, still sitting beside him. "Are you sure you want to take on my music?"

"I'll be off work for several weeks yet; I had a heart attack." She noticed his surprised look and explained, "Apparently, I had a faulty heart valve, but they've given me a nice new one. Besides, this will give me something to do. I'm not used to just sitting around doing nothing."

"I really appreciate this."

Valerie noticed a look in Quinn's eyes as he spoke to Dayna. He seemed like a kind, honest man, but she noticed something else. She'd seen that look in a man's eyes before. He was attracted to Dayna. Valerie wondered if Dayna was aware of it, if maybe she was feeling something, too.

"He's not the polished, sophisticated type that Dayna is normally attracted to," Valerie reasoned. *"But there's something in his eyes that doesn't match the rest of him. I feel like I've known him for years. Maybe that's what Madison sees, too. Children notice things like that; they're able to read people better than adults do."*

It was time to leave and they said their good-byes to Quinn. As they headed back to Dayna's room, Valerie commented, "What an interesting man."

"I like the pinano man," Madison declared.

"His name is Mr. Radford, sweetie."

"Mistu Wadferd," Madison repeated, in an attempt to pronounce his name. She looked up at her mother. "He likes us, too."

* * *

Rachael couldn't speak. Nearly overcome with emotion, she wasn't sure whether to laugh or cry. Then she looked into Brian's eyes and saw the question still waiting there. She laughed, "Yes. Yes! Oh my God, yes!"

As she threw her arms around his neck, she heard an audible sigh of relief. Rachael leaned back and looked at him. She stroked his face as she asked, "Did you think I might say no?"

"All this talk about being in the moment and then Dayna's husband cheating on her... I wasn't sure how you felt about marriage or planning for the future. I've wanted to ask you for weeks; I was just waiting for the right time."

"Brian, all I know is how I feel right now. I love you more than anyone else in the world. I want to be with you all the time; I miss you every moment we're not together. I love your family. I love your dogs. I love what you do. I love everything about you." She paused and kissed him, tenderly.

"And right now, the thought of being your wife fills me with more joy than I could have ever imagined." She couldn't stop the flow of tears. They were tears of joy and she welcomed them.

Brian took her in his arms and they held each other silently for a moment. Then, as the reality of it started to sink in, Rachael realized that the ring was still on Cassie's ribbon.

"Cassie, come here!" The dog had gone out of the bedroom, but came running back at the sound of Rachael's voice. "I want to see my ring!"

Brian removed the ribbon and untied the ring. He took Rachael's hand and slipped the ring on her finger. A brilliant, round-cut solitaire diamond, set on a band of yellow gold, it was the most stunning ring that Rachael had ever seen in her life.

"Oh, Brian!" she gasped. "This is beautiful."

"Do you like it?" he asked. "I've looked at dozens, but you know...this is one of the first ones that I saw and I liked it the best. It reminds me of you. You're so perfect; your beauty is natural and pure. This ring seems to reflect that."

Listening to Brian speak such loving words, Rachael silently thanked her Inner Being. She lay back down on the pillow and held her hand up in the air. The diamond caught the light, sparkling brilliantly as she turned her hand.

As she lay there, several thoughts surfaced at once. "Does anybody else know?"

"Tracy caught me looking at a ring catalogue one day, but I swore her to secrecy. I wanted us to tell everyone together."

"I thought she gave me a funny look, yesterday, when I told Gail that you had a surprise planned," Rachael laughed.

"So now..." she began to think aloud. "We get to plan when and where. I'm not sure where, but I know I don't want a long engagement."

"What do you think of a June wedding?"

June sounded good—not too far away, but enough time to plan and invite guests. "A June wedding," Rachael nodded. "That feels good."

"We have five Saturdays to choose from." Brian listed the possible dates.

"You have been giving this a lot of thought." Rachael loved that he'd spent so much time picking the ring and thinking about dates. "Let's check out possible locations and find out which dates will work. Do you have any ideas about where to have it?" she asked. Brian had lived in the city all his life and was more familiar with its amenities.

"It depends. Do you want a church wedding?"

"Not particularly," she shook her head. "Actually, I'd love an outdoor wedding."

They spent the next hour talking about possible locations and who would officiate. Brian knew of some officials who could perform the ceremony. He suggested a golf and country club as a possible location. He'd bought his dad a membership at one several years back. It was located just outside the city and had nice grounds around the clubhouse. Brian had even been to a wedding there once.

Rachael knew that all the details would fall into place. It would be fun to plan the wedding. She knew she wanted Gail to be her maid of honor; Rachael couldn't wait to ask her—and, of course, go shopping for the perfect wedding dress.

She couldn't wait to tell her family. They'd all be together tomorrow. Her mom was having everyone over at Dayna's and was putting on a big meal to welcome her home. That would be perfect!

"Let's surprise your mom and dad!" Rachael knew how excited Brian's parents would be. "Why don't we go over there and tell them right away?"

"Sure," Brian agreed. "Then let's take a drive out to the golf and country club. I want to see what you think of it. If we like it, we should book it right away."

Rachael got up. She took a moment to dance around the room before she went into the bathroom to get ready. She felt at home at Brian's now; she stayed there almost every weekend.

All of a sudden, a new thought occurred to her. "Where will we live?"

"I've given that a lot of thought, too," Brian replied. "To be honest, I'd live anywhere. I just want to be with you."

Rachael continued to think about it as she brushed her hair. It wasn't quite as easy as the other decisions had been. She loved Brian's place—living there made the most sense because of the dogs, but the thought of giving up her own cute, little house left her with a slight sadness.

The feeling didn't last, though. There was too much else to be excited about. She knew that they would find a perfect solution and she didn't want to spend any more time thinking about what wouldn't work. Besides, she felt the same as Brian. She just wanted to be together, wherever that was.

* * *

Chapter 17

Before Valerie left with Madison, they spent some time visiting with Dayna in her room. Dayna enjoyed the company and found it harder to say good-bye than she had on the previous days. She just wanted to go home. One more day seemed like an eternity.

She really didn't like being idle and was beginning to think that it might have been the reason she'd jumped at the chance to help Quinn with his music. Whatever her motivation, she truly was looking forward to it.

Dayna was also looking forward to her mom's home-cooked meal the following day. It would be nice to have her whole family there to welcome her home; she wanted to see them all. She wanted to thank them, too.

Valerie reminded her that it had been a year since her dad had passed away. Dayna's experience in the hospital made her realize how short life really was. She hadn't taken the opportunity to make amends with her father before he passed away—she would have to live with that. But the rest of her family was alive and she wanted to let them know how much they meant to her.

Dayna had been angry with her father for so long. She'd hated him. She'd let that anger affect every aspect of her life.

"All that bitterness and hate," Dayna closed her eyes, as if doing so would erase it from her experience. *"I thought I was justified in feeling that way. I became a hard, cynical person—only to find out that my father wasn't totally at fault."*

As for the things that her mom had shared, Dayna realized that she no longer felt any resentment toward her, either. It was in the past; she wanted to move forward now.

When it came to Mark, however, she wasn't sure that she could just forgive and forget. What he did hurt her deeply, but she knew she'd have to find a way to forgive him, too, and move on with her life. She didn't want to continue living in anger the way she had been doing. The cost was too great.

She remembered something she'd read in Rachael's book. She reached for it again and flipped through until she found the page. It talked about changing the basic pattern of one's thought in order to change circumstances.

"Is it really possible that my thoughts affect my circumstances?" she wondered.

Dayna knew that the mind was a powerful thing. She even believed in mind over matter to some degree. Now, she wanted to know more about the new ideas. She opened the book and began to read.

The more she read, the more she could feel the concepts in the book resonating with her and yet she still had so many questions. She wished she could talk to someone about it. The idea of talking to Rachael felt comfortable, now, but Dayna didn't know whether her sister would be stopping by or not.

She closed the book, feeling somewhat restless. The thought of spending time in the chapel, again, appealed to her. Hoping that she might find it empty on a Saturday afternoon, she decided to go. The nurse at the desk could always direct Rachael down there if she came to visit.

Hospital policy wouldn't allow her to venture very far unattended without a wheelchair—even though Dayna saw it as unnecessary. It was just one more reason that she would be grateful to be in her own home again.

Dayna closed her eyes and tried to imagine herself there already, seeing her girls every day, sleeping in her own bed, eating what and when she wanted to and playing her piano—how she missed her piano!

She'd taken those things for granted before, but now she knew that life's small pleasures were meant to be appreciated.

She walked to the nurse's station and informed them that she wanted to go down to the chapel.

The nurse looked at her watch. "They'll be setting up for tomorrow's mass. You can go down if you like, but you might not find peace and quiet, if that's what you're looking for."

"Oh," Dayna hesitated. "Maybe I'll wait until later, then."

The nurse smiled at Dayna, "The terrace is nice this time of day. There's still some sun, but there's shade also if it gets too warm."

"That sounds nice."

"You should be fine without a wheelchair. It's just down at the end of that corridor." The nurse pointed the way.

Dayna felt free, being able to go somewhere without a wheelchair or an attendant. It would be nice to be outside again, too. She found the terrace easily. It was a good size and had large pots with trees and flowers separating the benches. Wanting to feel the warm sun on her skin, she chose one that was drenched in full sunlight. As she sat down, she turned her face to the glorious rays and closed her eyes.

"It's my favorite place this time of day, too."

Dayna was startled by the voice. She hadn't seen anyone else when she arrived, but as she looked around, she noticed that just down from her, almost hidden by a large, flowering shrub, was another bench. Quinn was looking over and smiling her way.

"Hi, Quinn," she smiled back. "Yes, it is beautiful out here. I didn't know about this spot until today, or I would have taken advantage of it sooner."

"I was used to spending my days outside, so being indoors all the time was driving me crazy. Now, I come up here every chance I get."

"Do you mind if I join you?" Dayna asked. It was awkward, talking around the bush.

"Please do," he replied. "I'd like the company."

Dayna moved over to the next bench and sat down on the end opposite Quinn. She had to smile at his outfit. Under a brown velour robe, he was wearing blue pajamas with yellow and green musical notes all over them.

He noticed her smile and, with a slight hint of embarrassment, said, "My daughter looked all over to find this fabric. She made me these in her sewing class in school." Even as he blushed, Dayna could hear the pride in his voice again. He was obviously very close to his daughter.

"They're very nice," Dayna said, politely, not wanting to add to his embarrassment.

"I really enjoyed your music again this morning," she continued, changing the topic.

"Thank-you," he replied. "I looked over once and noticed that you had your eyes closed and your head was moving to the music. I almost lost track of where I was in the song, just watching you."

"I was listening for the notes and determining the intervals between them. If I'd had some staff paper with me, I would have written them down."

"I've obviously found the right person for the job," he said. "I know I said it already, but thank-you. This means a lot to me."

"Well, I haven't done anything yet." Dayna looked away; she'd always felt somewhat awkward with people showing gratitude, but she decided to add, "I am looking forward to it, though."

The uncomfortable moment was quickly forgotten when Quinn said, "You asked me the other day what it was like to nearly die."

"Yes."

"I was wondering..." he hesitated. "Did you experience that, too?"

"They said it was pretty serious." Dayna looked out at the city skyline as she spoke. "They never tell you the worst, but I know I'm lucky to be alive. I'm starting to look at life differently, now."

"In what way?"

Dayna wasn't sure why she felt comfortable with Quinn; she sensed it was because he could relate to the things that she had experienced.

"I didn't realize it before, but I had a lot of anger and unforgiveness—especially toward my family. I'd become cold and cynical about life…"

Dayna could feel her emotions close to the surface and, rather than try to suppress them as she had in the past, she decided to be honest—even if it meant being vulnerable. "I don't want to be like that anymore. I want to learn what it means to really live." Dayna felt a tear run down her face as she said the words. She wiped it away with her hand.

"I know what you mean." Quinn reached in the pocket of his robe, pulled out a tissue and handed it to her.

"Thanks." She dabbed at her eyes with the tissue. "This is new for me, too. I was always in control of my emotions before."

"I was a workaholic," Quinn admitted. "Every part of my life suffered because of it—my marriage, my relationship with my daughter. I missed most of her childhood because I was always busy. I guess I needed a wake-up call."

"Do you believe in God?" he asked after another brief silence.

She smiled. It was uncanny how he could relate to a lot of the same things that she was feeling. "Yes," she said, simply. "I do now."

"I have to admit, I'm confused about just who or what God is. The image I had of God, growing up, came from my religious grandparents. Their concept of God scared the hell out of me... literally," he laughed. "I spent so much time on my knees as a kid, it's a wonder I ever learned how to walk."

Dayna couldn't help but laugh; Quinn had a delightful sense of humor.

"But the things I experienced after the accident..." he continued, becoming serious. "They caused me to see things differently. I felt this all-encompassing presence that gave me confidence. I felt protected and loved. It was so different from the image that I had of God—which was outside of me, separate somehow, and always judging."

Dayna couldn't believe it; he had just described her own experience. She began crying again and Quinn reached over, gently touching her shoulder.

"You, too?"

All she could do was nod. It took her a minute to be able to speak. "I always thought of God as a crutch for weak-minded people who couldn't think on their own. But I felt what you just described and now… I feel like God is actually a part of me."

"I started hearing music." Quinn continued sharing his experience. "And it felt like it was coming from that new-found part of me. Now when I play, I feel like I'm connected to it—like I'm connected to God."

Dayna felt a connectedness when she played; she always had. Only now, she was beginning to understand what that feeling was and where it was coming from.

That understanding should have brought her comfort. Instead, it left Dayna with mixed emotions. The things that Quinn was sharing were remarkably similar to her own experiences. It was almost too much, though. Something was happening between them and it left Dayna feeling uncomfortable.

"Music does that for me, too," she replied, politely, trying to disregard the anxiety that was growing within her.

"I could tell." Quinn looked at her, pensively. "When I saw you playing in the chapel last night, I could feel it. I could hear it in your music—it made me feel the same way that I feel when I play."

Again, Dayna wanted to tell him about hearing his music when she was unconscious. The impulse was strong, but something was holding her back. It was too intimate, too personal.

She was feeling something toward Quinn and it was beginning to scare her. She wasn't attracted to him, at least not physically, but something about his personality, his openness and the way that they had just shared their experiences, left her in unfamiliar territory. It left her feeling vulnerable, as if she needed to protect herself, but she wasn't sure from what.

"Well, I should really go back to my room now," she said, almost abruptly. "It must be getting close to dinnertime."

She saw the surprised look on his face and added, "I really enjoyed talking to you, Quinn. I'll see you tomorrow. My mother is bringing the voice recorder. What time will you start playing?"

"Mass is at nine o'clock. It lasts about an hour. I usually start to play right after that."

"Okay, we'll see you then."

Dayna didn't know what had come over her, but she had to leave. She hadn't intended to be rude; she truly hoped that he hadn't taken it that way. She'd never in her life shared her feelings with anyone like she had just done, let alone a stranger, a man she barely knew.

"So why doesn't he feel like a stranger?" she questioned. *"Why do I feel comfortable enough to share my thoughts and deepest feelings with him?*

"And why, now, do I suddenly feel vulnerable?"

He'd touched her—not inappropriately—just lightly on the shoulder when she was crying. She didn't mind being comforted, but she realized, now, that it was the touch that had caused her to see him in a different light.

She'd been fascinated by his story, his sudden ability to play the piano. She'd seen him as a fellow patient, a gifted musician, someone who could relate to having nearly died... but she hadn't seen him as a man.

"Have I shared too much? Have I crossed some line, become too personal, too intimate? He's a married man—at least I assume he is. He's not wearing a ring, but that's not unusual for a hospital patient. He mentioned that his marriage had suffered, but he didn't say that it had ended."

Suddenly, she felt foolish for not having recognized it sooner. *"Married or not, the last thing I intend to do is lead him on. I'm not the least bit interested in him in that way. Our relationship is strictly business!"*

Dayna reproached herself and determined to be more careful in the future. She didn't want to send any wrong messages.

* * *

Rachael didn't know what time it was, but she was too excited to sleep, so she lay there thinking about the wonderful day that she'd just had. Brian's parents had been ecstatic when they'd told them the news. His mom had cried and hugged both Rachael and Brian, and his dad had welcomed her into their family.

They'd invited his parents to go with them for a drive out to the golf and country club. They'd all agreed that it was the perfect location and had booked it for their wedding and reception on June twenty-third.

"I'm getting married on June twenty-third!" As she made the proclamation in her head, she felt a fresh burst of excitement.

They'd started to make up a guest list. The facility could hold up to two hundred guests. Rachael couldn't even imagine inviting that many people. When she added up everyone that she knew on her side, including immediate family, relatives and friends, it only came to forty-seven. Brian, on the other hand, had a lot of relatives, as well as friends and close business acquaintances.

"We'll need to pick out invitations right away and get them mailed out." She began making a mental list of the things they'd need to do.

"Brian said he'd talk to someone about officiating the ceremony. We'll have to decide on live music or a DJ... I think I'd prefer live music.

"And my dress!" She stopped to imagine what style of wedding dress she wanted. *"Something sleek and elegant, or something out of a fairytale with lots of ruffles and lace?"* She wasn't sure, but she did know that her perfect gown was out there and she couldn't wait to begin looking.

There was no point in even trying to sleep. She thought about waking Brian and making passionate love. Just the thought of it made her smile.

Instead, she focused on the day ahead. She'd already talked to her mom to make plans for Dayna's homecoming. It had taken immense restraint not to share her exciting news. They were planning to stop by early in case her mom needed help with the dinner. She couldn't wait to pick Dayna up from the hospital in the afternoon, as well.

"When would be the best time to announce our engagement?" She pondered her options. *"I could hide my ring, then wait and tell everyone at the dinner table.*

"No" she resolved. *"I don't want to take my ring off—not even for a moment."* She gazed at her beautiful ring again. Even in the dim morning light, it sparkled.

Telling each family member as the moment presented itself felt better. She hated keeping secrets and didn't want to hide her excitement. *"Why wait a moment longer than I have to? I want to share this news with everyone!"*

Looking at Brian, she noticed a slight smile flash across his face and she wondered if he was dreaming about her. She couldn't resist reaching over to stroke his face; he was such a good-looking man.

As Rachael ran her fingers through his hair, he moaned slightly. She touched his shoulder, ever so lightly and then ran her finger down his chest. He moaned again and stirred.

He smiled, eyes still closed, and turned toward her. She kissed his forehead and nose. He put his arm around her and opened his eyes as she kissed his lips. He gazed into her eyes, for a moment, with a look that told of his unending love. Then he pulled her body close and returned the kiss.

That dear, wonderful man was to become her husband. He was hers and she was his. She loved every moment with him, but the closeness she was feeling in that moment, the uniting of body and soul—Rachael was sure that there was nothing on earth, or in heaven, that could compare to the ecstasy that she felt in his arms.

* * *

Chapter 18

Valerie awoke early. There was a lot to do in the hours ahead and she was excited. She had a big meal planned in honor of Dayna arriving home from the hospital, but even more exciting was the thought of her whole family being together. It was enough to bring tears to her eyes.

It wasn't even just the fact that they were going to be together, physically; it was more than that. What really excited her was all the change that had taken place—especially the openness in Dayna and the fact that Valerie had finally shared her secret with her girls. She still hadn't told Greg, but she hoped that the opportunity would arise as the day progressed. If not, she decided to make a point of visiting Greg and Amy in the upcoming week to tell them about Stephanie.

She got the turkey ready to go into the oven. There would be plenty of time to put it in when she got back from visiting Dayna.

Mark was planning to stay with the children until she got back. It had been awkward, at times, with him there all week, but Valerie knew that it was the best thing for the girls. She just hoped that the excitement of having their mother back home would keep Madison from questioning why her father had to leave again.

Dayna had called the evening before to remind Valerie to bring the voice recorder and to let her know that Quinn would be playing at ten o'clock that morning. Mark found the recorder in Dayna's office and checked to make sure the batteries worked. It was in her purse, now, ready to go.

Valerie made sure that she got to the hospital in plenty of time, so that she could spend a few minutes with Dayna before they went down to the chapel. When she arrived, Dayna had just come back from having a bath. The beaming smile on her face warmed Valerie's heart. It was so good to see her daughter smile. She was an attractive woman, but the smile really brought out her beauty.

"You look beautiful," Valerie said as she squeezed Dayna's hand. "And happy."

"I'll be even happier when I can walk into my house, sit on my sofa, eat at my table and sleep in my own bed," she laughed. "But you know what I've missed more than anything? Tucking the girls in at night."

"They've missed it, too."

The nurse entered the room as they were talking. "Dayna, the doctor will be in this morning to see you. Then, hopefully, you'll be free to go home."

"Do you know what time he's coming in?"

"Oh, no dear," she laughed. "And I can't predict the weather, either. Dr. Lee is one of the more reliable ones, though; he's usually within an hour or so of when he says he'll be in."

When she left, Dayna sighed, "I guess I won't be able to go down to the chapel. Do you think you could go down and tape Quinn playing?"

"Sure, honey. I don't mind, but I'm sorry you won't be able to go. Is there anything you need to talk to him about before you leave the hospital? Do you have a way of getting in touch with him if you have any questions about his music?"

"No. I just assumed that I'd be seeing him this morning. We should probably arrange something," Dayna replied.

"Maybe you could meet with him before you leave today. Do you know where his room is?"

"No," Dayna shook her head. "I don't, but I can ask at the desk."

Valerie looked at her watch. "I should go down; he'll be starting in ten minutes or so."

She took the recorder out of her purse. "Mark showed me how to use this, so I think I'll be fine."

As she turned to go, she added, "I'll tell Quinn that you'd like to see him before you leave."

"Thanks."

Valerie noticed her daughter's disappointment. It was obvious that she really wanted to hear Quinn play again. It was an odd connection that Dayna had with Quinn. She was helping him with his music, but Valerie sensed something more. She'd seen the way that Quinn had looked at Dayna.

"Dayna's not ready to be in another relationship; it's too soon," Valerie reasoned. *"And Quinn... he's a bit of a mystery. I wonder what his situation is. Still, there's something there—something in the music that seems to connect them at a deeper level. I wonder if Dayna even understands what's happening."*

As the elevator door closed, Valerie breathed deeply and allowed her thoughts to dissipate. She didn't want to worry or get caught up in the details of Dayna's personal life. She wanted to trust the Law of Attraction to work things out in the way that she knew it could.

Mass was still on when Valerie arrived at the chapel. Quinn was waiting outside the main doors. He smiled, politely, as she walked up, but his eyes looked past her.

"Dayna's doctor is coming in this morning to examine her before she goes home," Valerie explained. "She had to stay and wait for him. I brought the recorder."

"Do you know what time she's going home? I was hoping to talk to her before she leaves."

"She was hoping to see you, too. I guess it all depends on when the doctor comes. Maybe you could stop by her room after lunch," Valerie suggested, giving him Dayna's room number.

A few people were starting to leave the chapel, indicating that mass had ended, but many were staying to hear Quinn play. Quinn and Valerie made their way to the front of the chapel. Valerie set the recorder on top of the piano, turned it on and then sat down to listen to Quinn's music.

She'd been distracted the day before, by Madison on her lap and by watching Dayna's reaction to the music, but this time, Quinn had Valerie's full attention. She noticed the way he seemed to be at one with his music. The look on his face told her that he was completely absorbed in the task of playing; he looked serene. At times, his eyes were closed. He allowed himself to flow fully into the pieces that he played.

The songs were all different, but there was a quality about them that made them similar. His style was unique. It was more than just the combination of notes; it was how they were flowing through him. Valerie got the sense, just watching him, that it was some kind of spiritual experience. She could see why Dayna was so captivated by the music and by the man, himself.

* * *

As Dayna sat and waited for the doctor, she tried to think about going home; it was so close now. But her mind kept going to Quinn. She felt bad for how abrupt she'd been the previous day.

"Maybe I jumped to conclusions too quickly, yesterday. Quinn seems like a kind man and he's just had a life-altering experience. Why should I assume that, just because he's a man, there's anything other than friendship happening between us? And what's wrong with having him as a friend, anyway?" Dayna asked herself.

"I like how easy it is to talk with him. We could have a business relationship and a friendship, as well," she rationalized. *"I just don't like the thought of having to be guarded around him.*

"But really, there's no reason to feel I have to be," Dayna argued. *"Quinn hasn't done or said anything to imply that he's interested in more than friendship. I know how lonely it gets in here. If we'd met in any other setting, we likely wouldn't have had two words to say to each other.*

"I'm just being paranoid," she scolded herself. *We may not even see each other after today. Once I*

finish getting these pieces down on paper, who knows if he'll ask me to do any more."

Dayna was feeling better about the whole situation, although still a little foolish for becoming so irrational about it. She tried to let it go as she busied herself getting her things together. The flowers she'd received had been beautiful, but weren't worth taking home. The hospital could dispose of them. She put Rachael's book in her overnight bag, along with Madison's drawings. Valerie had brought in a picture of the girls. Dayna looked at her precious daughters, once more, and smiled as she put the picture in her bag.

When she was finished, she looked at the time and realized that it was almost noon. She felt a little frustrated, knowing that she could have gone down to the chapel and still have been back in time for her check-up.

She sat down and took a deep breath. *"I'm going home. Soon, I'll be at home with my girls. That's all I want to think about right now."*

Valerie walked in just then and, as she looked at Dayna, her eyes asked the question.

"No," Dayna shook her head. "The doctor hasn't come yet. I'm still waiting."

"That's too bad," Valerie replied, as she handed Dayna the recorder. "I hope this taped everything okay. Quinn said that he'd like to talk to you, before you go, so I gave him your room number and suggested he stop by after lunch."

Dayna realized that she was looking forward to seeing him, too. Not only did she need to make arrangements to get his music to him, but she also wanted to get past the feelings that she was having. She wanted to prove to herself that she was being irrational and that she could treat their interaction as a casual business relationship and nothing more.

"I need to get back and get the turkey in the oven," Valerie said. "Rachael and Brian offered to come pick you up. Should I just have them wait for your call?"

"I guess that makes the most sense. Hopefully, it won't be too long."

Valerie left and shortly afterwards, a woman came in with Dayna's lunch. As she ate, Dayna tried to imagine the delicious home-cooked meal that she would be enjoying later on. It helped to make the dry veal cutlet and plain white rice a little more palatable.

She noticed the voice recorder on the bed beside her and decided to listen as she finished her meal. As she turned it on, Quinn's distinctive music filled the room.

The sound quality was good. She could easily distinguish the notes he was playing and would have no problem with the notation process.

Pleased with the success of the recording, she hummed along with the music as she took the cover off her dessert bowl.

"The fruit salad's not bad today. I had three cherries in mine."

Dayna looked up to see Quinn in her doorway. She laughed, "I'm just glad it's not tapioca again."

"No, tapioca is Monday, Wednesday and Friday. Rice pudding is Tuesday and Saturday and fruit salad is Thursday and Sunday."

"Are you serious?" Dayna gasped. "Is it really the same every week?"

"It is," Quinn nodded. "I can tell you the breakfast, lunch and dinner menu every day, as well."

"Spare me, please," Dayna raised her hand in mock protest, enjoying the exchange.

"Sounds like the music recorded okay." He was still in the doorway, so Dayna invited him in.

"I'm sorry that I couldn't come down to hear you this morning," Dayna apologized. "I'm still waiting for the doctor."

"They're famous for making you wait in here," Quinn replied. "Why is it that time flies by so quickly in everyday life, but in here, it drags on forever?" Dayna detected a hint of sadness in his voice.

"Maybe part of us knows that we need to take time to slow down. It gives us the opportunity to remember things that we've forgotten." Dayna listened to herself say the words and realized that she didn't even know where they'd come from. Nevertheless, they sounded profound.

"I like that," he said. "Do you think that maybe there's some older, wiser part of us that knows all this stuff and is trying to remind us of it?"

"It's possible," she shrugged and then shook her head, "This is all so new to me; I don't really know what I think."

The doctor entered the room just then and greeted Dayna. "So who's ready to go home?"

"My suitcase is packed." She patted the bag on the bed beside her. "I just need your okay." Dayna turned off the recorder.

"That was really nice," the doctor smiled. "Who was it?"

"It's Mr. Radford, here," Dayna gestured. "He's been playing down in the chapel."

"I've heard about you." The doctor turned and shook Quinn's hand. "Congratulations. You've put this hospital on the map."

"Apparently, I have," Quinn shrugged and smiled weakly. "Thank-you." He seemed uneasy with compliments. Dayna felt for him.

"Dayna, I'll be out on the terrace."

"Okay, I'll stop out there before I leave."

The examination went quickly. Dayna was recovering well. She had to go and see the doctor in his office in a couple of days, so that he could do a complete exam. So far, he seemed to think that the operation had been a total success. All she needed now was a few weeks of rest before she resumed regular activities.

Dayna was elated. When the doctor left, she quickly changed into her clothes. It felt odd after being in bedclothes for a whole week. She realized that she'd lost a few pounds; her pants felt loose. She did up the buttons on the blouse her mom had brought her. Then she looked in the mirror. She'd already combed her hair, but now she decided to put on a bit of make-up. She was still rather pale from spending a week in bed and she didn't want to look like a hospital patient any longer.

Satisfied with the result, she stopped at the nurse's station to call home, letting them know that she was ready to leave and that she would be out on the terrace when Rachael and Brian arrived.

* * *

Chapter 19

Rachael and Brian arrived at Dayna's place, after going out for a nice brunch at their favorite sidewalk café. It had been lovely, but Rachael could hardly contain her excitement about telling her family the news.

They walked in the house, just as Mark was leaving. Madison had been clinging to her dad, but got excited when she saw her Aunt Rachael. Mark mouthed a thank-you to Rachael and slipped out quietly. He had an overnight bag in his hand. Rachael still found it strange to think that he didn't live there anymore.

Rachael's thoughts quickly turned to her nieces. She gave them each hugs and kisses. They were still a little shy around Brian; they'd only seen him once or twice. He knelt down to Madison's level and complimented her on her dress.

"My mommy's coming home today. I want to look pretty."

"You look very pretty," Brian said with conviction. That was all it took for Madison to warm up to him. She took his hand and began to lead him to the kitchen. "I'm helping Grammy make dinner," she said, proudly.

"Aren't you a big girl!"

Madison giggled at his compliment, as Rachael stood watching the interaction with excitement. She hugged Abigail tightly in her arms and kissed the little one, her mind filled with thoughts of having children one day with Brian. She'd seen him with his nieces and nephew; she knew he loved kids and couldn't wait to talk to him about it. There was so much to talk about, now that they had created a future pathway to walk down together.

Valerie smiled as the troop entered the kitchen. "I have lunch ready for the girls. Have you eaten?"

Rachael put Abigail in her highchair while Brian helped Madison into her booster seat. "Yes, we just went out for brunch."

She was bursting with her news and didn't want to wait a moment longer. Taking Brian's hand, she proudly announced, "Mom, Brian and I are getting married."

Valerie set down the fork full of macaroni she was about to feed Abigail. She went and hugged Rachael and then Brian. "I couldn't be happier for you both!" she cried. She took Rachael's hand and looked at her ring. "Oh, Rachael, it's stunning. Have you set a date?"

"June twenty-third, at Orchard Valley Golf and Country Club. We just booked it yesterday. It's really nice out there."

"I know," Valerie smiled. "It's where your dad and I had our reception."

"Really? How come I didn't know that?"

"It's changed names since then. It used to be called Ridgeholm, after the original owners."

"That's right," Brian said. "The new owners did a major renovation about five years ago. It was getting a bit run-down. That's when I bought the membership for my dad."

The phone rang and Valerie answered it. "That was Dayna. She's ready to come home."

Rachael looked at Brian, anticipation evident on her face. "Let's take the girls with us."

"Why don't you take Madison," Valerie suggested. "Abby needs a nap right away. I want her to be rested when Dayna gets here."

"Madison, do you want to come with us to pick up your mommy at the hospital?" Rachael asked, knowing what her response would be.

No words were needed. Madison squealed and bounced up and down, trying to get out of her booster seat. Brian went and helped her out. Then he picked up a napkin and wiped cheese sauce off her chin. Rachael smiled as she observed, again, how comfortable he was around children.

They were just about to leave, when Valerie called out, "Oh, I forgot; Dayna said she'd be waiting out on the terrace."

Madison was talkative as they drove, but in a quiet interval, Rachael leaned over and said softly to Brian, "I'm looking forward to having kids with you."

He glanced at her and smiled, "How many?"

"I don't know, two, maybe three." She looked up, thoughtfully, as if there were an image in front of her. "I'd really like a boy and a girl."

"Yeah, that's what I was thinking, too." He squeezed Rachael's hand. "You're going to make a wonderful mother."

Rachael sighed dreamily as she thought about all the exciting things that lay ahead of them. Getting married, having children—things that had seemed like a far-off dream just a few months ago, were now becoming a reality.

They arrived at the hospital and took the elevator to the fourth floor. When they walked out onto the terrace, Rachael was surprised to see Dayna talking and laughing with a man. As they walked up, Rachael realized that he was the man she'd seen in the chapel the day Madison ran in there. *"So this is the piano man."*

"Mommy!" Madison shrieked and ran straight into her mother's embrace. After a moment, Madison turned to Quinn, "Hi, Mistu Wadferd."

He smiled at her attempt to pronounce his name. "You can call me Quinn, sweetheart, if that's all right with your mommy." He looked at Dayna.

"I don't mind," Dayna replied. "It's a little easier for her to pronounce."

"Koo-win," Madison repeated, making two syllables out of his name. "We came here to bring my mommy home. Is somebody bringing you home today, too?"

"No, honey, I have to stay here a while yet."

"Why?"

He smiled at her innocence. "Well, sweetie, I hurt my legs real bad and I have to learn how to walk all over again."

"I showed my baby sister how to walk; it's easy. I could teach you."

"I'll bet you're a very good teacher," he laughed.

Rachael watched the heartwarming interaction between Madison and the man in the wheelchair. Madison seemed very comfortable around him. Dayna did, too, for that matter. Their mom had mentioned that Dayna was going to be helping him with his music, but Rachael was surprised that they had become such fast friends.

"Well," Dayna turned to Rachael and Brian. "I'm ready to go…" As she looked at Rachael, she gasped and reached for her sister's left hand.

"Rachael! When did this happen?" she asked, looking at the ring, gleaming in the sunlight.

"Yesterday," Rachael smiled. "We were going to tell you right away."

Dayna held on to Rachael's hand and gave it a squeeze. "Congratulations," she smiled. Rachael could hear the sincerity in Dayna's voice and noticed tears in her eyes.

Dayna turned to make the introductions. "Quinn, this is my sister, Rachael, and her…" she hesitated and then smiled at Brian. "Her fiancé, Brian."

They both shook Quinn's hand. "It's a pleasure to meet you, Quinn," Rachael responded.

"It's nice to meet you, too," he replied. "Congratulations."

"Have you decided when?" Dayna asked.

They told her the date and the location.

"I've heard it's really nice there, now, since they fixed it up," Dayna commented.

"I can vouch for that," Quinn added. "My company did that job."

"So you're in the construction business?" Brian asked him.

"I was," Quinn shrugged. "I own Metro Construction. I'm looking at selling the company now, though. It's not the same if I can't get my hands in there and get dirty. I don't have any sons to pass it on to, anyway."

As Rachael listened to Quinn talk, she wondered how hard it must be on him to have his whole way of life yanked out from under him like that. Yet he didn't seem bitter. In fact, he'd turned in a completely new direction—music. She couldn't help but wonder where that would take him... and what part Dayna would play in it.

"Mommy, let's go." Madison pulled on Dayna's hand.

"Yes, we should go." Dayna turned to Quinn. "I'll give you a call and let you know how I'm doing with the music."

"Thanks," he smiled. "Take care."

Madison ran and gave Quinn a hug. It seemed to catch him off guard, but he hugged her back. "Take care of your mommy, okay?"

"I will."

* * *

Valerie heard the door open and smiled at the sound of the familiar voices. Lacey ran to meet them, barking as she recognized Dayna's voice. Untying her apron, Valerie went to greet her family. She watched as Madison pulled Dayna by the hand, talking excitedly. Lacey was jumping up at Dayna's leg, trying to get some attention. Dayna's eyes were bright with tears as she looked at her mother.

Valerie went over to her and gave her a hug. "Welcome home, honey."

"I can't believe I'm finally here." She looked around as if seeing her home for the first time. As she walked in, she touched the things around her and then knelt down to pet her dog.

The commotion woke Abigail and she began to cry. Dayna looked up the stairs, her face portraying a mother's love and a desire to see her child. Valerie was about to go and get her, but Dayna gently touched her arm. "Let me go."

Valerie went with her to help with the baby; Dayna wasn't supposed to strain herself at all. Valerie lifted Abigail out of the crib and handed her to Dayna in the rocking chair.

"She has some juice left in her bottle; why don't I go and get it?" Valerie smiled at the picture of mother and baby rocking together. The look of contentment on both their faces was precious.

As Valerie looked down the stairs, she saw that Greg and Amy had just arrived. Amy was hugging Rachael, and Greg was shaking Brian's hand. Congratulations were being offered.

Joy filled Valerie's heart as she saw her family together. It was what she'd been missing. As she pondered how she could possibly leave them again, a powerful thought presented itself to her, *"I don't want to go back!"*

Suddenly, it became perfectly clear. *"This is where I want to be! I want to move back here and be close to my family."*

The new idea filled her with excitement. She had some close friends back home; she would definitely miss them, but it was the thought of being that far away from her family again that pained her the most.

She decided to discuss it with her kids, later; she wanted to begin making plans. She owned her own condominium and she still had her parent's house that she was renting out. It would make sense to sell them both, rather than have the hassle of dealing with renters over such a long distance.

Thrilled with the new direction of her thoughts, she went downstairs to welcome her son and daughter-in-law.

* * *

Chapter 20

Dayna heard the voices, but she was content to sit and hold Abigail a little while longer. She'd dearly missed the precious child. The baby held tight to her mother as she lay in her arms. Her eyes remained on Dayna as if she didn't want to let her out of her sight, proving that Dayna's absence had been hard on Abigail, too.

Dayna silently vowed that she would never take anything for granted again, not even the simplest of things. She looked around the brightly decorated room. A year had passed quickly. So much had happened. She didn't feel sad, though, or angry. In that moment, Dayna felt very peaceful.

When Valerie returned with the bottle, Abigail reached out for it.

"Do you want to stay here a bit longer?"

"No, we can go downstairs now." Dayna smiled at her mom, thankful that she understood how precious those moments alone with her baby had been. "I want to see everybody."

As they walked into the living room, Greg got up and came over to Dayna. "Welcome home, sis."

As she embraced her big brother, Dayna noticed that Amy was struggling to get up, but was having difficulty with her enormous stomach. She walked over and gave her a hug where she sat.

"I remember what it's like," Dayna laughed. "I looked like that a year ago. How are you feeling?"

"I feel great as long as I don't have to move around too much. The baby's dropped already. The doctor says it will likely come sooner than we thought."

"Maybe Abby and her new cousin will share a birthday." Dayna kissed Abigail's forehead as Valerie placed the baby on her lap. Madison crawled up beside Dayna, on the sofa, and the dog lay down at her feet.

"That would be great; we could get together and celebrate their birthdays every year." Amy was a sweet girl. She was almost ten years younger than Greg and came from a big family. Dayna had wondered at first if he was wise to marry someone so much younger, but Amy had proven to be a perfect match for him.

Dayna looked around the room at her family and was filled with gratitude as she thought about how much she loved them. She felt herself getting emotional, but it didn't scare her as it had in the past. It was actually a relief, knowing that she didn't have to try to control it anymore. She understood, now, that emotion wasn't her enemy.

"I just want to thank everybody...for being with me through this..." Dayna took a deep breath, swallowing hard. The others remained silent, waiting for her to continue. Rachael reached over and put a hand on her shoulder.

"You all mean so much to me..." Dayna couldn't go on; the emotion was too powerful. She wanted to express the depth of love that she felt for her family, as well as show her appreciation for the love and support that they had offered her. Instead, she simply looked at each one of them, silently sending the message that she couldn't verbalize.

Valerie was crying and Rachael had tears in her eyes. Amy was sniffling; even Greg looked choked up. Suddenly, the situation struck Dayna as funny; the laughter that ensued served as a welcome relief.

"I'm sorry," Dayna laughed through her tears. "I didn't mean to put a damper on things. This is supposed to be a happy occasion."

"It is," Valerie declared, adamantly. "It feels so good to be together as a family. I've been dreaming of this for a long time."

"Me, too," Rachael nodded.

"And our family just keeps expanding," Dayna added, wiping away her tears. "Brian's a part of it now and we'll get to meet a new little one soon." She smiled at Greg and Amy.

"It's good to welcome new members."

Looking directly at her mom as she said the words, she nodded her head in encouragement. Greg didn't know about Stephanie yet and Dayna was ready to hear more about her now, too.

* * *

As Valerie shared about Stephanie, Rachael realized how difficult it was for her mom and silently sent her love and support. Looking around her, Rachael noticed that the response was favorable; Dayna was smiling as she sat with her girls and Greg looked surprised, but not upset.

"She'd like to meet you all one day," Valerie concluded. "I've brought a letter from her. It's the first one she wrote, telling me all about herself. I can read it to you, if you like."

Dayna nodded and Valerie got up to get the letter from her room. Rachael looked around at her siblings and wondered what it would be like to have Stephanie as part of their family—a sister by blood, but one with whom they shared no memories.

Smiling, she asked Greg, "What do you think?"

"I'm not sure," he laughed, shaking his head in mock dismay. "I always wanted a brother. I'm really going to be out-numbered now."

They all joined in the laughter; it helped to break the tension. Greg was very easy-going. It was one of the reasons why Rachael loved him so much. She truly loved them all and, now, to be together as a family—laughing, joking and feeling comfortable with one another—Rachael realized that a long-held desire had finally manifested.

Valerie returned and began to read the letter. It was full of detail, painting a picture of Stephanie for them all to see. She'd had a good life and had been blessed with wonderful parents, but they were gone now. She was married, had two children and worked full-time as a nurse. Stephanie openly shared her feelings about being adopted and wanting to meet her birth parents. Rachael listened intently, feeling the emotion behind the words.

By the time Valerie finished reading, Rachael felt like she'd come to know her new sister; she couldn't wait to meet her in person.

Next, Valerie had some pictures to show them. Rachael took a long look at the picture of Stephanie. She could definitely see a resemblance. She was tall, like Rachael, but had blond hair. Both Rachael and Dayna had darker hair, like their mom.

It was a picture of Stephanie's daughter that really caught Rachael's attention. Brian was looking over her shoulder and noticed it, too. "Wow, her daughter looks a lot like you."

Dayna and Greg both looked at the picture and Dayna agreed, "She looks just like you did at that age, Rachael. Brian, there's a photo album on the shelf beside you, do you mind grabbing it?"

He pulled out the album, but before he could open it, Rachael took it from him. "I'm not sure I want you to see what's in here," she joked. "Let me look first."

"If I remember correctly," Greg said. "You were a tall, gangly teenager with braces."

"That's not nice." Amy swatted him.

They flipped through the pages and came across a picture of Rachael and Dayna. Rachael was about twelve or thirteen.

"Oh my," Rachael laughed. "That wasn't a good year."

Brian looked closer. "You look cute with pigtails and braces." He gave her a kiss on the cheek. "Very cute."

As they compared the picture with the one of Stephanie's daughter, the resemblance was uncanny. The girl even had braces.

Continuing to flip through the photo album, Rachael noticed a picture of their dad. Most of the pictures were of Dayna and her friends. There were some of Greg and Rachael and a few of their mom, but just the one of their father.

Rachael ran a finger gently across the picture.

"It was a year ago today," Greg said, softly.

Rachael looked at her brother, pleased that he'd remembered. Dayna was looking at the picture, also. It wasn't a close-up. It was a photo taken of their dad in the back yard. He had his shirt off and a hammer in his hand.

"He was building the tree house," Dayna commented. "I loved that tree house."

"I want a tree house!" Madison had been sitting quietly, but suddenly sprang to life. She went over to examine the picture.

Greg picked her up and set her on his lap. "Maybe we'll just have to build you one, squirt." He looked at Dayna. "You have some good-sized trees in your back yard. Maybe Brian and I could get together some Saturday and start building a tree house for the girls."

Brian agreed.

"Just don't build it too high," Dayna glared at her brother. "I don't want her to fall out and break an arm." Then she laughed, "At least she doesn't have a big brother to push her out."

"I didn't push you," Greg defended himself. "That was an accident."

More laughter followed, as they reminisced about their childhood years. Rachael remembered the fun that they used to have in the tree house. She hadn't been much older than Madison when their father had built it for them.

She looked at her father's picture again, silently thanking him for being a part of their lives. Rachael had brought along the framed pictures that she had made up after the funeral and decided that it was the perfect moment to give them to Greg and Dayna. She got up to get them.

"I had these made up last year." Rachael handed one to each of her siblings. "But I wasn't sure how you felt about the whole thing."

Dayna was silent for a moment. She wiped away a tear before she spoke. "He was a good father."

"Yeah, you're right," Greg agreed. "How did things get so messed up?"

Valerie had been sitting quietly watching her children interact, but she spoke up, "I have to take some of the blame for that."

"No, Mom," Dayna interrupted her. "Let's not blame anyone. You were right; the past is past. Let's remember the good times and move on. We have lots of exciting things to look forward to."

Rachael couldn't believe the words that she was hearing. Dayna really had changed; she was looking at life differently, now.

A timer went off in the kitchen. "I need to check the turkey." Valerie walked out, touching Dayna's arm, lovingly, as she went by.

"I'll help you, Mom." Rachael got up and followed her mother out to the kitchen.

"This is exactly what I've been dreaming of," Valerie said, excitedly, once they were alone in the kitchen.

"I know," Rachael agreed. "When I was first together with Brian's family and saw them sitting around laughing and talking like this, I really felt the lack in ours. I had to work at feeling better about it, but I was able to get to a place of loving everyone as they were and seeing our family as whole and complete, rather than broken."

"I have to admit, I focused on the brokenness for a long time," Valerie replied. "But once I learned about the Law of Attraction, I started to do what you just said—to see our family the way I wanted it to be, instead of the way it was. Now, it's even better than I dared to imagine."

"It's always so perfect the way the Universe works things out."

"I'm starting to see that," Valerie smiled.

They were both quiet for a moment. Rachael was elated about all that had taken place. She was on a new high and was reveling in the sensation of it.

"You know." Valerie finished basting the bird and put it back in the oven. "When I saw everybody together before, it made me realize how much I want to move back here."

"Really!" Rachael turned to her mother in surprise. "I'd love to have you close by."

"There's nothing keeping me there, now that Grandpa and Grandma are gone. I could sell both my condo and their house and buy a place here. I really want to be near you kids."

"Mom..." An idea presented itself and, immediately, Rachael knew it was the perfect solution. "You could have my place!"

"What?"

"It makes so much more sense to live at Brian's, but I love my little place... I was having a hard time with the idea of letting it go."

"If that's really what you want to do, I'd love to buy it from you. Your house would be perfect for me!" Valerie exclaimed.

"I don't care about the money; the Universe gave it to me for next to nothing."

"We can leave the details for another day." Valerie hugged her daughter. "This is all so exciting. I'm really beginning to create my own reality! And it's deliberate creation, not by default the way I did it for most of my life."

"I know. It's exciting when that starts to happen. Now you get to really start living."

* * *

"If you've got that figured out, I'd like to know the secret." Dayna said it jokingly, but deep down, she did want to know what it was that her mother and sister had learned.

"It's the Law of Attraction," Valerie smiled as Dayna joined them in the kitchen. "I'm just beginning to understand it. Rachael's the expert."

"The book you left me at the hospital..." Dayna was finally ready to discuss it; the time seemed right. "It talks about the power of our minds and about our thoughts affecting our experience. Is that what the Law of Attraction is?"

"Yes!" Rachael replied, eagerly. "It's actually a simple concept. Our thoughts are really just energy vibrations. We're like a radio transmitter, sending out signals and then attracting whatever is on the same frequency.

"The secret is that we have the power to change our frequency, by changing our thoughts. I discovered it a couple of years ago. It's completely transformed my life. I've come from depression..." she smiled, "to bliss."

"I watched your life change and I was happy for you, but I didn't understand how it was happening. Do you really believe that your thoughts have affected your circumstances?"

"Absolutely. I've been proving it over and over, in all areas of my life."

"I'd like to talk to you some more about that."

"I'd love to," Rachael beamed. Dayna could tell that it was something her sister was very passionate about; she looked forward to discussing it more.

"Dinner's ready," Valerie announced. "I set the table earlier, so all we have to do is dish the food."

"Mom, I really appreciate you going to all this work. Thank-you."

"You're welcome, honey," Valerie smiled. "Say, do you have your voice recorder handy. I thought we could have some dinner music."

Dayna got the recorder and turned it on as the family came and sat around the table.

"Is that Mr. Radford's music?" Rachael asked.

"You can call him Koo-win," Madison reminded her. "It's easier."

"Yes, that's right," Rachael laughed.

"He's very good," Brian added.

Dayna saw the puzzled look on Greg and Amy's faces and filled them in.

"And this guy never played before?"

"Just a few lessons when he was a kid."

"Wow!"

"I wonder if he'd do weddings?" Rachael asked, suddenly, looking at Brian, "I'd love to have piano music at the ceremony, maybe even during the reception." She turned to Dayna. "I was thinking of asking you, but you're family and I want you to be able to relax and enjoy yourself. Plus, you'll have the girls with you."

"As far as I know, Quinn can only play the pieces that he's composed. He may be able to pick up something by ear, but he doesn't read music.

"I could play a few specific songs if you want," Dayna offered. "And maybe Quinn would be willing to play some of his, too. I'll ask him. He should be out of the hospital long before that."

At the mention of the word 'hospital' Dayna realized that her time there was already beginning to feel like a distant memory. She felt for Quinn, having to stay there for weeks yet. He really did have a good attitude about it; she admired him.

As for Dayna, she was thrilled to be at home and glad to have her family around her table. The food was delicious. It was hot and flavorful and she savored every mouthful. As she listened to her family's conversation, she tapped her foot in time to Quinn's music.

The song ended and the next one to play was the same one that Dayna had first heard from her hospital bed. She still didn't know how it was possible, but she couldn't deny it; it had happened. It gave her an odd feeling every time she heard it.

Dayna still questioned whether she should have said something to Quinn about it. The problem was, she didn't know what to say. It was so far beyond anything that she'd ever experienced before. There was a strange connection between them that she didn't understand. In all honesty, it scared her a little.

But she didn't want to focus on that now. Turning her attention to her family, she smiled as she listened to Greg teasing Rachael, again, about her pigtails and braces. She was pleased to see Brian engaged in an animated conversation with Madison, as he cut up her turkey. Abigail was resisting Valerie's help and, in an attempt to feed herself, had managed to get cranberry sauce up her nose. Dayna laughed. It was good to be home.

* * *

Part II

*"Once you remember who you are,
and deliberately reach for thoughts that hold
you in vibrational alignment with who you are...
well-being will show itself to you
in all areas of your life experience."*

ABRAHAM-HICKS

Chapter 21

As Quinn watched her walk away, he felt an emptiness start to grow deep inside. He silently questioned how the woman could have such an effect on him. He'd only known her a couple of days, but now to watch her leave, not knowing when he would see her again, left him with an ache that reached down into the depths of his soul.

He looked at the card she'd left him.

"Dayna Adams-Hargrath, 22 Carlyle Lane. That's a nice area. She must be well off. She mentioned that she was an assistant professor. I wonder what her husband does...

"She's a married woman. What's the matter with me?" Quinn reproached himself, *"God, I have no right to feel this way about her."*

He'd felt it the moment he walked into the chapel and heard her play. He'd felt it when he saw her wipe away the tear after she'd stopped playing. He'd felt it when he saw her eyes closed and her head moving in time to his music. He'd felt it, just now, when he said good-bye, but he knew he had to stop feeling it.

Suddenly, he longed to play the piano—to find a quiet place and play—all alone. He usually didn't mind others listening, but there were times when his music felt so personal that he just wanted to be alone with it.

"Two hours a day just isn't enough," he sighed. *"I need more than that. I'll go crazy, having to stay in here another few weeks, if I can't devote more time to my music."*

He'd asked, but there was no other piano in the building. He didn't own a piano, himself. His ex-wife had taken the one they had when they were married. At the time, he didn't care; he'd never even tried to play it.

"What if I was to buy one and have them deliver it here?"

The scheme intrigued him. He didn't care about the cost. He would be getting one for his own place when he got out of there, anyway.

"Surely, there must be a room somewhere I could play without disturbing others and without being disturbed. I don't care if it's a linen closet."

Inspired, he decided to go and ask. He turned his wheelchair and headed through the terrace doors, into the hospital. He'd be glad to get out of the chair, but he had to admit, he was pretty good at getting around in it. He'd always had a strong upper body, from all the physical work he'd done, but now, he noticed his arm muscles getting even stronger since he'd been moving around in the chair on his own.

He went down to the nurse's station on the second floor, where his room was located. They had obliged him by putting him in a room close to the chapel. The floor was mainly for geriatrics, but he didn't care. He could be very persuasive when he wanted something and, when all else failed, money talked. It was how he'd succeeded in his business. He was an honest man, but he didn't take 'no' for an answer.

Quinn knew all of the nurses on his floor and got along well with them. As he wheeled up to the desk, he noticed that Helena was on duty. She had a heart of gold; if anyone would help him get what he wanted, it would be her.

"Helena, my love," he teased. "I have a proposition for you."

"Mr. Radford, I'm a married woman!" she retorted, grinning.

"I want you to do something for me; you can name your price."

She frowned at him for a moment and then burst out laughing. She was a plump, jolly woman who couldn't stay serious for long.

"Mr. Radford." All the nurses called him by his proper name, even though he'd asked them numerous times to call him Quinn. "What are you up to?"

"I need to play the piano. Two hours a day isn't enough; I'm going crazy."

She gave him a sympathetic look. "I've already asked, honey. They won't budge."

"I realize that, but I've had another idea. Is there a room that I could play in, if I was to have a piano brought in?"

"Well, now," she scratched her chin as she thought for a moment. "That might just work. Let me see what I can do."

"Thank-you, my dear," he said. And with his most charming smile, he added, "You know you're my favorite."

She laughed again, shaking her head, as she turned back to her desk.

Satisfied that he'd done his best, he went back to his room. The next task was to see about getting a piano. He'd had the hospital install a phone in his room; he had been lost when they wouldn't let him use his cell phone to make calls. Quinn trusted his supervisors to keep the jobs running smoothly, but he still liked to touch base every few days.

He liked to talk to his daughter as much as possible, too, but she hadn't called him in several days. He was really hoping that she might stop by before the weekend was over.

Entering his room, his face brightened as he saw his daughter lying on his bed, foot crossed over her knee, watching television.

"Hi, Daddy. Where were you? I've been waiting almost ten minutes." She jumped down and gave him a hug.

He resisted the urge to point out that ten minutes wasn't a long time. "I'm sorry, sweetheart. I didn't hear from you, so I wasn't sure you'd be in today."

"Did your mom drop you off?"

"No, I took the bus."

He decided to lie on the bed. He was tired of sitting and needed to stretch his legs. With a little help from his daughter, he managed to get on the bed and get comfortable without calling for help. Brianna promptly sat down in his wheelchair and began wheeling around the room.

"Hey, you're not bad," he observed.

"We got to try them out in gym class one day. They brought some chairs in and we played around. We even tried to have a game of volleyball."

"I guess that's so you'll be more sympathetic toward people in wheelchairs."

"I guess," she shrugged.

He smiled. Teenagers didn't seem to use any more words than absolutely necessary when talking to adults. He'd seen her talk on the phone to her friends for hours at a time, but as soon as she was around an adult, the flow of words dried right up.

Still, it was a dramatic improvement. Before the accident, she'd been almost impossible to talk to. She was rebellious and was getting very good at playing her parents off one another. He and his ex-wife had to start communicating, just so they could stay sane.

Since the accident, however, she'd changed radically. He had almost died and the first day she was allowed to see him, she'd hugged him and cried—even apologized for being such a bad daughter. He'd never thought of her as bad, just a typical teenager. Having divorced parents hadn't helped matters, either.

Now she was more open and loving. She came to see him often and called several times a week. He didn't know what he'd do without her.

"Did you play this morning?" she inquired.

"I did," he smiled, feeling honored that his daughter cared to ask about that important part of his life. "I even found someone who's going to write my music down for me. She recorded me playing and now she's going to work on it at home."

"Who is she?"

"Her name is Dayna Adams-Hargrath. She came down to hear me play one morning. She's a talented pianist and has even played professionally."

"Hmm," Brianna responded, already sounding a little bored with the conversation.

After a short silence, she asked, "Dad, are you going to be on Oprah?"

"Where did you hear that?"

"Some kids at school said they heard you were."

Quinn laughed, "Well, it's news to me."

"Would you, if they called you?"

Quinn let out an extended breath as he contemplated the question. "I don't know." He'd been a little uncomfortable with the interview he had done for the local TV station and it wasn't even in front of a live audience.

"But Dad, you can't say no to Oprah!"

"I'll make that decision if, and when, it happens." Personally, he didn't think it would. His was a sensational story, but they usually ran out of steam pretty quickly. People were always ready to move on to the next one.

Brianna looked at her watch and jumped up out of the wheelchair. "I gotta go."

"Where's the fire?"

"My bus comes in five minutes; I'm meeting my friends at the mall." She gave him a quick kiss on the cheek and ran for the door. "Love you, Daddy!"

In a flash, she was gone and he was alone again. He'd been in the hospital for nearly two months already, but never had he felt as lonely as he did that afternoon.

In the emptiness of his room, images of Dayna began to flood his mind. She was at home—probably sitting down to a nice dinner with her family. He recalled the way she had looked earlier. Until then, he'd only seen her in her gown and robe, with no make-up. Even so, he found her easy on the eyes.

But when she'd walked out on to the terrace wearing pants and fitted shirt, hair styled and make-up on, he could hardly take his eyes off her. She was a beautiful woman. He wondered how old she was. Her mother was an attractive woman, too, and she didn't look to be much more than fifty.

The little girl, Madison, was an adorable child. She reminded him of Brianna at that age—curious, outgoing and always asking questions. He wondered if Dayna had a happy marriage...

"Damn it! Why am I torturing myself?"

Turning resolutely back to his mission, he pulled a business directory from his bedside table and opened it to look for piano dealers.

After getting a couple of voice recordings, he saw a name in the book that he recognized. His company had done renovations on the store a few years earlier. It was some kind of music superstore, but they were listed under pianos, so he gave them a call. A woman answered.

He inquired about getting a piano, telling the woman as little as possible about his situation. She quoted him prices and delivery costs. He didn't care about that; he just wanted to know how soon they could deliver it. The woman assured him that he could have one in a week or so.

That wasn't soon enough for Quinn. He asked to speak to a manager and within several minutes, had tentatively set up a delivery time for the following day on a floor model they had. It was a small upright—he couldn't bring in anything too big. The manager assured him that it was a good make, but Quinn wished that he could ask Dayna's opinion. She would know by the name if it were a quality piano or not.

"I'll just have to trust that it is," he decided. *"All I need to do now is convince the hospital that it's a good idea. I'll pay for the privilege if I have to. Maybe I can rent a room—somewhere out of earshot of other patients so I won't disturb them—somewhere that I can have the privacy to play whenever I want."*

He called the nurses' desk and Helena answered, "Mr. Radford, I have some good news for you. I talked to the hospital administrator. She's willing to let you use the auxiliary room. It's empty most of the time. Volunteer groups use it when they come in. If somebody needs it, you might have to vacate it for part of a day, that's all."

"Helena, I love you!" Quinn said, feeling triumphant. "I'm going to come out there and give you a big kiss."

"Mr. Radford," the good-humored nurse chuckled. "Don't you dare!"

"All right," he conceded. "Just tell them I'm having a piano delivered tomorrow afternoon."

"You don't waste any time!"

"No, I don't." He hung up and called the store back to confirm the delivery. Then he sat back and nodded his head in satisfaction. He liked the feeling of making things happen; he just wished it were that easy in other areas of his life.

* * *

Chapter 22

Dayna woke up in her own bed. Smiling, she ran her hand across the smooth sheets and hugged her plump, soft pillow. It was heaven. As she looked around her room, she offered a silent prayer of appreciation for everything in it.

She'd left the sliding door to her balcony open a crack, the night before, and now a breeze was playing with the sheer curtains. The sun was beginning to peek in, as well, casting a golden glow on everything it touched. Dayna's feeling of gratitude expanded to include the beauty that was being painted on a canvas right before her eyes—beauty that she had, up until that moment, taken for granted.

It was still early, but she couldn't sleep, so she got up, put on her robe and walked out onto the small balcony. As she looked down on her back yard, she smiled at Greg's offer to build Madison a tree house. She had no doubt that he would; he was true to his word. He was a good brother.

Dayna was reminded, again, of how much she loved her family. Her mom had gone to so much work preparing the meal the day before. Rachael had given her the framed picture of their father, for which Dayna was deeply touched. Moreover, they had all laughed and cried together like a normal, loving family—and for that, Dayna was overjoyed.

So much had changed in her life in such a short time—she'd become a single mother and had just spent a week in the hospital, recovering from a heart attack—but it wasn't those external changes that stood out in her mind; it was the change that had taken place inside her that seemed huge. She didn't even feel like the same person anymore.

She remembered the discussion she'd had with her mom and Rachael the previous day. Rachael compared thoughts to radio frequencies, attracting things with similar vibrations. Dayna had to admit that it made sense. She'd noticed that when things were going well, they often seemed to continue that way, but when something bad happened, it could easily keep spiraling in that direction, too.

"So, what causes life to begin going in one direction or the other?" she pondered. *"And does a person really have control over that?"*

Rachael seemed convinced of it. Her life was an example of things going well and continuing that way and she definitely had a positive outlook on life. Dayna couldn't say the same; she'd allowed the circumstances in her life to control her, making her pessimistic and distrustful of others.

She'd read in Rachael's book that a person's thoughts create their limitations.

"Does that mean that my thoughts have attracted the circumstances that brought about my marriage ending and my heart attack? That's putting the blame solely on myself."

"No!" She felt herself getting frustrated. *"I'm not to blame for the things that have happened to me!"*

Dayna stopped and took some deep breaths to calm herself. As she did, she realized that there was some truth to the concept that she just couldn't deny.

"If I could take responsibility for having created the circumstances in my past," she allowed. *"Then maybe, somehow, I could have control over what happens in my future, too."*

The thought was powerful; she could feel it resonate. *"Is this the power that Rachael and Mom have discovered in their lives? Is this the secret that Rachael was talking about?"*

Something told her that it was. Wanting to know for sure, she added it to a mental list of questions that she had for her sister. Dayna looked forward to sitting down and talking to Rachael in the near future.

She began to feel chilled, so she walked back into her bedroom. The voice recorder on the nightstand caught her eye. Her mind had been so full the night before, thinking about all that had happened, she couldn't fall asleep, so she'd turned on Quinn's music and it had helped her to drift off to sleep easily. Suddenly, she was anxious to get started on his songs. She got dressed and tidied her room.

Dayna tiptoed into Abigail's room and took a moment to gaze at her sleeping daughter; she looked so peaceful. Then she peeked into Madison's room; she was still asleep, as well. They'd both stayed up later than usual, having fun with their aunts and uncles.

Brian had impressed Dayna by how natural he was with the girls. She knew that Rachael wanted children one day and it seemed obvious that Brian did, too. Dayna smiled at the idea. It would be nice for her girls to have more cousins to play with.

As she walked quietly down the stairs, Lacey came up to her. The dog was wagging her tail in expectancy, so Dayna sat down on the bottom stair and stroked her soft curls.

"I missed you, too," she whispered.

In the kitchen, she put on a pot of coffee and then went into her office, looking for a blank book of staff paper that she had tucked away somewhere.

With the notebook in one hand and a steaming cup of coffee in the other, she retreated to the small room just off the main entry. Her piano welcomed her.

The sunny turret room at the front of the house had once been open to the main foyer, the staircase and the surrounding rooms, but after buying the house, Mark had closed it off, installing French doors so that Dayna could play the piano and not disturb anyone else in the house. He'd never really appreciated her music. Occasionally, if she forgot to close the doors before she sat down to play, he would get up, close them, and then go back to what he was doing. It was one of the many things, she realized now, that they didn't have in common.

Dismissing the notion, she sat down at her piano and set the coffee and book aside for a moment as she ran her hands over the beloved keys. They were like dear, old friends and she had sorely missed them.

Dayna began to play, uniting with the familiar melody that she had chosen. With her eyes closed, she was carried off to an enchanted place—an alluring setting like the one she'd experienced in the hospital. She continued to play, not so much aware of the music, as the feeling that it evoked.

Before long, she realized that she was playing Quinn's song, rather than the piece she had begun. Having heard it quite a few times, she had obviously picked it up by ear. It still had a peculiar effect on her—even more so as she played it herself. Strangely, it was no longer just Quinn's music; somehow, it had become a part of her.

Thoughts of Quinn filled her mind and, this time, they felt good. She was beginning to see that meeting him had been a gift—one that she didn't quite understand, but she felt appreciative, just the same.

"It was nice being able to talk openly about the things we experienced; I'll miss that."

Dayna didn't know if she'd even see him again and the realization left her feeling a little disheartened. *"I could take the music to him when I'm finished, rather than just courier it. I could call him—I did say that I'd call him and let him know how it was going.*

"It might be different seeing him again, though," she cautioned herself. *"What we shared in the hospital was based on us both having a near-death experience, but beyond that, big as it was, we'd probably have nothing in common."*

"Except the music," a voice reminded her.

"The music! How could I have overlooked that?" Music had brought them together, but she couldn't explain why the connection was so strong, or why that particular song had become a part of her.

With her eyes closed, Dayna felt herself being drawn to the magical place again as she listened to the music emanating from her piano. She was in a valley, standing beside a tranquil stream, just as before. This time, however, she was aware of her senses. The fragrant air was warm on her cheek and the dew on the lush grass felt cool on her bare feet.

Dipping her toes in the sparkling water, she was delighted as the water bubbled up around her, gently caressing her with a warm mist.

Fully immersing herself, she relaxed in the effervescent warmth, as if a hand were supporting her. Although she was alone, she felt a presence. It had no form, but it felt loving and warm—not like the sun, coming down from above—it was a warmth that not only wrapped around her and held her, it seemed to be radiating from within.

And the music! It was all around her and it danced as if it were alive. She breathed deeply, wanting to hold on to the captivating dream.

After several minutes, Dayna stopped playing and opened her eyes. She wasn't sure what had just happened to her, or where she'd gone. The images were the same as the ones that she'd seen in the hospital, but this time, they were so much more vivid and detailed.

"Did I add to it now, or did I just remember more of it?" she questioned.

As wonderful as they felt, the extraordinary things that she was experiencing scared her. Dayna wanted to understand them, but she wasn't sure that she could share them with anyone.

"Have mom or Rachael ever experienced anything like that? Could they relate?"

"Quinn could," a voice interjected.

"How do I know that?" she argued. *"He hasn't shared anything like that with me."*

Despite efforts to convince herself of the contrary, Dayna was certain that Quinn had experienced something similar. She didn't know why or how she knew, but she did. Not only that, but the knowing was combined with a desire to talk with him about it. It was a desire that she wasn't ready to act on, however, so she attempted to file it away.

Determined to put it out of her mind, she played the first few notes of his song again. Then she opened her notebook and began to mark down the notes on paper.

* * *

Quinn watched her. She was beautiful, almost angelic. Her head was tilted back, her eyes were closed and she was smiling, as she playfully splashed the water with her toes. She looked like a goddess. He called out to her, but she couldn't hear him. It was as if they were in two separate places.

After a moment, he began to hear music. It sounded different from his other songs. It had a soulful quality to it, a sad but beautiful tone. As before, he not only heard the music, he felt himself playing it. He felt his hands on the keys, striking each note.

Suddenly, something caught his attention and he looked up. The woman by the stream turned his way and smiled. It was Dayna.

Quinn opened his eyes. He'd been dreaming. Just as the dreams he'd had before, it felt real, but this time, Dayna was in his dream—she was the beautiful woman by the stream. He'd seen her many times, but he could never quite make out her face.

The woman hadn't been aware of him in the past. He'd always called out to her, but she had never responded—until now. He didn't even know if she could see him, but she could hear his music. Dayna had responded to his music.

Quinn turned to look at the time on the clock radio beside his bed. It wasn't even seven yet. He lay his head back down on the pillow and closed his eyes. The music in his head began again.

"Why does it sound so different from my other music?" he wondered.

The desire to play was as strong as ever. Sometimes, he felt like the constant yearning to play was more of a curse than a gift. He'd be glad when he had his own piano and a private place to play.

He tried to think of something else—anything else. The image of Dayna in his dream was still fresh. He recalled how she'd looked the day before, out on the terrace. He remembered her laugh. He saw a tear run down her cheek and saw her wipe it away.

He knew that it was wrong, but he didn't stop. He allowed himself to think of her, rationalizing that it was only himself he was hurting; he knew that he could never act on his feelings. As images of Dayna adorned his thoughts, however, the music continued and the desire to play taunted him.

He struggled to sit up in his bed, as he entertained the idea of going down to the chapel.

"It's far enough away from the nurse's station that they might not hear me if the chapel doors were closed. Most of the patients on this floor are hard of hearing, anyway."

He decided to do it. Quinn looked from the wheelchair to the walker and decided to take the walker, even if it was slower. He needed to use his legs as much as possible to get his strength back.

As he made his way to the chapel, he could notice a slight improvement in his legs. He was going to physiotherapy every day, now, except for Sundays. The therapist worked him hard and Quinn felt the discomfort, but he didn't complain. He knew that it was what it would take to get full use of his legs again.

Quinn believed that he would fully recover. The doctor had told him that he would likely always have some difficulty. He'd said that the best Quinn could expect was to be able to get around with just a cane, but that wasn't his style. He was determined to resume full use of his legs. He was only forty years old and wasn't willing to settle for becoming an old man, or looking like one, before his time.

The chapel doors were closed but not locked. He walked in, shut the doors behind him and slowly made his way up to the piano at the front of the room. As he sat down on the bench and lifted the cover, he took a deep breath. Sitting in front of a piano was like being home.

As he closed his eyes, he began to hear the music from his dream, earlier. At first, he picked out the melody with one hand and then slowly started adding chords with the other. Just like after his accident, he was aware that his playing sounded childlike and awkward, but as he got into the music and let it flow, it began to sound just like the music in his dream.

Quinn could feel that the music he was playing was different from his other music and he couldn't help but think of Dayna as he played it. There was something significant about her being in his dream. He recognized the fact that he couldn't reach her—life presented too many obstacles—but he could touch her through his music and she could be his, even if it was only in his dreams. As he played, the tone of the music reflected the solemn reality of his circumstances.

* * *

Chapter 23

Brian had just left and Rachael missed him already. He was going to pick up the dogs at his mom and dad's, then go back to his place.

In the quiet of her cozy living room, she enthusiastically replayed the details of the incredible weekend they'd just had. Rachael loved the way that Brian had proposed. The ring was breathtaking—she stopped to admire it again. Telling their families had been so exciting. The location they'd booked was perfect...

"I'm getting married!" she cried, reveling in the excitement of it.

Suddenly, she realized that she had yet to tell Gail. She didn't just want to show up at work the next day and have her best friend find out at the same time as everyone else in the office. Glancing at the time, she decided to call.

"Hey, what's up?" Gail asked. "How was your weekend? Are you back at work tomorrow?" The way that Gail was firing questions at her, Rachael knew that she hadn't caught her friend sleeping.

"My weekend was light years beyond amazing," Rachael said, passionately. "And yes, I will be at work tomorrow."

"Everyday is amazing for you," Gail laughed. "What could be so far beyond that?" She was quiet for a moment. "Rachael, is this what I think it is?"

"If you're thinking a sparkling, solitaire diamond, you're right."

"Oh, my God! He asked you? When? How?"

Rachael filled her friend in on all the details and then added, "I want you to be my maid of honor."

"Of course," Gail answered. "But June. Wow! That doesn't give you long to plan. At least you have the place booked. What's it like?"

"It's perfect." Rachael described the facility and the beautiful grounds surrounding it. "We have the choice of outdoors or inside, if the weather's bad."

Gail laughed, "Like you're going to attract bad weather on your wedding day!"

Rachael had to agree. She could picture the day already. They were outdoors and the sun was shining brightly. Brian was standing by the altar watching her walk down the long, grassy aisle. He looked incredibly handsome in his tux. He was smiling...

"Hey, where'd you go?"

"Sorry," Rachael laughed. "I just got caught up visualizing the ceremony."

"Were you surprised," Gail asked, "when he proposed?"

"Totally! I was getting so good at being in the moment, I didn't think about the future. I mean, I did vaguely. I hoped it would happen someday. But this soon? I had no idea!"

"Where are you going to live?"

"His place." Rachael felt good about it now. "My mom is moving back here. I told her that I want her to have my place."

"That's great," Gail replied. "Then you won't have to let go of it completely. I know how much you love that little house."

"Yeah," Rachael agreed. She was excited about the idea of her mom having her place, but even more wonderful was the thought of moving in with Brian and making his house their own.

"What about your dress?" Gail asked with an urgency that made Rachael laugh. Her friend had suddenly remembered that important detail—one which Rachael had expected to be at the top of Gail's priority list.

"I want you to help me find one."

"We should start right away! If you find one you like and have to order it, it could take weeks.

Hampton's and Rose Claire are the best, but we should check at some of the smaller bridal boutiques, as well."

Rachael smiled to herself, knowing that she was in good hands. She sat back and put her feet up on the coffee table as they continued their conversation. She told Gail about the family dinner that her mom had put on for Dayna and how they'd all had had such a wonderful time together.

Rachael still couldn't believe how much Dayna had changed. She'd become open and sensitive and was even willing to forgive. The part that excited Rachael the most, however, was that her sister had asked to hear more about the Law of Attraction.

* * *

In the week following her hospital stay, Dayna appreciated her time at home more than she ever had before. Madison went to preschool three mornings a week. Dayna enjoyed those mornings alone with Abby and spent time with Madison in the afternoons while Abigail was sleeping.

It was nice having her mom there; Dayna could appreciate her now. Valerie insisted on making all the meals, doing the cleaning and being available to do any lifting. She told Dayna of her desire to move back and Rachael's offer of her house. Dayna was pleased to hear it. She was looking forward to having her mom close by and getting to know her better.

Mark came by regularly to spend time with the girls and Dayna noticed that having him there was less awkward now. She even found herself being able to talk with him about things that related to the girls or work or how she was recovering. She eagerly told him about Rachael's engagement and her mom's plans to move back to the city.

She wondered what the difference was—time, maybe; they say it heals all wounds. Somehow, she felt that it was more than that. She noticed that she didn't feel so angry with him, anymore, and she liked the freedom of not carrying that around with her.

Dayna tried not to speculate about her future. She didn't know what it would hold, but she felt like she was beginning to trust in something bigger. Her experience in the hospital had taught her that each moment was precious and now she wanted to enjoy each moment to the fullest.

Working on Quinn's music provided some very enjoyable moments for Dayna. She could appreciate talent when she saw it and Quinn's musical gift amazed her. By the end of the week, she had almost half of his songs down on the pages of her notebook.

There was a computer notation program that she'd heard about once. As she researched the internet, she found that there were, indeed, several good programs available to do that sort of thing. She decided to pick up a program that would print out Quinn's music in a professional looking format, before she gave it back to him.

She hadn't called him yet—there really wasn't a need to. The work that she was doing was straightforward, so there was nothing specific to ask him. She decided to wait until she had his songs completed.

Saturday morning, Mark came by to pick the girls up. Dayna was planning to go out and do a bit of shopping with her mom, when the phone rang. She was greeted by her brother's excited voice.

"Dayna, it's Greg. Amy's in labor!"

"That's great! Are you at the hospital?"

"Yeah, I just got through all the paperwork. They're setting Amy up in a labor and delivery room. Her water broke at home this morning; and the contractions are coming quickly now!"

"Hopefully it'll be soon, then. Mark just picked up the girls, so Mom and I can come right away." Dayna could see Valerie nodding her head.

"That would be great," Greg replied. "Can you let Rachael know, too? I gotta go. See you soon."

Dayna hung up the phone and smiled at her mom. "It looks like this little one's birthday won't be too far off Abby's after all."

Abigail's first birthday was one day away and they were planning a party for her. Rachael and Brian were going to be there and Mark was bringing his parents. Greg and Amy were invited, too, but now it looked like they would probably have their hands full.

Dayna called Rachael at Brian's to tell them the news. They all agreed to meet at the hospital. Then, she called Mark to let him know where they were going, in case he got back with the girls before they returned.

"Okay, I guess we can go." Dayna announced, grabbing her keys, but as she reached the door, she had an idea. "I think I'll bring Quinn's music along. Maybe I'll have a minute to stop in and show him what I've done so far."

Arriving at the hospital the same time as Rachael and Brian, the four of them went up to the maternity ward together.

"I don't miss this place!" Dayna shuddered, as she stepped into the elevator.

"At least you're not wearing your robe and slippers," Rachael laughed. "And you can leave any time you like. The place is starting to become rather familiar, though; the parking attendant greeted us like we were old friends!"

"I can't believe that Greg is going to be a father," Dayna remarked. "He was an elusive bachelor for so long, but I've noticed how he is with my girls since Amy's been pregnant. There's a big difference in him. I think he'll make a great dad."

"Hey," Brian joked. "Don't knock elusive bachelors. I've been one for a long time, too. We're not elusive, we're just extremely selective." He squeezed Rachael's shoulder and kissed her hair.

The small space filled with laughter. Dayna really liked Brian. He was a good match for Rachael and seemed totally at ease with the rest of their family. Not only that, but Rachael was happier than ever. Dayna was truly pleased for them both.

The elevator door opened and they went to the desk to inquire about Amy.

The nurse looked up. "I'll find out how she's doing and let them know that you're here. Are you Greg's family?"

"Yes," Valerie answered.

"Amy's family just arrived. They're waiting in family room 'C'. It's just down that hallway, halfway down on your right," she pointed.

They joined Amy's parents and two of her sisters in the waiting room. They hadn't seen each other since the wedding, but Dayna felt very comfortable around them. They exchanged pleasantries and settled in to wait for some news.

Dayna was impressed that the hospital had private waiting rooms for the families; it was the first time that she'd been in one. In fact, it was the first time she could remember being in that hospital as a visitor rather than a patient.

Greg came into the room, just then, and told them that they were still waiting, but that things were progressing well.

"They gave her an epidural, so she's not in too much pain. She's about six centimeters, now. The monitor's showing that the baby's heart rate is nice and strong."

He was absolutely glowing. Dayna smiled to herself; she could feel his joy. After the quick report, Greg went back to be with Amy.

"It could be a little while yet," Dayna announced, looking at her watch. "I think I'll go down and see Quinn."

She didn't know whether she would find him in his room or in the chapel at that time of the morning. She decided to ask at the nurses' station.

"Mr. Radford is down in the auxiliary room. It's on the main level." The nurse gave Dayna directions to get to it.

Dayna questioned why he'd be down there rather than in the chapel; it was almost ten o'clock. She decided to go and see for herself. The room was easy enough to find; it was down a corridor marked, 'Staff and Hospital Volunteers Only'. The door was clearly marked, also, but she hesitated, looking in the window before she entered.

Quinn was playing a piano. It was in the corner of a large, empty room. The piano was facing the door, but Quinn's head was down and it looked like his eyes were closed. He was definitely caught up in the music that he was playing. Dayna wasn't sure if she should disturb him or not.

As she listened, she could hear the music faintly through the door. It wasn't anything she'd heard him play before. It was new and it sounded different from his other music. It was beautiful, but in a sad sort of way, like a poignant love song. He played it with such passion. She wondered if he was thinking of someone as he played—maybe his wife, maybe a past love.

* * *

Quinn savored the sensation of his fingers on the keys. He was enjoying having his own space, his own piano. There were subtle differences in the way his new piano played, in the way it sounded, but overall, he was quite happy with it.

Most of all, he was happy to be able to go down and play anytime he liked. He could go early in the morning or stay late into the night. He even cut back on going to the chapel every morning. He only went there three or four days a week now. Lately, he preferred his own space and time alone with his music.

His newest songs were already so familiar to him; he'd been playing them all week. He continued to play his original ones, too, not wanting to forget them—although he didn't see how that could ever happen—they had come from somewhere deep inside of him and he was sure that they flowed out from that same place each time he played.

He began with his favorite. It was the one he'd heard in the dream—the one that had caused Dayna to turn and look. Closing his eyes, he saw her as she'd looked in the dream. She was smiling. She was beautiful.

Quinn let himself think of her, now, as he played. He knew he shouldn't, but he reasoned that if he could convince himself she was just a dream, just his inspiration, then maybe his heart wouldn't get so involved. He had to justify it somehow, because not thinking of her wasn't an option.

Dayna seemed even more real that morning than she had in past days, so he channeled the intensity of the feeling into his music. When the song ended, he opened his eyes and looked up. Dayna was standing in the doorway. He blinked, convinced that he must be dreaming.

The vision smiled and started walking toward him, sounding very real as she said his name.

"Hi, Quinn."

"Dayna," he spoke carefully, hoping that his voice would convincingly hide the shock that he was experiencing. "It's so good to see you."

"My brother's wife is having a baby," she explained. "We were all just waiting around, so..."

"How are you?" he asked, trying to ease the awkwardness that loomed between them.

"I'm starting to feel like myself again. It's good to be home."

"I can only imagine," he laughed.

"I see you've found another place to play."

He told her about his idea to buy a piano and have it delivered to the hospital. "I've been coming down here all week. It's nice being able to play whenever I want now."

"Are you still playing in the chapel?"

"Not every day." He noticed her eyes as they talked. Outdoors, they had looked hazel, but in that light, they were brown, with a ring of gold around the pupil. "I prefer it here."

"The song that you were playing just now," she inquired, "it's new, isn't it?"

"Yes," he smiled, wanting to tell her that she was his inspiration, but he knew that he couldn't. "I have several new pieces."

"It's so beautiful! I think it's even better than your first ones, if that's possible."

"Thanks," he replied, longing to tell her that it was a reflection of her.

"It still amazes me how this came to you so suddenly after the accident. If you were to record these, you'd have a hit album. They're really good."

"Thanks. It still amazes me, too."

"I wanted to show you what I've done so far," she said, surveying the room. The only chairs were stacked in the far corner, so she turned to Quinn and gestured to the piano bench that he was sitting on, "Do you mind if I sit down?"

"Not at all." He moved over to the far left half of the bench, leaving her the right side. There was room for two, but just barely. Her arm rubbed against his as she reached in her purse and pulled out a notebook. He could smell a hint of her perfume as she put the book on the ledge in front of them and opened it up.

"It looks kind of messy in a notebook like this," she apologized. "But I found a computer program that I can transfer it to. Then, I can print it out and have it look professional."

He looked at the pages of notes that were his songs. They weren't messy at all, by his standards. He realized, suddenly, the amount of work that Dayna had put into it.

"Dayna..." he hesitated a moment before deciding to go ahead and ask. "I was wondering...why do you want to do this for me?"

"I..." she started and then paused to take a deep breath. "I don't know, Quinn. You asked me. I was very impressed by your music and I truly enjoy working on it."

It wasn't the answer that he'd hoped for. *"What was I expecting anyway—that she'd tell me she's doing it because she's in love with me? God, I'm being such a fool!"*

She was quiet for a moment and then turned to him, "Quinn, that's not the only reason."

He had no idea what she was about to say, but he felt like his heart stopped beating, as he waited for her to continue.

"It's your music...the way it makes me feel. It's hard to explain." Dayna paused, searching for the right words.

"Something happened to me after I had the heart attack—when I was unconscious. I felt peaceful, just like you described. I was in this wonderful place. I felt warm and loved and protected. And then..." She hesitated again. "I heard music playing.

"I didn't think much of it until some other strange things began to happen. My sister, Rachael, told me that she had a vision while they were waiting for me to come out of surgery. She saw herself lying in my place and she heard the music, too. That's when the nurse told us about you.

"Then my husband told me that Madison had seen you on TV and that she kept talking about the 'piano man.' She even drew several pictures of you.

"As strange as that all seemed, I probably could have dismissed it as coincidence, but I decided to go down and hear you play that morning..." Dayna stopped again and Quinn looked at her. Whatever it was that she was trying to tell him, it was hard for her; she looked uncomfortable.

"The first song that you played..." she continued with difficulty, "was the same song that I heard when I was unconscious. It was this song right here." She pointed to the page that was open in the notebook in front of them.

Quinn remained quiet, stunned by what Dayna had just shared with him.

All of a sudden, he thought of something. "Tell me about your dream," he said, "...when you heard the music."

She described a beautiful valley with a sparkling stream. She told him about bathing in the bubbling water, feeling tranquil and hearing the music dance around her.

"I know I experienced it when I was unconscious—that's when I first heard your song.

"But the other morning…" She thought for a second. "It was the first morning that I was home from the hospital. I had the same vision again, as I played my piano—only this time, it was more vivid. That's when I saw the details of the valley and noticed how the water felt.

"Quinn, this is all so strange," Dayna shook her head. "I don't understand it at all. I don't even know why I'm telling you this."

"Do you have a pen?" Quinn disregarded the common sense that was trying to prevail and followed his intuition. The problem was that he had no idea where it would lead.

She looked at him strangely, as she handed him a pen from her purse.

Quinn carefully wrote, *'Dayna's Song'* on the top of the page of music before them.

"I don't understand," she said, cautiously.

"I don't understand it either, but you've been in my dreams, even before I met you. Ever since the accident, I've had this recurring dream with a woman in it. I could never quite see her face, until the other morning—Monday morning."

"And you saw my face?"

There was something in Dayna's eyes and in the sound of her voice that Quinn recognized. It was the same panic that he'd seen the other day when she'd left the terrace so abruptly.

He nodded.

Neither of them spoke for several long seconds and the silence threatened to suffocate Quinn. A wave of anxiety washed over him. He'd said too much. Telling her about his dream had been inappropriate and now he desperately wished that he could take it back.

Dayna stood up. "Quinn, I should get back to my family. Who knows?" she laughed, weakly. "I may have a new little niece or nephew by now." She quickly put the notebook back in her purse and started to walk away.

"Dayna?"

She turned back to look at him, the panic still evident on her face.

"I don't want things to get weird between us, because of this; I value your friendship."

"Me too," she nodded, smiling slightly. As she turned toward the door, she hesitated a moment before she put her hand on the handle. Then, she pulled the door open and walked out without looking back.

* * *

Chapter 24

Rachael noticed Dayna's face when she returned to the waiting room. There was an odd look in her eyes. Dayna smiled and asked about the baby, but Rachael sensed that something had just happened to upset her.

"We're still waiting, but they just started the delivery a few minutes ago," Valerie answered. "So it won't be long now."

Dayna excused herself to go and find a restroom. When she was gone, Rachael leaned over to her mom and whispered, "Is something going on between Dayna and Mr. Radford?"

"I'm not sure. I saw the way he looked at her the other day. I think that he's attracted to her, but I don't know if she feels anything toward him."

"Quinn doesn't really seem like her type. Plus, she and Mark just separated," Rachael responded, shaking her head. "I wonder what just happened; she looked upset."

"I know," Valerie concurred. She sat back in her chair for a moment and then looked at Rachael. "Quinn's different than you'd think. I'm not sure what he was like before his accident, but now, he seems kind and sensitive. There's something in his music that Dayna feels drawn to. I don't know," she said, thoughtfully. "This may be bigger than either of them realize."

Rachael reflected back on the strange things that had taken place since her sister's heart attack. She'd had a feeling, too, that the mysterious and fascinating occurrences meant that something big was happening. Taking a deep breath, she released any negative thoughts and reminded herself that everything was under control.

Dayna returned and sat down with Rachael and Valerie. Brian had struck up a conversation with Amy's dad on the other side of the room. Amy's mom was too excited to sit; this was her first grandchild. She and her two younger daughters had gone to pace the corridor.

"How's Quinn?" Valerie asked.

"He's fine." Dayna shrugged her shoulders. She really seemed affected by whatever had happened, but she put on a smile and said, "He had a piano brought in, so he could play whenever he likes. They found a room for him down on the main level."

"That's great," Valerie said. "It'll make the time pass more quickly for him."

"Mmm," Dayna nodded, visibly distracted.

Rachael put her hand on Dayna's arm. "Daynie," she said softly, addressing her sister by her childhood name. "Is everything okay?"

As Dayna looked up, she smiled at Rachael, but her eyes were filled with tears. "You haven't called me that in years."

"Do you mind?"

"No, it reminds me of the good times we used to have together."

"Did something happen with Quinn to upset you?" Valerie asked.

Dayna shook her head as if to say no and then sighed, "Yes, something's been happening the whole time—since before I met him, but I don't understand what it is.

"I've felt this pull—not so much to him as to his music, right from the start—that's why I agreed to do the notation for him.

"Today, he asked me why I was doing this for him and I told him about hearing his song when I was unconscious."

"What did he say?" Valerie asked.

"He's been having dreams, too, ever since his accident. That's where he hears his music. There's always been a woman in his dream, but he couldn't see her face clearly—until the other day. He said the woman turned to look at him... and it was me."

"Wow." Rachael didn't know what else to say. It was all pretty amazing.

"And now his music—it's different, slower. It's beautiful, but sad, like a bittersweet love song."

"He's just playing what he feels. Do you think maybe he's in love with you?"

Dayna looked up at Valerie in shock. "No, he's..." she shook her head, adamantly. "No, it's not that. I think he's just as confused by this as I am."

Their conversation was cut short as Greg came in the room with a huge grin on his face and announced, "It's a boy!"

* * *

Quinn knew that he had to let Dayna go, even if it meant losing her friendship. That look in her eyes told him that things were going in the wrong direction and if he didn't put a stop to it, he would lose her altogether. He knew that he had to put her out of his mind and even more difficult, he had to put her out of his heart.

Deciding to focus on rehabilitation, rather than relationships, he began to push himself harder than before. He even refused to use his wheelchair.

He refused to play the piano, too, knowing that it would only remind him of her. It tortured him, because he couldn't shut off the music in his head. He couldn't stop the dreams, either, and Dayna was always in his dreams; as soon as he started playing the piano, now, she would turn and look his way and then smile.

After a day or two, Quinn began to hear a new type of music in his dreams. It was strong and dramatic. He could feel the force of his fingers on the keys; it felt good, giving him a sense of relief. The music was drawing him again and he couldn't resist it. He got in his wheelchair and went down to the auxiliary room to play his piano.

Seeing his piano again was like reconnecting with an integral part of himself. He sat down and let the new music begin to flow out of him. Quinn let his emotions pour out, too, making him aware of just how frustrated he was—frustrated that he'd let himself fall in love with Dayna in the first place and frustrated with life for not allowing her to love him in return.

He continued playing, losing all track of time and, gradually, he felt his emotions lift. It felt good to connect in that way again.

By refusing to play, he had shut off the part of him that he'd found after the accident. That part was life to him—he understood that now—and he never wanted to let it go again.

After he played, contentedly, for some time, Quinn's hunger began to demand his attention. He decided to return to his room, hoping that he wasn't too late for breakfast.

Entering his room, he saw that the breakfast tray was still on the table at the end of his bed. He moved to the bed and took the cover off the tray to find that the porridge was still warm and the coffee, drinkable.

Quinn felt a renewed sense of peace. Life was short and he didn't want to live with regrets. He also didn't want to spend his time longing for something that could never be; he knew that he could get past it. He understood, somehow, that the Source his music came from was the same Source that could help him to feel joy again.

A knock at the door interrupted his thoughts. He invited whomever it was to enter and was surprised to see Dayna's mother standing there.

"I hope I'm not bothering you, Mr. Radford."

"Please, call me Quinn. It's Valerie, isn't it?"

"Yes." Valerie smiled as she answered him and he couldn't help but observe that she and Dayna had the same smile.

"I thought I'd come down and hear you play this morning. I'm just here visiting my daughter-in-law and my new grandson."

"Congratulations."

"Thank-you," she smiled and turned to leave. "Well, I should let you finish your breakfast."

"No, please stay," Quinn insisted. "I enjoy having visitors."

Valerie sat down on a chair at the side of the bed. Quinn set the remainder of his breakfast aside. It was cold now, anyway.

"I asked the nurse if you'd be playing this morning. She mentioned that you haven't been playing at all, lately."

Quinn didn't know how to reply. He couldn't very well tell her that he'd stopped playing because he was lovesick over her daughter.

"I decided that I wanted to focus more on my rehab," he told a half-truth. "I want to get my legs back in shape, again. Then, maybe I can get out of this place a little sooner."

"Your music seems to have a healing quality to it." She looked him in the eye. "For you and for others who hear it, as well."

"It saved my life," he said, honestly. "You're right; it does have a healing quality. I went downstairs to play this morning and I found that connection again. I've missed it lately."

"Quinn," she hesitated. "I'm not sure if it's my place to say this or not...it's just that...I couldn't help but notice that something's happening between you and Dayna."

"Shit! How do I respond to that? Confess my feelings or deny them?" He decided that truth had always served him in the past.

"Dayna's a very special woman," he admitted. "It was nice to talk to someone who could relate to the things I've gone through. We had a connection." He stopped there, not knowing how much Dayna had shared with her mom about their conversations.

"Is there anything more than that?"

"God!" he flinched. *"Can this woman see right into my soul?"* Part of him felt relieved, however, to be able to admit his feelings.

"Is it that obvious?" he sighed.

"I could see it in your eyes when you looked at her—that morning in the chapel."

"I don't know what to say." He felt like a child that had been caught with his hand in the cookie jar and yet she didn't seem to be upset at him.

"She's an amazing woman, not to mention beautiful and talented."

"Quinn, you might have to give her some time. I'm not sure, but I think that she may have feelings for you, too. She's just really confused, right now."

He thought he must have heard wrong. *"Did she just say that Dayna may have feelings for me? Is she actually condoning a relationship between her married daughter and me?"*

"Are you saying that there could be more than just friendship between us?" he asked, cautiously.

"I don't know for sure, Quinn; that's up to both of you," Valerie replied. "And maybe I'm wrong in telling you this, but if she pulls away, I don't believe it's because she doesn't care. I think she's just scared of how much she does care.

"Dayna's really vulnerable, right now," Valerie added. "She's trying to come to terms with a failed marriage, plus she's just had a life-threatening experience. It's a lot to deal with."

"Failed marriage?" He looked at her, shaking his head in disbelief. "I didn't know... I've been beating myself up because I thought I was falling in love with a married woman."

Valerie sent him a look of compassion. "Quinn, I'm sorry; I just assumed you knew."

"But he was with her in the chapel that day," Quinn frowned, "and she referred to him as her husband, the last time I talked to her." He thought back to all the things that had led him to believe that she was married.

"It's only been a few weeks," Valerie explained. "She probably said it without thinking. And they do still see each other, for the girls' sake. They want to make it as easy on them as possible."

"Wow." He blew out a long, slow breath as he took in the new revelation. Dayna was free to fall in love with him. That didn't mean that she would; she was obviously scared of whatever feelings she was having, but it did give him hope.

Quinn heartily thanked Valerie for her visit and invited her to come and see him anytime.

Afterwards, as he sat alone in his room, he couldn't keep the smile from his face. He felt like he'd just been given the key to a hidden treasure. He felt more alive than he had in a long time.

Suddenly, he wanted to play the piano—he needed to play—and he didn't care who watched him. Looking at the time, he realized that he could still go to the chapel for an hour. He grabbed his walker and headed out the door. A song was already playing in his head. It was joyful and upbeat. It was 'Dayna's Song.'

* * *

Chapter 25

Dayna was enjoying a quiet morning alone with Abigail. Valerie had dropped Madison off at preschool and was going to the hospital to visit Amy and the new baby, Jackson Nathaniel Adams.

Her father would have been proud to know that his first grandson was named after him. Dayna wished that he could have lived to see little Jack. He never got to meet Madison and Abigail, either.

Dayna blinked back the tears. She wasn't sure what to do with past regrets. She felt the pain, but it was such a powerless place to be, when no amends could be made. She'd been so proud, so stubborn, so determined to be right—and it had cost her dearly.

Her only consolation was in hoping that he knew somehow, from the place he was now, that she was sorry, that she would gladly go back in time and do things differently.

She glanced over at his picture, now sitting on top of her piano. It had obviously been taken in recent years. He'd grayed somewhat and had lines in his face. Dayna felt strange as she looked at him. He was familiar and yet a man that she scarcely knew.

Thinking about her father, Dayna strengthened her resolve to live in the moment and appreciate life more fully. She vowed never again to let a misunderstanding sever a relationship. As she heard the words in her mind, she thought of Quinn. She remembered the look on his face when he called her name and told her that he didn't want their friendship to end.

"Friendship." She closed her eyes and sighed. *"He said it himself; that's all it is. I'm the one who's reading more into it. I'm the one who's getting all freaked out by the strange things that are happening. He's done nothing wrong."*

She didn't know what had possessed her to share with him that it was his song she'd heard the day of her surgery. And when he told her that he'd seen her face in his dream, she simply hadn't known how to respond.

"Friendship." She listened to the word again.

She didn't mind the thought of it. Quinn made her laugh and he could understand what she'd been through. Not only that, but she enjoyed his music and was happy to put it on paper for him.

Abigail was playing contentedly, so Dayna got her notebook from the piano and went into the office. She'd picked up a notation program and had loaded it onto her computer, but hadn't tried it out yet. It took her a few minutes to learn the program, but she soon discovered that she could bypass the pencil and paper method altogether. She could simply pick out the notes on the computer screen and have it compile them for her.

Transferring one of Quinn's songs from her notebook onto the computer program didn't take long at all. When she was finished, she clicked the 'play' button and it immediately began playing his song. She marveled at the technology.

Dayna clicked 'print' and when she turned to her printer to look at the result, she was thrilled to see a page of printed music like any she might buy in a music store. The only thing missing was the title. She went back to the computer and checked a few of the program's drop-down buttons. Sure enough, she could add a title to the work.

Suddenly, she had an idea. Turning to the page that Quinn had titled, 'Dayna's Song', she began to transfer the notes on to the computer. When she was done, she entered the title and printed off the finished piece. Then, on a facsimile cover sheet, she typed a quick note.

Dear Quinn;

Please forgive my abrupt behavior the other day. So many strange things are happening; I guess I just needed time to process them. I value your friendship, too, and I know that we can find a way to get past the 'weird' stuff that is happening.

I just thought that I would send you a sample of what this computer notation program can do. I'm having fun with it.

Take care of yourself.

Your friend, Dayna

Satisfied with what she had written, she typed the hospital name, along with Quinn's name and room number, on the top of the paper. Then she found a fax number for the hospital, compiled the pages and sent them off.

Dayna glanced out the doorway of her office at Abigail, who was still playing contentedly with her toys. Dayna went and sat down on the carpet beside her. As she watched her daughter, she marveled at the refreshingly uncomplicated world that small children seemed to inhabit. To be in the moment, so in awe of the simple things around them, was something that adults would do well to remember.

"Can Mommy play with your toys?"

Abigail looked up at her mother with a smile and generously handed her the toy that she'd been playing with.

* * *

Quinn left the chapel feeling better than he had in a long time. Sharing his music with others was truly fulfilling; he'd missed that. Several people had approached him, telling him how much they'd enjoyed his music. Some had even been visibly moved by it.

He liked knowing that he made a difference; it was like touching other people's souls. Valerie claimed that his music had a healing effect on others, as well as on himself. He could see that more clearly now.

As he walked back to his room, he hummed a song. He smiled as he met another patient in the corridor. He couldn't really explain the change, but whatever the feeling was, he wanted to hold on to it.

He knew that it had to do with Dayna, but it seemed bigger than that. No matter what happened with Dayna, Quinn wanted to find a way to continue feeling good. Life had given him another chance and he didn't want to waste it. Life had given him a very special gift and he knew, now more than ever, that he wanted to share it.

In his room, he noticed some papers on his table that hadn't been there when he left. Picking them up, he read Dayna's note on the front. He stared at the page of music, amazed by how professional it looked. It was the title, however, that moved him. By adding that, it seemed that Dayna was ready to acknowledge what had taken place between them. He read the note again.

"Friendship," he nodded. *"That's all Dayna has to offer right now. I can be content with that."*

She'd drawn a little smiling face beside her name. He was touched by the gesture; it was her smiling face that was the inspiration for his music.

Closing his eyes, he pictured her beautiful face. He realized that he felt free, now, to think about her. Guilt no longer plagued him. It was replaced by hope.

* * *

Dayna sat down at the table with her girls. Valerie brought the casserole from the oven and joined them.

"I saw Quinn today."

Dayna was surprised. "How is he?"

"I had intended to go down and hear him play, but the nurse said that he hadn't been playing at all for the last few days."

Dayna frowned. It had been a few days since she'd been there to see him; she wondered if it might have something to do with that.

"I was curious, so I stopped by his room."

"Is he okay?" Dayna was concerned.

"Yes. He's fine. He's been trying to focus more on his rehabilitation, but he said that he went down to play his piano this morning and realized how much he missed it."

Dayna wondered if that was the only reason. She knew how much his music was a part of him.

"I sent him a fax today," Dayna informed her mom. "I wanted to apologize for being abrupt the other day. Plus, I sent him a sample of what the computer program can do. It's remarkable. It will really save me a lot of time."

That's great. I'm sure he was glad to hear from you, too."

"It gets pretty lonely in there," Dayna acknowledged. "One week was too long for me; I can't imagine having to stay as long as he does."

"He seemed really happy that I'd stopped in."

"I do miss visiting with him," Dayna admitted

"Why don't you go and see him one afternoon? Madison might like to go with you. I'll look after Abby," Valerie offered

"Yeah," Dayna nodded, liking the sound of her mom's suggestion. "I might."

"Can I go and visit Quinn?" Madison asked. She'd been practicing saying his name and had it down to one syllable now.

"Would you like that?"

"Yes, yes, yes!" Madison started bouncing in her seat.

"Maybe you could make a special picture to take to him."

Before she'd even finished the sentence, Dayna realized that she shouldn't have mentioned it before her daughter was done eating, because now, Madison wanted to go and start on it right away.

"I want to go draw a picture for Quinn," Madison insisted. Dayna knew that there was no use in trying to convince her to eat. Her mind was already made up.

"Okay, sweetheart, you can go," Dayna smiled. Her daughter was very determined, but Dayna had been like that as a child, too. Valerie helped Madison out of her booster seat and she shot off like a rocket to go and start her project.

They all enjoyed their meal in silence for a few minutes. Every time Dayna loaded Abigail's little spoon, the child would take it from her mother and attempt to feed herself. It was comical to watch, because more went on her face and in her hair, than in her mouth.

"The friendship that you have with Quinn is special, you know." Valerie broke the silence. "But it doesn't have to be anything more than that—not unless you both want it to be."

"I know." Dayna was beginning to like the prospect of a friendship with Quinn. She didn't feel so apprehensive anymore. In fact, she was beginning to see that it was something special—a gift, even—and she didn't want to risk losing it over a misunderstanding.

"I think I'll get a few more of his songs printed out and take them to him." She realized that she was actually looking forward to seeing him.

"Did you ask him about playing at Rachael's wedding?" Valerie inquired.

"No, I totally forgot the other day. I should do that soon, though. Rachael will need to make other arrangements if Quinn isn't comfortable doing it."

Dayna got up to start clearing the table, but Valerie objected, "Dayna, let me do that. Why don't you go and work on some of Quinn's songs?"

"Mom, I'm feeling fine. Really. I can do some of the work around here. You don't have to do it all."

"I don't mind," Valerie replied, graciously. "You go on. I'll just clean up here quickly; then Abby and I will go and see how Madison's picture is coming along."

Dayna gave in and went to her office. She was being utterly spoiled, but she didn't mind. Her mother seemed very happy to be able to do it for her.

Sitting down at her desk, she began working on the music. She was pleased at how easy it was.

Before long, she had the rest of the songs from her notebook entered onto the computer.

It was exciting to be able to give Quinn his music on paper like that. He had an amazing gift and she felt honored to be a part of it. He had some new songs, now, too. She contemplated taking her recorder with her when she went to visit, in order to record his new work, but she decided that it would be better left for another day.

Taking a minute, she looked over her day-planner. She had a doctor's appointment in two days and then it was the weekend. Madison really wanted to go with her and Mark would be taking the girls out Saturday. Amy's parents had invited them all out to their acreage for a barbeque on Sunday. They'd have to go the following day or else wait until the beginning of the week. She realized that she didn't want to wait.

She decided that it would probably be a good idea to call and let Quinn know that she was coming to visit. In her purse, she found the phone number that he'd given her. She wasn't sure if it was the best time to call, but she dialed, hoping that she might catch him in his room.

"Dayna?"

"Either you have call display, or you're psychic," she laughed.

"Thanks for the fax today. The song looks great. I'm glad you added the title."

"You should think of titles for all your pieces. You'll need them if you record a CD."

"I guess I haven't thought that far ahead. Maybe I should hire you as my manager."

"I'm sure I haven't the expertise you'd need for that," Dayna laughed, "but it's not a bad idea. You really should have someone to represent you."

"I guess," he conceded, somewhat hesitantly. "It's just...you don't know how much thinking like that messes with my head. I'm just getting used to the fact that I can even play something that doesn't sound like a cat walking across the keys."

Dayna laughed again. That was exactly what she'd missed—the lighthearted joking and his delightful sense of humor.

"Quinn, the reason I called is that I was thinking of coming by to see you. I have several of your songs finished and printed out; I can bring them in for you. Madison wants to come, too. She's working on a picture for you, as we speak. Tomorrow works best for us. Is the afternoon okay? Say around one-thirty?"

"Jeez, let me check my schedule. I'm having lunch with the mayor tomorrow, then a meeting with the city planning committee at three, but I should be able to squeeze you in."

It took Dayna a second to realize that he was joking; he could be so serious about it.

"I've missed that," she laughed.

"What, my 'BS'ing?'"

"I guess you can call it that," she replied. "You make me laugh and that's something I need to do more of."

"What are friends for?"

His words warmed Dayna's heart. She felt so much better about their friendship now; she was truly looking forward to their visit.

"Do you want to meet out on the terrace if the weather's nice?" she asked.

"Sure, that works."

"I noticed a Starbucks when I was there the other day. Why don't I stop and get us some lattés before I come up?"

"Oh God, Dayna," he teased. "I'd never be able to drink the hospital brew after that! I'd be spoiled. I'd have to hire some cute little orderly to bring me lattés all the time."

"Is that a yes or a no?"

"Oh, it's definitely a yes," he laughed. "Actually, I spied it myself when I first went down to the main floor to play my piano. Just tell them to make Quinn's special."

"Are you serious?" Dayna couldn't tell any more, but she was enjoying the challenge.

"It's a triple grande, light classic, whole milk, extra hot, no-foam latté—but don't worry about remembering all that; they know me down there."

Dayna wondered what kind of a man Quinn Radford was, that he could command attention the way he did. She'd been amazed at the way he'd arranged to get a piano delivered in just a day. He ran a successful construction company, too. It wasn't just a small family business, either. Both Brian and Greg knew of it.

"Okay, Quinn's special it is!" Dayna declared. "I might just have to try one, myself, to see what's so special about it."

"It's good. Not too sweet. And none of that non-fat crap—I like to taste the milk. It packs a punch, though; you might want to back down to a double."

Dayna couldn't help but laugh. Quinn seemed to be in a very good mood. Either that, or he was trying harder to keep things light between them. In any case, it felt good.

"Oh yeah, while I'm thinking of it, Rachael asked if you might be interested in playing at her wedding. She heard some of the music that I had recorded and she really liked it.

"Don't feel pressured, though. I offered to play any specific favorites that she wanted. She just thought that yours would be nice background music while guests are being seated and things like that."

Quinn was quiet on the other end of the phone. She hoped that he wasn't feeling obligated because of the work she was doing for him.

"Quinn, please don't feel like you have to."

"No, Dayna, I'd be honored. It's just another one of those weird things I'm trying to get my mind around. Before this, if I was asked to do anything for a wedding, it would be to build a gazebo or a sound stage, not play music."

"I guess I can't really relate to having those kinds of life-altering changes. My life is still much the same on the outside since my heart attack. It's just inside that I feel like a different person."

"At least I can talk to you about it. That means a lot to me."

"I'm glad," Dayna smiled to herself. "And I'm looking forward to tomorrow."

"Ditto."

* * *

Chapter 26

Quinn awoke early to the music playing in his head. Once again, Dayna was in his dream. This time, however, she started walking toward him. He lay there wondering what his dreams meant.

"Are they guiding me? Are they showing me the future? Or is it just that I want something to happen so badly, I'm creating it in my dreams?"

There was no use in trying to go back to sleep. He decided to get up. He'd had a hard time falling asleep the night before, too. In his mind, he kept replaying the conversation that he'd had with Dayna. He didn't want to read too much into it, but she was coming to see him, with no other reason than to visit. She could just fax him the rest of the music when she finished it. He wasn't in a real rush for it anyway. As much as he appreciated the work she was doing, it was all just circles and lines to him.

He was beginning to realize that he wanted it to be more than that; he wanted to learn to read music one day. It would open up a whole new world for him. Dayna would be the obvious choice to teach him, but he wasn't sure if he wanted to ask her. For now, keeping their relationship at a place that was comfortable for her was more important.

Valerie's visit had certainly given him hope and he was extremely thankful for it. It had helped him to put things into perspective, knowing that it was just a matter of weeks since Dayna's marriage had ended.

"I wonder what happened between them. How could her husband not see and appreciate what I see in her? The girls are so young, too. One's just a baby. God! It must be hard on her. No wonder she looks like a scared rabbit when things get awkward between us."

Quinn put his thoughts on hold and went for a shower. He wanted to keep himself busy. One-thirty was still several long hours away.

He played the piano in the chapel after breakfast. He performed for the full two hours and then stayed to chat afterwards with some people who'd come to see him for the first time.

When lunch was over, Quinn made his way up to the fourth floor. It was only one o'clock, but he didn't mind being early. He took his wheelchair, but once outside, he got up and walked the short distance to a bench.

It was quiet on the terrace. He was glad to have it to himself for a moment. As he listened to the beautiful sound of a bird singing, he realized that he'd never stopped to appreciate things like that before. He noticed the flowers on the shrub beside him. They were so delicate—each petal folding around the next in an intricate pattern radiating outward from the center.

"What created this beauty? What holds it all together? It can't be the same God that I learned about as a child."

He thought about the power that he felt flowing through him as he played the piano.

"Could the power that I've felt be the same power that created all this beauty?"

He wanted to talk to Dayna more about that. She'd mentioned feeling the same things.

As he looked up, he saw Madison running toward him with a smile on her face and a paper in her hand. She ran right into his arms and gave him a hug, just as she'd done the last time he saw her. Then she handed him the awkwardly folded paper that she was holding.

Before he opened it, he looked up to see Dayna smiling at him. That smile—it made his heart yearn. He looked at her for a moment, before turning back to Madison.

"Quinn, I made this for you." Madison unfolded the picture for him and went on to explain what was on it.

"This is me," she pointed, "and this is my baby sister. This is my house and my back yard and this is my tree house. Uncle Greg is going to build me a tree house."

The drawings of herself and her sister were large. The house was quite small in comparison. The tree, however, took up the whole height of the paper and the tree house was a brightly colored box that sat precariously on one branch. It was delightful. He could tell that she'd spent a lot of time making it and he was touched.

"Thank-you, Madison." As he gave her a hug and kissed the top of her head, he was reminded of his own daughter at that age. He'd forgotten how nice small children smell. Madison giggled and continued to stay by his side.

Dayna handed Quinn his latté before she sat down. She had one for herself, also, and a small slushy drink for Madison.

"You're getting quite the reputation down there," she smiled. "The girls seem to know you well."

Quinn wasn't sure he wanted Dayna to think of him as a flirt or a ladies' man, but he had been down there quite often and, if it wasn't busy, he liked to hang around and talk with the girls.

He simply shrugged his shoulders and smiled, "What can I say?" He held up his latté. "Thank-you for the drink."

"You're welcome." She took a sip of hers and commented, "It's very good."

Madison took her drink from her mother, sucked on the straw and then made a face. "It's very, very cold," she informed them, pouting. "It makes my head hurt."

"Just suck it slowly, then," Dayna advised. "Or let it sit in the sun, here, so it can melt a bit."

Madison chose the latter and went back to lean against Quinn's knee.

"Quinn, is yours very, very cold, too?" It was cute the way she said his name.

"No honey, it's very, very hot."

The child climbed up on the bench beside him. Setting his drink aside, he looked at her picture again.

"This tree house your uncle is building—it looks really nice," Quinn said. "I built my daughter a tree house like that when she was little."

"Is she still little?" Madison asked, innocently.

"No sweetie, Brianna's just about all grown up now. She's seventeen."

"Is that old?"

"That's how old Caitlyn is, sweetheart," Dayna informed her.

"Caitlyn baby-sits me and Abby when Mommy and Daddy go out," Madison explained. Quinn saw a pained look flash across Dayna's face at the reference to her husband. It was all still so fresh. He wondered if she was still in love with him.

Dayna opened her bag and pulled out a thick coloring book and some large, colorful markers. She handed them to Madison and the little girl immediately jumped down and spread out her things on the carpeted surface near their feet.

Dayna turned to Quinn, "Their father and I are separated. It happened just before my heart attack."

"Dayna, I'm sorry. It must be hard on you; the girls are so young."

"Yes," she admitted. "It has been. I don't think she really understands it yet." Dayna looked at Madison as she said the words.

"My wife and I split up when our daughter was five. It's hard on kids. Brianna went through a few rough years, but she seems to have come around now. She's a good kid."

Dayna watched Madison coloring for a moment. "He left me for another woman," she said, softly.

Quinn felt anger flare up inside of him. *"What kind of goddamned bastard would leave a woman like this and two adorable kids?"* He wanted, more

304

than anything, to reach out and comfort her, but he knew that it would scare her away. What she needed right now was a friend—a friend who could understand what she was feeling.

"He's a fool." As soon he said it, he wished he could take the words back. If she still had feelings for her husband, she might resent the insult toward him.

She looked at Quinn and smiled, "It's not totally his fault. I was different before. I'm not sure I really knew how to love."

Quinn found that extremely hard to believe. The woman before him seemed so open, so caring, so capable of love.

"Do you love him now?" He had to ask. He needed to know.

"Probably not in the way you mean. I think I'm beginning not to hate him, though," she laughed.

"That's a good start," he said, enjoying her laugh.

"What happened with your marriage?"

"We married young. She was pregnant with Brianna. I thought we could make it work, but she resented having to give up her career plans. I ended up working even harder to provide for them, but it also meant that I wasn't home a lot. We just drifted apart."

"It's amazing how we can live so much of our lives, not really living."

"I know what you mean. Today, for the first time, I listened to a bird singing and I noticed the way the petals are formed on these flowers. How is it possible to live forty years and not notice those things?"

"I've just begun to realize for the first time what a wonderful family I have," Dayna said. "We weren't close at all, before. Now, they feel like my lifeline. I don't know what I'd do without them."

As they shared their experiences, Quinn realized that he'd never talked so openly with anyone before. Yet with Dayna, he felt he could share anything. For that reason, he knew he had to be careful. It would be very easy to let it slip how he felt about her.

"When I look at these flowers and how perfect they are, I can't help but wonder about God. What, or who, created such beauty, such perfection?" He was looking at the flowers, but he couldn't help thinking about her.

"I've been listening to Mom and Rachael talk about God as an energy Source, rather than a being. They describe it as a power that's in us and through us—something we're made up of, as well.

"Rachael really believes that we can access this power to change our lives—deliberately. Not just be changed by it, but actually have control over what happens in our lives."

Quinn had heard similar words before. "I have a guy working for me—one of my foremen. He talks about stuff like that. I've had a hard time with some of the things he says, but he's a decent guy; I respect him. He believes we can control our circumstances by our thoughts. He called it the Law of Attraction."

Dayna looked at him, "That's what Mom and Rachael call it, too. Rachael describes thoughts as energy—like radio transmitters, sending out signals. Do you think it's possible?"

"Mommy, I have to go pee."

"Okay, sweetie." Dayna took Madison by the hand. "Quinn, we'll be right back."

Quinn mulled over the things they'd just talked about. Something about it resonated with him. He'd experienced the supernatural with his music, so he knew there was a lot more going on than what he understood.

Dayna returned. Madison sat down between them and sipped on her drink.

"The part I have a hard time with is if we can control what happens to us, then why don't we? Why do these kinds of things happen to us?" Quinn looked down at his legs.

"I was just thinking about that the other day," Dayna said. "When I first heard the concept that our thoughts are responsible for what happens to us, I felt angry. I wasn't willing to take the blame for the way my life had turned out—for my husband leaving me, or for me having a heart attack.

"But then the thought occurred to me, that if I had attracted those things by my thoughts, maybe I could attract different things, if I changed the way I was thinking. It gave me a sense of power."

"Mommy, I'm all done coloring." Madison's attention span was beginning to wear thin.

They changed the topic of conversation and focused on Madison. She wanted to know if Quinn had learned to walk yet, when he was going home and what his daughter's name was. She wanted to see the tree house that he had built. She also invited him to help her uncle build her a tree house.

Quinn answered her stream of questions and thanked her for asking him to help with her tree house. He told her that he would consider it.

The questions finally ran out and Dayna said, "Well, we should probably get going."

Quinn was sorry that their time was up so soon. He wanted to talk to Dayna some more about the topics they had touched on.

Dayna seemed hesitant to leave, also. "Quinn, I enjoyed this. I'd like to talk to you again about some of these things."

"Stop by anytime," he said. He wanted to make their good-bye easier, so he added, "I'm training for a marathon in a couple of weeks, so I'll be busy, but for you, I'll make time to visit."

She smiled and shook her head as she held out her hand. He took it and held it for a brief moment. Then he squeezed it and let it go.

Madison had another hug for him.

"Thanks for the picture, Madison. I'm going to put it up in my room."

"Good-bye, Quinn. I love you," Madison waved.

"I love you, too," he admitted silently, as he watched Dayna and her daughter walk away.

* * *

Rachael was thrilled at how the details for the wedding were coming together. They had found invitations that she and Brian both loved. The front of the card was a casual photo of the two of them printed in burgundy and white. It gave the picture the look of an old-fashioned photograph, but had a modern, romantic feel.

She and Gail had gone shopping for her dress and she'd found one that she really loved. It was the perfect combination of chic and elegant, and fairy-tale romantic. A strapless satin gown, the skirt wasn't too full, but it had a generous train on the back. The bodice was covered with intricate lace and beading and there were matching details down the back and onto the train.

When she tried it on and came out of the change room to look in the full-length mirror, she was convinced. Gail had gasped and a woman across the room said, 'Wow!' Rachael knew that she had found the perfect dress.

They'd booked live music for the dance. It was a band that Brian had heard about from a friend. He took her to see them play at a nightclub one evening and Rachael really liked their style of music.

Quinn had agreed to play at the wedding and reception, in addition to the pieces that Dayna was playing. Rachael had a favorite song that she wanted to walk up the aisle to; the rest of the song selection, she was leaving to Dayna and Quinn.

The invitations had come back within a week; they were now in the process of addressing them and sending them out. They had just spent an evening at Brian's parents working on them and were planning to do the same with Rachael's mom.

There was little else that needed to be done. They were meeting with the caterer the following week to decide on the food for the reception. They'd already met with the official who would be performing the ceremony. She was a lovely woman; Rachael liked her right away. She'd asked them about vows. There were standard ones that they could use, of course, but Rachael liked the idea of writing their own. She wanted their wedding vows to reflect their personal beliefs.

Rachael sat back and rested her head against Brian's shoulder. "Everything's falling into place effortlessly." As she closed her eyes, she thought of one more thing. Turning to him, she asked. "Did you book the tickets?"

He smiled and kissed her forehead. "It's all taken care of."

They were going to be spending two weeks in Tahiti at a romantic resort. Their accommodation was to be a thatched-roof bungalow out on the water where they could actually look below and watch the sea life beneath their feet. The package included a three-day, two-night cruise to the surrounding islands. It sounded so exotic; Rachael could hardly wait.

"What about our vows? Do you want to work on them together, or should we each write something separately?"

"I have some ideas of what I'd like to say." Brian caressed her arm. "But it might be nice to work on them together, so they have a similar tone."

That sounded perfect! Brian was truly amazing. It was uncanny, sometimes, how he could read her thoughts, or she, his. So far, they'd agreed on every detail of the wedding. They each had unique tastes, yet they blended together perfectly.

"What ideas do you have?" she looked up at Brian and smiled.

He was quiet for a moment and then turned to face her. He gently took her hands in his own. "I'd tell you that since you came into my life, you've made me happier than I ever believed was possible. I'd tell you that your outlook on life is amazing and that I learn from you every second that I'm with you. I'd tell you that I don't know for sure what our future holds, but that I'm happy to walk beside you and experience each moment as it unfolds."

Rachael looked into the eyes of the man she adored. The words that he had just spoken brought tears to her eyes. They were absolutely the most beautiful she'd ever heard in her life.

"Write that down," she implored, lovingly. "Don't change a word."

"I have." Brian wiped a tear from her cheek. "I've gone through several drafts already."

He leaned back then and looked at her for a moment. The grin on his face and the look in his eyes made Rachael curious.

"What?" she smiled.

"I got you a wedding present."

She wasn't sure how to respond. He was always giving her gifts, but she had a feeling that this was something else altogether.

"Do I get to open it before the wedding?"

"Yes."

He was being too mysterious; it was driving her crazy. "Are you just trying to torture me," she laughed, "or are you actually going to tell me?"

"Why don't I show you?" He stood up and offered her his hand. The dogs came to life at the sign of activity and Brian asked, "Do you two want to come for a ride?" Cassie barked and Duke ran to the front door and back again.

"Where are we going? It's ten o'clock at night."

"We could go tomorrow."

"Are you kidding?" she replied, excitedly. "You've got my curiosity piqued now."

They all got into Brian's SUV and, as he drove, she watched him, trying to figure out what he was up to. They headed in the general direction of Rachael's place, but before they got there, Brian turned off the main road, onto a side street. It wasn't too far from her house. Rachael had gone for walks in the area; she liked the beautiful homes, the big yards and the tall trees.

Brian made one more turn and then pulled up in front of a house. It was one that she'd never been to before. She wondered if it belonged to someone that Brian knew.

He didn't move to get out of the vehicle. He just looked at her with that same look on his face.

"Are you going to tell me?"

"This is your wedding present," he replied, simply, glancing at the house that they were parked in front of.

Rachael looked at him and then back at the house that, she now saw, had a realtor's sign on the front lawn. The truth was beginning to register, as she looked back at Brian.

"You bought me a house?" Her words were barely audible. She was in shock. Her mind was trying to absorb what just happened.

"When? How?" she started to ask, but instead of waiting for the answers, she said the words again, "You bought us a house?" This time the excitement was evident in her voice, although Rachael still couldn't quite believe what she was saying.

"The deal's not final yet." Brian reached for her hand. "I wanted you to see it, first. You have to love it, or we'll keep looking for something else."

Rachael turned to look at the house. It was an older, two-storey home. It had beautiful stonework on the front and shutters on the windows. There was an elegant, stone walkway, leading up to impressive-looking double doors at the front entry. A large weeping birch stood majestic and dignified in a well-manicured front yard.

Even in the dark, Rachael could tell that it was a beautiful house. If the inside were anything like what she was seeing on the exterior, she knew that she would love it.

"Brian, it looks beautiful!"

"Wait until you see the inside. It has hardwood floors throughout, a modern kitchen and the backyard is fenced, with lots of big trees."

"If you like it, then I know I will, too." Rachael squeezed Brian's hand. "I can't believe you did this! How long have you been looking?"

"A couple of weeks," he grinned. "I've looked at four houses right in this area and two others further away, but I like this one the best."

"Brian, I just have to say I would have been happy living at your place. It's a really nice house; you've put so much work into it."

"I wanted something that wasn't mine or yours. I wanted something that would be ours, a house that we both love. I want this to be a place that we can start a family one day."

"I want that, too." Rachael leaned over and kissed Brian. He pulled her close and returned her kiss with one so full of passion that it took her breath away.

After a moment, she murmured, "Brian, let's not wait." She looked deeply into his eyes, asking a question and she could see the answer reflected there. "Let's not wait long to start a family."

* * *

Chapter 27

As Dayna listened to the dialogue at the table, she noticed that her sister's face was shining with incredible joy. Knowing all the years that Rachael had suffered with depression, Dayna was truly glad that she'd found happiness.

"So everything's gone through?" Valerie was inquiring. "The house is yours, then?"

"The deal's done," Brian declared, smiling at Rachael. "We take possession on the first of June."

"That's great!" Valerie replied. "It will give you time to get settled in before the wedding."

The group turned as Madison came down the stairs in her pajamas and walked into the dining room. "Mommy, I can't sleep," she said, rubbing her eyes.

Dayna didn't mind. She was about to say that Madison could stay up for a bit, when Brian offered, "Why don't I read you a story? Do you have a favorite?" Madison took his hand and they went up the stairs."

"I definitely see kids in your future," Dayna smiled at Rachael.

The look in Rachael's eyes as she watched Brian follow the child up the stairs was ample proof that she agreed with her sister.

Dayna was reminded, again, about how perfectly Rachael's life seemed to be unfolding. Still wondering how Rachael could be responsible for the amazing things that kept happening in her life, she decided to approach the subject.

"Rachael, I'd like to know more about this teaching that you talk about."

The question got her sister's full attention.

"Quinn mentioned it the other day, too," Dayna said. "It's hard to understand how we can control the things that happen to us."

"It's all about focus," Rachael explained. "Your thoughts are powerful. If you could be aware of your thoughts every moment—if you could set up a system to monitor them—you'd see a direct correlation between the thoughts that you think and what's happening in your life.

"The problem is that most people aren't aware of their thoughts, or the fact that they're mostly negative."

Dayna had to agree that what Rachael said made sense. Before her heart attack, had she been aware of her thoughts, she would have noticed that they were ones of anger, resentment, cynicism and skepticism. Hindsight offered her that awareness, but now she wanted to learn how she could use the teaching to affect her future in a more positive way.

"There's a powerful, Universal law at work that's attraction based," Rachael continued. "In simple terms it means that 'like attracts like.' Because each thought has its own vibrational frequency, this law is constantly matching our thoughts with circumstances and events that are vibrating at the same frequency."

"Can it really be that simple?"

"I think everybody has to prove it for themselves. But I've seen enough evidence in my life to know that it works that way."

"So we change our circumstances by changing our thoughts?" Dayna really wanted to believe it.

"It's easier if you understand what part your emotions play in this." Rachael went on to tell her about the emotional scale.

"Thoughts evoke emotions. You may not always be aware of what you're thinking in the moment, but you know how those thoughts make you feel. Your emotions are an incredible guidance system. They help you to know if you're moving in the direction you want to go."

Dayna sighed, "I always thought my emotions were something that I had to keep under control. But you're saying that this whole time they were trying to tell me I was moving in the wrong direction?"

"Yes," Valerie interjected. "But once you understand how this works, you can leave the past behind and start being in the moment. That's when you realize that life is yours for the living and happiness is yours for the having. The reason we seem to stay 'stuck' is that we stay focused on the mistakes we made in the past."

Brian came down just then. "It took four books, but I think she's out for the count." He looked at the pile of invitations, barely touched. "Looks like you ladies got side-tracked."

"Dayna asked about the Law of Attraction," Rachael smiled.

"Uh-oh," Brian joked. "I know where that leads. I naively asked her about that subject once, and look where it's gotten me." He kissed Rachael and, becoming serious, looked deep into her eyes. "It's made me the happiest man in the world."

Dayna watched the encounter and was touched by the depth of love that she saw between them. Rachael truly had created the wonderful things that she was experiencing; Dayna's heart was telling her that what she heard tonight was true.

She wondered if Quinn would agree. They'd touched on the subject, but really hadn't had a lot of time to talk when she and Madison visited. She toyed with the idea of calling him.

Brian and Rachael said their good-byes, leaving some of the invitations unfinished. They had finalized a list, however, making the rest of the process easier. Valerie offered to work on them the next day and then excused herself to go up to bed.

Dayna looked at the time, wondering if it was too late to call Quinn. He didn't seem like the type that would be asleep early, but in the hospital, she wasn't sure. Wanting to talk to him while the ideas were fresh in her mind, she decided to take a chance.

He answered on the first ring. "Quinn's Pizzeria. We're open twenty-four hours to serve you."

Dayna laughed. She never knew what to expect from him; he definitely wasn't predictable.

"Hi, Quinn. It sounds like I didn't wake you."

"No, I was just watching TV. I'm getting hooked on these reality shows. I'm even thinking of signing up. I can't sing or dance, but I sure wouldn't mind being the bachelor. I wonder if they've found anyone for next season."

"Really? Having to decide between all those beautiful women?" Dayna joked. "I don't know, Quinn. I think it would be harder than it looks."

"Probably," he agreed. "Besides, I'm not sure how many women would be willing to fight over a middle-aged, ex-construction worker who can't even walk properly."

She caught something in his voice. It wasn't bitterness, but it had a tone of sadness. She realized that she had never thought of him in that way. He had so many good qualities.

"That's not what I see, Quinn. I see a man who's built a successful business. I see a good father, a man who finds humor in adversity, not to mention a gifted pianist."

"Keep going. I like your version better."

Dayna smiled. *"Maybe Rachael is right. Maybe it is all about focus."*

"You have a lot of wonderful qualities," Dayna assured him. "It's just a matter of what you choose to look at. I was talking to my sister tonight about the Law of Attraction." Dayna touched on some of the things that she and Rachael had talked about. "I don't know, Quinn, but I think there's something to this."

"With all the weird stuff that's happened to me, I wouldn't rule anything out. Tell me more."

Dayna reiterated more of what she had learned from Rachael earlier that evening, while Quinn listened intently.

"So basically," she summed up. "Our emotions are a guidance system; they can guide us to the things we want in life, if we learn to listen to them."

"Wait," Quinn interrupted. "Is that like saying, 'If it feels good, do it?' My grandmother would roll over in her grave if she heard that and yet I'm not sure I can argue with it."

"All I know is that I've been trying to control and even deny my emotions all these years." Dayna twisted the phone cord around her finger. "I thought they were a hindrance. I didn't listen to my heart; I listened to my head. All the while, my emotions were telling me, 'No, go this way.'"

"I think maybe there's a connection here," Quinn concluded. "Between this power that we've both felt inside and what you're talking about."

"Yes!" Dayna agreed, her thoughts heading in the same direction. "Because if we're connected to this power and we have an internal guidance system, then it makes sense that we would have at least some control over the direction our life takes."

"It sounds good in theory."

"I'd have a harder time believing it, but I've seen so much evidence in my sister's life, the last couple of years." Dayna filled Quinn in on what Rachael had gone through in the past. "She might still be battling depression if she hadn't found this.

"Now, her life seems to be one amazing experience after another. And it's not just the outward things, either; she's happy—all the time.

"Too happy, I used to think," Dayna added. "Some days it really pissed me off."

Quinn began to laugh, heartily. "Dayna, you are good for the soul."

"What are friends for?"

He was quiet on the other end and, as Dayna looked at the time, she realized that they had talked for nearly an hour. She also realized that she'd thoroughly enjoyed herself.

"Well, Quinn, it's getting late. I should go."

"Thanks for calling, Dayna. I enjoy talking like this. I think we nailed down philosophy tonight," he joked. "Maybe next time we can tackle world hunger and global warming."

"Good night, Quinn," Dayna laughed, feeling greatly uplifted by their conversation. "Take care."

* * *

Quinn looked forward to Dayna's calls, as the weeks passed. They often talked late into the night about all kinds of topics. He was trying not to delude himself; he still had no reason to believe that Dayna wanted anything more than friendship, but he could live with that for now. As long as he had hope, he knew it would sustain him.

It was fascinating to hear all of the things that she was learning from her sister. Quinn was becoming more and more convinced that it was truth, as well. He was even beginning to apply some of it in his life.

Dayna was reading some books that she'd borrowed from Rachael and, occasionally, she'd read parts to him over the phone. One phrase in particularly had stuck with him.

> *"Your habit of resistant thought is the only thing that ever keeps you from allowing the things you desire."* [19]

Quinn couldn't help but wonder how much of his own life he'd spent in resistant thought.

"What if I'm resisting the very things that I desire?" he asked himself. *"What do I really want out of life anyway?*

"Dayna." The answer was loud and clear.

It was true; he thought about her day and night. Her beautiful face was always in his dreams. He could see her smile, hear her laugh. He could even feel her warm, soft hand in his own. He imagined touching her hair and caressing her face, but he wouldn't let himself go beyond that. He was torturing himself enough as it was.

He was in love with her and he wanted, more than anything, for her to feel the same way, but he knew that he had to be realistic.

"What if Dayna never wants more than the friendship that we have now? What if I profess my love to her one day and she doesn't feel the same? Would it ruin what we already have?

"Could I be content with friendship and nothing more?" he asked, feeling frustrated.

"Damn it." he shook his head. *"I don't know if I can do that."*

Suddenly, it occurred to him that the very thoughts he was thinking were the kinds of resistant thoughts that the book was talking about. He was imagining the worst, assuming that they could never move past friendship, when in truth, he wanted so much more.

He remembered Dayna explaining that in order to change a circumstance, he had to change the way he thought about it—he needed to focus on it in a way that felt better.

When he thought about Dayna, it was easy to feel good, but he always seemed to counter those positive thoughts with doubts about their future, which didn't feel good at all.

"Is it possible that my thoughts are cancelling each other out? The positive thoughts are bringing my desire closer, but the negative ones are pushing it away. If that's true, then my work is to think only good thoughts about Dayna," he concluded, feeling triumphant. *"I can do that."*

Satisfied with his plan, he went on to examine the other areas of his life.

"What else do I desire?"

He was determined to walk normally again and he was doing well; the doctors were impressed with his progress. Since the accident, he'd refused to entertain the idea of being crippled. It wasn't an option.

Whenever he thought about his physical well-being, he tried to imagine himself healthy and strong—self-sufficient too. It had been a long journey, but now he was looking forward to going home in less than a week.

Playing the piano was a given. He had no lofty desires of fame, but he liked the idea of sharing his gift with others. He saw himself playing in front of audiences and felt comfortable doing so. He didn't know how to make that happen, but he wasn't worried. Somehow, he knew that there was a greater power in control of things like that.

"So why am I not trusting this power to work things out with Dayna?" he questioned.

Immediately, the answer became clear. *"This greater power—this God that I've been feeling within me—has been in control the whole time!*

"Meeting Dayna...the fact that she heard my music from her hospital bed. The dreams and all the 'coincidences'...they weren't coincidences at all!

"That's it!" he concluded. *"It all makes so much sense now."*

Quinn closed his eyes and felt a surge of appreciation for the loving, guiding presence that had made itself so powerfully known. He felt like a weight had been lifted from him as he realized that the same powerful presence was organizing the details of his life much better than he ever could.

* * *

As Rachael packed up the last of her belongings, she looked around her cute little house. She'd be seeing a lot of it in the future; her mom would be moving in shortly. Rachael had sold some of her furniture, but the rest, she was able to leave. They'd moved all of Brian's things to their new place earlier in the day. His house was empty now, ready for its new owners.

Her house held so many wonderful memories. There was appreciation for her father and his amazing gift to her. There was the fun she'd had with Gail, especially the crazy cooking lessons—they always had a little too much wine!

She remembered the first time that Brian had come to pick her up at her place—how nervous and excited she'd been. She reflected back on all that she had learned there and the precious moments she'd spent alone with her Inner Being. They were all such treasured memories.

Turning around, she saw Brian standing in the doorway, smiling.

"I didn't want to disturb you. It looked like you were having a nostalgic moment." He came over and put his arm around her. "How are you doing?"

"I'm fine," she replied, gazing at her fiancé, lovingly. "I was just remembering all the wonderful times I've had here. But I'm looking forward to making memories in our new house, too."

"So am I."

"Well," she glanced toward the box that she had just packed. "This is the last one. I didn't realize I had so much stuff."

Brian picked it up and held it with one arm as he took Rachael's hand.

She smiled up at him, "Let's go home."

* * *

Chapter 28

Dayna was fully recovered. The doctor had given her a clean bill of health and she could now resume all normal activities. Ironically, her body was the only part of her that was back to what it had been; the rest of her would never be the same again. She was forever changed.

She wouldn't wish what she had experienced, physically, on anyone; but in her heart, she was actually thankful for what she'd gone through.

"My heart..." she mused. *"It's interesting that it was that part of me that was affected."*

With the understanding that she'd gained recently, it did make sense. *"My heart—the emotional center of my being—was closed off. No wonder it cried out in pain. It was being starved.*

"I think that what happened to my physical heart corresponded to what was happening to my emotional heart. It makes perfect sense." She couldn't wait to share her insights with Quinn.

He'd been home from the hospital for a couple of weeks, now, and was managing fine with the help of a woman he'd hired, who took on the roles of nurse, housekeeper and chauffeur. He still had some physical limitations; he wasn't able to drive yet, but he was confident that he would in time. Dayna greatly admired his determination.

She had visited him once more in the hospital, before he was released and, having recorded his new music, was working on it in her spare time. They talked on the phone regularly and Dayna always looked forward to their uplifting conversations.

Having returned to teaching, Dayna was limiting herself to three days a week, with the option of going back full-time in the fall. It felt good to get into a busier routine again, but now, she set aside more time for herself. She took more walks, read more books and enjoyed life more fully. She appreciated moments alone, quality time with her girls and time spent with her family.

She missed having tea with her mom in the evenings, however. Before moving into Rachael's house, Valerie had gone back home to get her things organized and sell her properties, so it had been a couple of weeks since they'd had a chance to sit down and talk.

It was good to see the positive changes in her mom's life. Moving back seemed like the perfect plan for her; Dayna had never seen her happier.

Dayna was enjoying her friendship with Quinn. She could share anything with him. He made her laugh and it was fun to learn new things together.

It was an odd relationship in some ways. If she was honest with herself, she would have to admit that she loved him—he'd become very dear to her. Nevertheless, telling him so would seem awkward.

It was funny how children used the word so freely. Whenever Madison talked to Quinn, whether on the phone, or in person, she never hesitated to tell him that she loved him.

Dayna didn't quite understand the way she felt toward him. It wasn't a physical attraction—not that Quinn was unattractive. He had so many other qualities that attracted her; she just never gave much thought to his looks.

She really didn't know that he felt any differently toward her, either. There had been a couple of times when he'd looked at her and she thought she saw something more in his eyes. But then he'd tell a joke and make her laugh and she'd convince herself that she was just imagining things. Honestly, she liked things the way they were. She only hoped that they could stay that way.

Rachael's wedding was less than three weeks away. Dayna had already talked with Quinn about song selection and they had determined which ones would be best. She would be playing three songs during the procession. Quinn would play before the ceremony, as people arrived, and again, afterwards. The process had helped them to come up with names for some of his songs and to the rest, they'd assigned numbers for easy reference.

She'd been thinking that it would be a good idea to get together with Quinn once, before the wedding, and go over the song selections—both his and the ones that she was going to play. It would give her an overall feel for the arrangement.

Dialing his number, she prepared herself for the bizarre way he had of answering the phone. He always knew that it was her and would say whatever came to mind. She decided to fool him, this once, and keep her number from showing up. She stopped before she pressed the last digit of his phone number and re-dialed, keeping her number private.

"Hello," he answered, sounding normal.

"Hello?" he repeated, when she didn't respond.

Dayna smiled as an idea came to mind. She disguised her voice and told him that she was from the prize department of a local radio station. She informed him that his name had been drawn and that he now qualified for a trip for two to Mexico. All he had to do was answer a skill-testing question.

"Great. What's the question?"

"How do you spell... onomatopoeia?"

"On a mat of what?" he asked, incredulously. "Is this for real?"

A Song of the Heart

Dayna couldn't contain herself any longer; she burst out laughing.

"Shit, Dayna! You had me going. I can't believe it. I never fall for pranks like that!"

"I can't believe you did," she responded, feeling giddy. "I was having a hard time not laughing."

"You could have at least used a real word."

"Quinn, that is a real word," she retorted. "You learned it in elementary school. Don't you remember your language arts?"

"No, I was too busy shooting spitballs. What the hell does it mean?"

"It refers to words that imitate sounds," she explained, "like 'buzz' or 'pop' or 'click'."

"That's it? A big word like that to describe a word like 'buzz'. Boy, someone had way too much time on their hands."

Dayna was nearly in tears from laughing so hard.

"You realize this means war!" he declared.

"Are you kidding? I was just paying you back for all the weird and bizarre ways you answer the phone when you know it's me."

"No way," he countered. "A practical joke like that is in a whole different league, but I've pulled a few good ones in my day. The trick now, is to catch you when you least expect it."

"Oh, no," Dayna groaned. "What have I started?" She was having more fun than she'd had in a long time. She'd never in her life been a practical joker—rarely even the recipient of one, but it was quite exhilarating. Not only that, but she realized that she was actually pretty good at it.

"Seriously, though," she said, still trying to catch her breath. "I wanted to see if we could get together in the next few days. I'd like to go over the songs that we'll be playing for the wedding and see how the arrangement sounds."

"Sure. What works for you?"

"I'm working tomorrow," she replied. "Thursday's the best; I'm home all day, but I'll have the girls. Would you mind coming here? If Lucy can drop you off, I'll run you home later."

"Yeah, that's fine. What time?"

"Why don't you come over for lunch? Abby sleeps in the afternoons and Madison can keep busy; we should be able to get some work done."

"Great, I'll see you Thursday."

Dayna hung up the phone and laughed again. Playing a prank like that had been so unlike her and yet it felt natural and good. It was as if a new part of her was just beginning to come alive.

* * *

The doorbell rang and Madison darted to open the front door. Dayna picked up Abigail and followed. She stood, transfixed, for a moment, staring at Quinn, unable to believe the change in him. She'd only seen him in the hospital, wearing a robe and pajamas. Now, he was wearing blue jeans with cowboy boots and a t-shirt that showed off his muscular arms.

The biggest change of all, however, was his face; he'd shaved off his beard. As he stood there smiling at her, Dayna realized that she was staring.

"Quinn, I'm sorry. Come in. It's just that you look so different. I'm not sure I would have even recognized you if I passed you on the street."

"It's nice to wear regular clothes, again. These are new; I lost about twenty pounds in the hospital, so I had to buy myself some new threads."

"It's the beard. I can't believe how different you look." She knew she was repeating herself, but she was having a hard time adjusting to the change.

"I let it grow in the hospital; it was easier just to keep it trimmed," he replied. "I've always had a moustache. I tried a goatee once, but I was wearing my glasses, reading the paper one night and my daughter told me I looked like Colonel Saunders evil twin, so I got rid of it."

"Kids can be brutally honest," Dayna said, grateful for the small talk as she dealt with her shock.

"I know! And teenagers can be downright mean. Brianna lived with me one summer, a couple of years ago, and she informed me that I had no taste in clothes, my moustache was 'way not cool' and nobody wears cowboy boots anymore. Oh, and I had to drop her off two blocks from her friend's house because I drive an 'old piece of crap'."

"What do you drive?" Dayna laughed.

"In the summer, I drive my T-bird. It's a '56 convertible. Mint condition. I've had some sweet offers on it, but I'm not ready to part with it yet."

They moved into the kitchen and Dayna put Abigail in her high chair.

"Quinn, you get to sit by me." Madison took him by the hand and led him to the table.

He sat down and Dayna served the honey-glazed chicken wings and pasta salad she had made.

"Quinn, can I get you something to drink? I made juice for the kids, but I have beer if you'd like." She didn't normally keep beer in the house, but she'd picked some up. He seemed like he would be a beer drinker.

He surprised her by declining. "Juice is fine. Thanks, Dayna. This chicken is really good."

Dayna tried not to stare, but she couldn't help stealing a glance at Quinn every once in a while. The change in him was affecting her in a way that she hadn't expected. She realized that she found him physically attractive and she wasn't quite sure what to do with the new feeling. She tried to ignore it.

"So how is your housekeeper working out?" Dayna asked, trying to keep the conversation going.

"Not bad. Her English is still a little rough, but I've learned a few words in Portuguese, so we manage." Quinn seemed to be slightly uneasy, as well, and Dayna wondered if her reaction to him had made him uncomfortable.

"Your sister must be getting excited; the wedding's just around the corner."

"Quinn, I get to be a flower girl at Auntie Rachael's wedding," Madison informed him.

"I'll bet you have a pretty new dress."

"It's pink with fluffles on it, but I can't wear it yet. I have new shoes, too. Mommy, can I show Quinn my dress and my shoes."

"Let's show them to him after lunch," Dayna suggested, glad to have the kids as a distraction. She didn't like feeling uncomfortable around Quinn; he was still the same man that she'd come to know. They were good friends; she knew that she could get past the awkwardness. She was even a little annoyed with herself for the way she was feeling.

As lunch progressed, Dayna found herself beginning to relax. Afterward, she went and put Abigail down for her nap and brought Madison's dress and shoes down to show Quinn.

Madison held the dress up in front of her and paraded around the room. They applauded when the fashion show was finished and then Dayna set the clothes aside. She had a new video to entertain Madison while she and Quinn went over the music.

"Well," she turned to Quinn. "Let's get started."

"Lead the way," he replied, following her into the front room.

"We should play the songs in the order that they'll be at the wedding," Dayna stated, getting down to business. "I have five pieces down for you to play before the ceremony starts. I'm going to make note of how long they last in total. We may have to modify the last song to blend in with the piece that I begin with for the processional."

There were to be two pianos, one on either side of the wedding party, facing the guests. They would be sitting on platforms allowing her and Quinn to see each other, as well as providing them with a clear view of the center aisle. Madison would be the first to walk down the aisle and Dayna didn't want to miss a single detail.

Quinn sat down at the piano and began playing the pieces that they'd selected. Dayna stood back, noting the time as he played.

"Quinn, I just had an idea." Without thinking, she moved to sit on the piano bench beside him. "Play the final song again."

He proceeded to play and, part way through, Dayna instructed, "Okay, stop there." She then began to play the song that Madison and Brian's nephew would be walking down the aisle to.

"That sounded great," Quinn exclaimed. "The notes I stopped on were the same ones that your song began with."

"Now, play it again," Dayna said. "Stop at the same place, but repeat the last bar twice over. I think it will give the song a sense of being finished rather than just ending in the middle."

They each played their piece again. The songs sounded exactly as Dayna had hoped they would. They blended together perfectly.

"Amazing! How do you do that?" Quinn asked.

"Years of practice," she smiled, feeling satisfied in the accomplishment.

"I've been thinking I'd like to learn how to read music. I don't remember much from the lessons I took as a kid. I'd have to start from scratch."

"The best way would be to learn to play your own music," Dayna recommended.

"Say what?"

"What I mean is, play your songs with the sheet music in front of you. Here." She took a copy of 'Dayna's Song' and set it in front of him. "Now play the song slowly and I'll point out the notes on the paper as you play them."

Quinn played the first few bars of his song. "I see what you mean. If I do that enough, I'll train myself to recognize the written notes that correspond to the sounds I'm playing."

"Exactly," she smiled, feeling pleased that she could impart some of her musical knowledge. "Start by playing one hand at a time, so that you can hear each individual note. You'll pick this up quickly, but I can give you some lessons, too, if you want and it wouldn't hurt to learn some basic theory."

Back on task, they played the remainder of the songs for the wedding. Dayna made a few changes to the order of the songs, but overall, she was very pleased with how they sounded.

"I think we've got it," Dayna said, exuberantly. "I think it's going to sound wonderful!"

Still sitting next to her on the piano bench, Quinn put his arm around Dayna, giving her shoulder a squeeze. "I know it is."

He took his hand away, but she could still feel the heat through the fabric of her blouse. She felt a ripple of panic in her chest. It was simply a friendly gesture—something her brother would do.

"No," she objected, silently. *"My brother's touch would never make me feel this way!"*

"Quinn, I…" She got up and walked a few steps away from the piano. "I should really go and check on Abigail."

She hurried up the stairs and down the hall, stopping outside of Abigail's room. As she caught her breath, a plethora of thoughts bombarded her.

"This is crazy! What's wrong with me? There's nothing more than friendship happening between us. Quinn isn't acting any differently; it's just me. What am I going to do?"

Taking some deep breaths, she began to think of the things that Rachael had taught her. Reaching for thoughts that felt better in the moment, she reminded herself that Quinn was her friend and that they'd just had a good time playing music together. She was even looking forward to teaching him. There was no limit to what he could do, if he could read and write music himself.

"But if we were to let ourselves pass the point of friendship…" Her mind went back to what had just taken place. *"If it didn't work out, there'd be no going back; we'd lose everything."*

She strengthened her resolve. *"Nothing happened to jeopardize our friendship just now and nothing will—I have to make sure of that!"*

Dayna composed herself and went back downstairs. Quinn was in the living room with Madison. He looked up as she walked in.

"Everything okay?"

"Yes, she's a sound sleeper." Dayna went in and sat down on the edge of an armchair.

"So what's the plan?" he asked, somewhat abruptly. "Do you think we need to meet again, before the wedding, or is this good enough?"

"You'll need to be at the rehearsal. I'll call and let you know the details. I can even pick you up."

"Okay, that sounds fine." He stood to his feet. "Well, I guess I should be going."

"But I was going to drive you…"

"Don't worry about it; your daughter's still sleeping. I called Lucy. She was just out doing some shopping. She's on her way over."

As he walked toward the door, Madison ran after him. "Quinn, I didn't get to show you my tree house tree!"

"Your tree house tree?"

"She has the tree picked out that she wants her tree house built in," Dayna explained, hoping that he might reconsider and stay a little longer.

"Well now," Quinn smiled at the child. "I can't very well leave without seeing your tree house tree."

Madison took his hand and led him out to the back yard. Dayna watched out the window as Madison pointed to her tree. Quinn nodded and made some comments. Madison began to laugh and they both started to walk toward the house.

The front doorbell rang as Quinn walked into the kitchen. "That must be Lucy," he said. "Thanks for lunch, Dayna." He looked her in the eyes, but didn't smile or offer his hand. "Give me a call."

Knowing that she had offended him, Dayna reproached herself. *"How can I call myself a friend and yet treat him this way?"* He was within arms reach; she wanted to touch him, to let him know that she cared, but she couldn't. She simply watched him walk away.

* * *

Quinn went silently out to his car and got in the passenger seat. As Lucy drove, he put his head back on the leather headrest and closed his eyes.

"What just happened?" he asked himself. *"I touched Dayna—as a friend, on the shoulder. But the way she froze and then got up so quickly...and the excuse to check on the baby..."*

Something had snapped inside. He needed to distance himself from her; he needed to think.

"What am I doing here? I'm not being honest with myself or with her. I want more than friendship. Obviously, she doesn't.

"I'm in love with her, but I can't show her my true feelings," he sighed. *"She's no closer to warming up to me than the first time I touched her. God, this is torture!*

"Is she repulsed by me?" He had to ask, but he didn't think that was it. He saw the way she'd looked at him earlier—she'd never looked at him like that before. He caught her looking at him during lunch, too.

"Is she that afraid of her own feelings? Is she afraid of loving? Afraid of getting hurt?" He knew that it was still early for her to be entering into another relationship, but he felt that if he could just have some assurance that things would move in that direction, it would be enough.

Quinn knew that he was doing it again. His thoughts were moving in the wrong direction; it didn't feel good. He quickly reminded himself of the things that had happened to bring them together. He thought back to the things that Valerie had told him. She seemed convinced that Dayna had feelings for him. He truly hoped that she was right.

* * *

Chapter 29

Dayna put the girls to bed and went downstairs to sit in the living room. Quinn was on her mind that evening. He'd been on her mind all week. She hadn't called him since his visit and she missed their talks. She desperately wished that she could go back and undo what had happened between them.

"It's ironic," she concluded, after agonizing over the situation. *"I was scared that entering into a romantic relationship would jeopardize our friendship, but I've done it myself, just by my fear of it. I haven't been honest with him, either. Maybe I should have told him from the start how I was feeling about it. If he knew my concerns, maybe we could have talked about it and brought it out into the open.*

"And what about the feelings I had when I saw him the other day?"

She could still see him in her mind, standing in her doorway, looking incredibly sexy in his blue jeans and t-shirt. He definitely had a nice body, but it was his clean-shaven chin, his rugged good looks, that had mesmerized Dayna. Still, she didn't want to let herself go there; she didn't think it was wise.

"Is it too late? If I were to be honest with him now, what would happen to our friendship?" At that point, Dayna didn't think that she had anything to lose, but still, she hesitated.

"Should I say something before the wedding?" She really didn't think that Quinn would back out. In fact, she knew that he wouldn't. She had to try.

Dialing his number, she attempted to disregard the growing knot in her stomach. The phone rang several times and she was about to hang up, relieved, when she heard him say hello.

"Hi, Quinn."

"How are you?"

"I'm fine." As she listened to the words, she realized that it wasn't the truth. She'd called to be honest with Quinn and decided it best to start now.

"Actually, Quinn, I'm not fine. We need to talk."

* * *

Quinn didn't like the sound of those four little words. He'd heard them before; they had always preceded the termination of a relationship.

"I don't want this relationship to end," he asserted, inwardly. *"But maybe it's better that we talk now. The question is—can I be honest with her, without scaring her away completely?"*

She didn't say anything right away, so he decided to take the lead. "Dayna, I'd like to know how you feel about our relationship."

He could hear her take a deep breath before she responded. "Quinn, I'm scared."

"I thought so, but I'm not sure what it is you're scared of." He was pretty sure he did know, but he wanted to hear it from her.

"At first, I felt so drawn to you—to your music. I didn't understand what was happening and that scared me. I'd never experienced anything like it.

"Then, as we started to become friends, there were times that I saw you as a man and I didn't know what you were feeling toward me. My marriage had just ended and I was overwhelmed trying to deal with everything...

"But now, our friendship has become something special. I can't begin to tell you what you mean to me.

"Actually," she paused. "I can... I love you. I listen to Madison say it all the time and I wonder why it's so hard for me to say. I do love you, Quinn. You're a dear friend and your friendship means so much to me. I don't want it to end."

"She loves me." Quinn knew it wasn't the kind of love that he was hoping for, but the words soothed his soul. He wanted to tell her that he loved her, too, but he sensed that she had more to say.

She didn't continue, so he asked, "What are you afraid of now?"

"I'm afraid that if we were to let our relationship move beyond friendship, we might lose what we have altogether."

"Have you thought about that?" he asked, cautiously. "About us being more than friends?"

"Yes," Dayna replied, ever so softly.

It was the answer that he wanted to hear, but it left him confused—he needed to know more. There was so much that he wanted to say, as well, but he didn't know where to start, or how much he should share with her.

She gave him the opportunity. Whether he was prepared or not, it was her turn to ask, "Quinn, how do you feel about me?"

"I love you," he said, tenderly.

She didn't respond right away. Again, he listened to her breathing.

"What do you mean by 'love'?" she asked, finally.

He knew that he couldn't turn back now; it was all or nothing. "Dayna," he replied. "You mean so much to me. You've become more than just a friend; I feel like we're soul mates. I wasn't complete until I met you. To be honest, you're the inspiration for my music and the reason that I've worked as hard as I have to recover…but it's even more than that.

"Dayna…" he paused. "I'm in love with you."

He let the words sink in. The moment seemed like an eternity, as he waited for her to respond. As he listened, he thought he could hear her crying.

"Dayna?" he asked, softly.

"Quinn…" she sniffed. "I'm not sure I can love you in that way. I'm not even sure I know how."

"Dayna, I know you've been hurt and I know you need time to heal. But if I could just know that there was hope—that someday, you could learn to love me as more than just a friend."

He closed his eyes. *"I've really done it, now. I've thrown everything on the line; there's no going back. Dayna was right; our friendship will never be the same again, either. God! Why does it have to be like this?"*

They'd opened up their hearts to one another and now they lay exposed and vulnerable. It was torture. He could hear her sobbing and he desperately wanted to take her in his arms and comfort her.

"I don't know…" she responded with difficulty, her voice shaking. "Quinn, I just don't know… if I can promise you that."

"Please, Dayna..." He resorted to begging. "Please try. That's all I'm asking."

He sat listening to her cry, dangerously close to tears himself, feeling more helpless than he had ever felt in his life. His heart was being torn out slowly, painfully and, at the same time, he was the villain; he was the reason for her tears.

"Quinn, I have to go," she said, after a few minutes. "I'm sorry... I'm so sorry."

* * *

Dayna lay in her bed and stared at the ceiling. It was Friday morning. The wedding rehearsal was at six, followed by a dinner. She had sent Quinn an e-mail, letting him know the details and had even signed it, 'Love, Dayna', in an attempt to mend the rift in their relationship—if that were possible. Quinn's response was brief, but at least she knew that he would be attending.

They hadn't talked since their distressing conversation a week earlier. More than once, she'd picked up the phone and even started to dial his number, but she didn't know what to say. Nothing had changed; she was more confused than ever.

Dayna knew that she loved Quinn as a friend, but she didn't know if she could give him what he asked—assurance that she would ever love him the way that he loved her.

She got up and went to tend to Abigail. Mark was coming by that morning to pick up the girls. He'd taken the day off, giving Dayna the freedom to help with last-minute wedding preparations.

The girl's breakfast was finished and Dayna was starting to clean up, when she heard the front door.

"Daddy!" Madison went running to meet him. He came into the kitchen carrying her.

"The girls are almost ready. Madison," she instructed her daughter. "You need to go and wash up and then bring your bag down. Did you remember to pack your new book?"

Madison ran off and Dayna went to lift Abigail out of her highchair.

"Here, let me lift her," Mark said.

"I'm fine, really. I lift her all the time, now."

"Sorry." Mark sounded sincere. "But I worry about you, since... you know."

She looked at him with skepticism.

"Dayna, I know our marriage ended," he responded to her frown. "But you're the mother of my children. I still care what happens to you."

She wasn't really in the mood to listen to her ex-husband become sentimental, but, since they were on the topic, there was something that she wanted to ask him.

"Mark," she said, feeling intensely vulnerable and yet compelled to ask. "Why do you think our marriage failed—what was the reason?"

He looked at her, surprise evident on his face. Then he shook his head. "I don't know, Dayna. I've asked myself that question, too. Don't take this the wrong way, but I think, maybe, it could have worked if you hadn't been so scared to let yourself love me."

Tears were building and one slipped, unbidden, past her lashes. She quickly turned away before he could notice.

"I'm sorry, Dayna," Mark continued, now with a defensive tone in his voice. "But you keep a part of yourself so carefully hidden away—you just don't let people in."

Madison ran back into the kitchen and their conversation was cut short. That was fine with Dayna; she'd heard enough. Hearing Mark confirm what she already suspected, hurt deeply.

Dayna kissed the girls goodbye and reminded Mark to have Madison at the rehearsal before six.

As she shut the front door after them, Mark's words echoed in her head. *"He's right—I was scared to let myself really love him. Now, I'm afraid to love Quinn. I married Mark anyway and it didn't work out. I won't let that happen with Quinn. I won't hurt him like that."*

* * *

Rachael wanted to spend time with her mother and sister before her big day, so she'd invited them both out for brunch, Friday morning. She wanted to thank them for their love and support and tell them how much they meant to her.

She picked up her mom and they arrived at Dayna's just as Mark was leaving with the girls. They talked with him for a moment and gave the girls hugs and kisses before they went inside.

When they walked in the door, they noticed that Dayna had been crying.

"Honey, what's the matter?" Valerie reached out to comfort her daughter.

"I'm sorry," Dayna replied. "I don't want to put a damper on the wedding. I'm just trying to sort some things out."

"Why don't you let us help you," Valerie urged. "Is this about Quinn?"

Dayna looked at her mother in surprise. "How did you know?"

"It's not hard to see that he's in love with you."

"I couldn't see it," Dayna admitted. "I was too scared. Now that I know, I'm more scared than ever."

Dayna told them about the conversation she'd had with Quinn. She also told them what Mark had just said to her.

"I can't do that to Quinn," she said with conviction. "It wouldn't be fair."

"Daynie, what is your heart telling you?" Rachael asked, softly.

Dayna looked at her sister, blankly. "I'm not sure that I even know."

"Let's figure it out then," Rachael replied, knowing that she could help Dayna find the clarity that she needed. "Which feels better—ending your friendship with Quinn and never seeing him again—or walking forward, slowly, one step at a time, into a relationship with a man that you already love as a friend?"

"Rachael, of course the idea of being with him feels better than never seeing him again," Dayna retorted. "But there's more to it than that!"

She could feel Dayna's frustration, but decided to continue. "There doesn't have to be, not if you choose to live in the moment."

"But my past has affected this moment," Dayna argued. "And the decisions I make in this moment will affect my future."

"But don't you see," Rachael smiled, lovingly, at her sister. "That's all the more reason to make your decisions based on your internal guidance system—your heart."

"I want to believe that," Dayna sighed.

"All right," Rachael continued. "You said that being in a relationship with Quinn is preferable to never seeing him again. Now, choose which feels better—a romantic relationship with Quinn that is wonderful and fulfilling—or one that brings you pain and heartache?"

"I'd kind of like to take a chance on wonderful," Dayna smiled, weakly. "But how can I know that it will be?"

"You can trust that your guidance system is leading you to joy, no matter what the circumstances," Rachael explained. "Because the truth is, you don't choose circumstances that bring you joy—you choose joy and then joyful circumstances will follow.

"Dayna, don't base your current decisions on what happened in the past. This is a different relationship and you're a different person. This relationship has the potential to bring you more joy than you ever thought possible—but only if joy is your focus. You'll never find joy in any area of your life as long as you're holding on to thoughts of what could go wrong."

"Focus on joy," Dayna repeated. "Is it really that easy? I just focus on joy and I'll attract joy? It doesn't matter what my circumstances are?"

"Yes! People can be joyful in a hut or in a castle. They can be single or married, rich or poor and still be happy. It's all about focus."

Dayna breathed deeply. Her face brightened and a smile began to form, "And when joy is my focus, then I just live my life moment-by-moment and make decisions based on what feels best in that moment."

Rachael knew that her sister understood; she reached to give her a hug. "Dayna, I'm so excited for you!" She held her close for a moment, elated at what had just taken place. "You have so much joy waiting for you, if only you could see it.

"I want to give you something." Rachael reached in her purse and took out a small laminated card. "Here." She handed it to Dayna. "This will help remind you of what can be."

Dayna read the words,

"Once you remember who you are,
and deliberately reach for thoughts that hold
you in vibrational alignment with who you are,
your world will also fall into alignment
— and well-being will show itself to you
in all areas of your life experience." [20]

"Thank-you, Rachael," Dayna smiled at her sister and then turned to Valerie, who was beaming at her daughters. "Thank you both so much for knowing this... and," she added, "for being patient with me until I could understand it, too."

"What say we celebrate this over brunch?" Rachael suggested.

"There's just one thing I need to do first." Dayna went to the phone and began to dial a number. Rachael smiled, knowing it was Quinn that her sister was calling.

* * *

As Quinn arrived at the rehearsal, he saw a small crowd of people casually mingling. He watched a man in front of him approaching the group. Quinn recognized Dayna's ex-husband; he was holding Madison's hand and carrying the baby.

Quinn noticed Valerie, too, and nodded a greeting, but his eyes continued to search the crowd until he saw Dayna. Everyone else had turned to Madison as the child ran up to the group, but Dayna was watching him and smiling.

She had on a blue, sleeveless dress that fell to just above her knees and showed off her figure, beautifully. High heels emphasized her shapely legs. She looked incredible.

While his eyes were on her lovely form, his mind kept replaying the words that she'd left on his answering machine that morning, 'Quinn, I know what I want now. I'm willing to try.'

He wasn't totally sure what she meant by knowing what she wanted, but the fact that she was willing to try was all he needed to hear.

Quinn's heart swelled as he walked up to her. He longed to give her a hug, but he hesitated, deciding that it would be best to let her make the first move. She offered her hand and he took it in his.

A woman began to organize everyone, instructing the family members to have a seat and the wedding party to take their places.

Dayna turned to Quinn. "Showtime," she said with a smile and a squeeze of his hand. Then she walked over to one of the pianos, while Quinn took his place at the other.

The wedding organizer had them run through the ceremony exactly as it would happen the following day. Everything went smoothly and it was over in no time. She dismissed everyone but the bride and groom. Rachael and Brian took a few minutes to talk with the official who would be performing the ceremony.

Quinn remained at the piano, watching Dayna as she approached her ex-husband and spoke with him for a minute. She kissed her girls and waved to them as they left with Mark. Then, she turned to Quinn and walked over to where he was sitting.

"That was easy," he said. "What now?"

"We're going out for a rehearsal dinner. You're invited, of course."

He hesitated. It was a family time and, as much as he wanted to be with Dayna, he didn't want to intrude on their evening. He was about to decline, saying that he'd see her at the wedding, when she put her hand on his.

"I'd like you to come," she said, simply.

He was touched by her invitation; her eyes had conveyed so much more than even her words, but there was still something that he needed to ask.

"Dayna," he said. "On your message, you said that you know what you want now. What is it? What do you want?"

"I want joy," she replied, sounding confident. "I want to focus on joy and let the circumstances take care of themselves."

"I want that, too, Dayna—for both of us."

As they arrived at the restaurant, Quinn held the door for Dayna, putting his other hand on her shoulder. His heart was overjoyed when, instead of freezing or pulling away as she had in the past, she turned to him and smiled.

* * *

Chapter 30

Rachael stood beside her best friend. She took Gail's hands in hers.

"Sweetie, you're shaking," Gail said. "You're not nervous, are you?"

"No, I'm just excited!" Rachael assured her. "I can't believe this day is finally here."

They had a few more minutes to wait while the guests were being seated. Rachael looked around the room, which was actually a large tent set up for the members of the wedding party.

Her mom was straightening Madison's dress. Brian's sister was trying to keep her young son occupied; he was to be the ring bearer. Greg had just arrived and was standing alone, looking out of place with all the women. In another tent beside theirs, Brian and his best man, Jim, were waiting with the wedding official.

"Weather's nice," Gail winked.

"It's perfect," Rachael smiled, thinking back to the conversation they'd had when she told Gail that she and Brian were engaged.

Then, glancing over at her brother, she asked her friend, "Gail, it's not awkward for you being around Greg, is it?" The two had dated; it was how Rachael had first met Gail.

"Not at all," she replied, easily. "I talked to him at the rehearsal last night. Their baby is so adorable!"

As they listened to Quinn play the piano, Gail commented, "He's really good. He seems nice, too. I hope something happens between him and Dayna; she deserves to be happy."

"At least now she knows the secret to happiness."

Valerie came over and looked, affectionately, at her youngest daughter. "You look beautiful, honey."

"Thanks, Mom."

Madison followed and proceeded to hug Rachael's knees. She looked so cute in her pink ruffled dress and shiny white shoes with bows. Her hair was done up in dozens of tiny ringlets. A basket of rose petals completed the picture; she made an adorable flower girl. Rachael smiled at her precious little niece.

As she looked around at the people she loved dearly, Rachael felt appreciation for all of them. She was happier than she'd ever been before and she wanted to capture each perfect detail in her mind.

It was her day; she would remember it forever. In a few minutes, she was about to walk down the aisle to become Mrs. Brian DeWaltt.

The wedding planner poked her head in the doorway and announced, "Two minutes!"

Rachael couldn't resist; she peeked out the door of the tent and her eyes scanned the assembly of people that had joined them to help celebrate their wedding. There was a reverent hush over the crowd as Brian and Jim began walking toward the front of the outdoor 'room' that had been set up for the occasion. The space was defined by Georgian pillars, with streamers draped between them. The front was decorated with flowers and ribbons. Brian and Jim took their places beside a large trellis covered with pink and white roses.

Quinn's song ended and Dayna began playing her first piece. Rachael stepped aside as Valerie and Gail helped usher Madison out of the tent, followed by Brian's nephew. Madison took her time and sprinkled the rose petals just as they had rehearsed. In fact, she did it with the flare of a ballet dancer. Rachael could hear the comments from the guests as they watched the charming performance.

The music stopped and, when Dayna began the next piece, it was Valerie's turn to head down the aisle. Gail winked at Rachael, then followed as Valerie passed the halfway mark. Everything was perfectly choreographed.

Greg walked up to Rachael and held out his arm, "Are you ready, sis?"

They still had a moment to wait before Rachael's song began and Greg said, "I'm sorry Dad couldn't have been here instead of me."

Rachael squeezed his arm. "I feel like he is here with us and, anyway, I'm glad you're here. I love you, Greg."

Greg kissed her forehead and then smiled at her as they heard Dayna play the bar of notes that was the signal for everyone to rise. It was time!

Rachael felt a flutter of excitement as the curtain was drawn back and Greg led her out of the doorway of the tent. She glanced around, taking everything in. It all looked amazing.

It was a cloudless day, with a slight breeze that felt refreshing on her face. All eyes were on her and Rachael smiled as she saw the faces of people she loved. She noticed the roses on the seats that lined the aisle, as they slowly made their way to the front. It was a long, grassy aisle, just as she'd imagined; it looked magical with the rose petals sprinkled on it.

As they passed the halfway mark, which was indicated by pink ribbons on the seats instead of white, she looked toward the front and her eyes did a quick scan of the setting. She noticed Dayna at the piano watching her and smiling as she played.

She looked at Gail, then at Jim and at the children, before she let her gaze rest on Brian. When it did, she couldn't take her eyes off him. He looked incredibly handsome in a charcoal grey tuxedo with tails. He had on a black cummerbund over a crisp, white shirt. His hair was shorter; it looked as though he'd just had it trimmed that morning.

Brian's eyes were on her, as well, and he was smiling. He had love written all over his face. Rachael had to take a deep breath to keep the tears from welling up.

As they reached the front row where her mom was seated, Rachael stopped. Greg gave her arm a loving squeeze and went to sit beside Amy. Valerie stood up and mother and daughter embraced.

"I love you, Mom." Rachael saw the glint of tears in her mother's eyes and smiled, as she tried to blink away her own; they'd promised each other they wouldn't cry.

Rachael turned to Brian again. He'd moved toward her and, now, his hand was outstretched. She put her hand in his and, together, they walked the last few steps to stand under the trellis of flowers.

The wedding official began to speak. She'd met with them twice before the wedding and had asked them all kinds of questions. The words she spoke reflected what she had learned about them, their views on marriage and on life.

When she finished speaking, it was time for the vows. Rachael and Brian had written them together, but each added a line or two on their own to make them personal and unique.

Brian began first. Turning to face his bride, he lovingly took Rachael's hands in his own.

"Rachael, today I stand before you and before our families and friends, to declare my love for you.

I believe that life is to be lived in the moment and right now, in this moment, my life is fuller and richer because you're in it.

You're my lover, my teacher, my soul mate and my friend. You inspire me, challenge me and encourage me—but above all else, you love me. Your love is unconditional and true.

You are a ray of light shining down from the purest Source and as that light joins mine, together, our light shines brighter; together, our love radiates further; and together, our lives become a beacon to those around us.

Rachael, I can't tell you what our future holds, but I promise you that moment-by-moment, I will walk beside you and discover together with you, the joy that each moment has for us."

Brian's eyes were shining as he finished. Rachael wiped the tears from her own eyes, took a deep breath and began.

"Brian, today I stand before you, and before our families and friends, to declare my love for you.

I believe that life is to be lived in the moment and right now, in this moment, my life is fuller and richer because you're in it.

I made a decision, once, to choose joy above all else and because of that, joy has come to me in so many ways. Now, joy has come to me in the form of a man. Brian, you are that joy.

You love me, you make me laugh, you inspire and encourage me. You're generous and caring and you love to serve others. You are a gift to all who have the privilege of knowing you.

You're a ray of light shining down from the purest Source and as that light joins mine, together, our light shines brighter; together, our love radiates further; and together, our lives become a beacon to those around us.

Brian, I don't know what our future holds, but I promise you that moment-by-moment, I will walk beside you and discover together with you, the joy that each precious moment has to offer."

The official then asked for the rings. Brian's nephew stepped forward and held up a small pillow. There were two gold bands tied on with white ribbons. She took the pillow and held it out to Brian and Rachael.

Brian took Rachael's ring, gently slipped it on her finger and said, "Rachael, in this moment, the thought of becoming your husband fills me with more joy than I've ever known. Please accept this ring and wear it as a symbol of my love and devotion." He smiled and added softly, "I love you."

Then, Rachael took Brian's ring and carefully placed it on his finger. She repeated the words that Brian had spoken to her.

Rachael looked into the eyes of the man that she loved with a love so deep, it took her breath away. The words that they had used to declare their devotion were beautiful, but they paled in light of the love, itself.

In that moment, Rachael felt the Source of all love wrap itself around them and radiate through them. She felt at one with Brian and with the universe and with all that existed.

* * *

Dayna listened as Quinn's song came to an end and she sent a smile his way. Then, she began her first piece, watching with pride as Madison danced down the aisle, enthusiastically sprinkling her rose petals along the pathway.

Looking out at the guests, Dayna noticed Mark. His eyes were on Madison, as well. Abigail was asleep in his arms. The woman beside him turned to whisper something in his ear and then put her hand on his arm; she was obviously his girlfriend. She was a pretty blond with a kind face; they made a nice looking couple.

Mark turned and met Dayna's eyes and she looked at him for a brief moment. She realized that she no longer had any anger toward him. He had a right to happiness, too, and she wished it for them.

Dayna began the next piece and watched as Valerie walked toward the front. Her mother looked beautiful and extremely happy.

As the guests rose and she began to play the song that Rachael had chosen, Dayna's eyes were drawn to her sister. Rachael looked radiant. She was absolutely beautiful and her dress looked stunning. Her hair was partly up, held in place with tiny rosettes. She'd chosen not to wear a veil, claiming that she wanted to see everything clearly. She carried a single, long-stemmed rose, adorned with pink and white ribbons and a spray of baby's breath. Brian had a matching rose on his lapel.

Watching the interaction between Rachael and their mother, Dayna was filled with a deep sense of appreciation—not only for a loving family, but for the awareness of how truly blessed she was.

Finally, Rachael and Brian stood before the official, ready to take their vows. Their love for one another was evident on their faces. It was as if no one else existed for them in that moment.

As she listened to the words that they'd written for each other, she looked across at Quinn. He turned his head and, as their eyes met, she saw love there.

"Has it been there all along?" she wondered. *"Did I just miss it?"*

Dayna wasn't sure. What she did know, however, is that she didn't feel afraid anymore.

Rachael's words to Brian about choosing joy above all else, reminded Dayna of her decision to do the same and now she was excited about where that decision would lead her.

She heard them vow to walk beside each other and discover the joy in each moment together. Dayna realized that a relationship with Quinn no longer frightened her at all, when she thought about taking it one moment at a time.

After the exchange of rings and the lighting of the unity candle, it was time for the wedding party to sign the register. Quinn began to play.

Dayna looked at him in surprise. It wasn't the song that they had planned. He was playing 'Dayna's Song,' watching her as he played. She smiled at him, realizing that nobody else would notice the change in music; he had done it for her, alone.

The ceremony concluded as Brian and Rachael were declared man and wife. The guests slowly followed the married couple as they walked back down the aisle. Quinn began to play again and continued to play until all the guests had moved to the reception area.

Dayna stayed seated at her piano, watching him. She couldn't help but notice his appearance. He had on a perfectly tailored, three-piece suit and looked strikingly handsome in it. Before the last song was finished, Dayna sent a warm smile his way and began walking toward him.

He stopped playing as she approached. "Sorry, I lost track of where I was. The way you smiled and walked toward me—it was exactly the way you looked in my dream. I always wondered…" he began, tentatively.

"Wondered what?"

"The dream always ended there and I couldn't help but wonder…"

"What happens next?" Dayna offered, finishing his sentence as she sat down on the bench beside him.

"It's not just a dream anymore. We get to decide what happens now," she said, softly, yet feeling the strength of her conviction. No longer afraid of what the future held, Dayna was ready to live—really live and she knew that she could trust her emotions to guide her in doing just that.

Quinn searched her eyes for a moment before touching her hair and then slowly stroking her cheek with the back of his fingers. His hand felt strong and masculine, yet at the same time, gentle. She welcomed his touch.

In the peaceful, outdoor sanctuary, he kissed her—softly, almost reverently. Then he looked into her eyes, silently asking permission to continue.

Dayna smiled and caressed his handsome face, gazing lovingly at the man who was both her friend and her soul mate. Her only thought was of the moment and the rapturous joy that she was feeling. In that perfect moment, she wanted to let Quinn know that his kiss was not only welcome, it was something she truly longed for.

The End

The following is a preview
of book three in the
'Law of Attraction' trilogy.

HEARTS
Reunited

by JEANE WATIER

Stephanie wasn't sure what to pack. She'd be gone several days and spring weather in that part of the country meant she could require anything from snow boots to sunscreen. As she was making her final decisions on what to take, her daughter, Katie walked in and plunked herself down on the bed.

"I still don't see why you want to meet this guy."

"I want to get to know him better," Stephanie replied. "Plus, I'm curious to see what he looks like and find out if I'm like him at all."

"Yeah, but you don't know much about him," she replied. "What if he's a real creep? He could even be a serial killer."

Stephanie laughed. Katie had an active imagination. "You watch too much TV. I'll be fine. Besides, I'm not meeting him in a back alley or a dark nightclub. If I do feel uncomfortable around him, I'll just cut the visit short. Now go and get ready for school."

Katie gave her a look that told her she wasn't convinced, but she left the room and Stephanie went back to her packing.

"Are you ready?" Graham walked in as she was closing the zipper on her suitcase.

"I think so," she smiled at her husband. "I can't believe how nervous I am."

"Are you sure you want to do this?" he asked.

"I'll be alright."

Stephanie said good-bye to Graham and the kids and headed out the door to the cab that was waiting to take her to the airport.

That evening, she would be meeting Daniel for the first time. As much as she was looking forward to it, she was more nervous than she'd ever been. Her anxiety started to increase as she neared her destination.

By the time the plane touched down, Stephanie's apprehension had accelerated to the point that she felt ill. Taking a deep breath, she walked a bit before she went to claim her luggage. She was extremely tired and her legs ached from the long flight.

Daniel had offered to meet her at the airport, but she decided that she'd rather take a cab to her hotel and have a couple of hours to herself, before she met him. Instead, he was meeting her that evening in the hotel lobby and they were going out for dinner.

At the hotel, Stephanie tried to rest, but as she lay down, it seemed that sleep was out of the question. Her mind was full with all that lay ahead. She replayed the conversations she'd had with Daniel, reminding herself of how nice he had sounded on the phone and how comfortable he'd made her feel.

"Finding something to talk about shouldn't be too hard. I have my whole life I can fill him in on, if he's interested..." she yawned. *"Besides, we have some things in common; he likes horses..."*

Stephanie awoke and looked at the time. She'd fallen asleep after all and now she needed to start getting ready for the evening ahead. Daniel would be arriving in an hour to take her to dinner.

After showering, she put on the new outfit that she'd bought for the occasion and did her hair and make-up. With fifteen minutes left to spare, she decided to go down to the lobby. It was better than pacing her hotel room in nervous excitement.

As she watched people come and go, she silently questioned if she'd recognize Daniel. He'd described himself, telling her that he'd been blond when he was younger, but now, his hair was completely white. Based on that, she hoped that it wouldn't be too hard to pick him out.

Her attention was drawn, momentarily, to a woman with a small child. The child was making a scene and the mother was trying to settle her down. As Stephanie turned back toward the lobby entrance, she saw him.

Daniel had yet to notice her, so she watched him for a moment. She had expected him to look older, but as she observed his face, she noted that he looked far from old. He was a very good-looking man.

He was well dressed and the white hair gave him an air of distinction, but something else was even more evident. She could see a resemblance to her son, Tyler.

Suddenly, their eyes met. She smiled and began walking toward him. Stephanie was about to meet her father.

* * *

Dan paused a moment to look in the mirror in the hallway before he went out the door. He looked at his own face and wondered if she would look anything like him. He was looking forward to their meeting, but he was still a little nervous.

Stephanie seemed nice, based on the two conversations they'd had on the phone, but the fact that she was a daughter he'd never met, left him in unfamiliar territory.

In his line of work, he was always meeting new people, prospective clients, business men and women, CEOs and officials. Public relations was his specialty, but this was different. This was personal. Not only that, it opened a door to his past.

He'd played over their meeting many times in his head to try to quell his anxiety. Despite the nervousness, however, his curiosity was stronger.

There was so much he wanted to ask her, but most of all he was just intrigued with the idea of seeing his daughter. Vali's daughter.

As he walked into the hotel lobby, his eyes scanned the room. He noticed a woman with a noisy child. There were a few couples and an elderly woman carrying a small dog. Then he saw her.

Stephanie was looking at him, smiling. He couldn't believe it. Her hair color was the same as his own when he was younger. Her height was from him, but other than that, she was Vali—the same eyes, the same smile.

He hadn't given much thought to the possibility of Stephanie looking so much like her mother. He felt a strange sensation as memories of Vali flooded his mind. In an instant, he was reminded of their youthful plans and dreams and how scared they'd been when she found out she was pregnant. He remembered, too, the pain of losing her.

Suddenly, he realized that their meeting was about more than just seeing his daughter for the first time—it was about coming to terms with his past.

"Daniel?" She held out her hand to him.

"Stephanie... hi." He shook her hand and there was an awkward moment, as he questioned whether to embrace his daughter or not. They looked at each other for a few seconds and then, he could resist no longer. He smiled and opened his arms.

He noticed tears well up in her eyes, as her mind processed what he was offering. She eagerly accepted and Dan felt a lump in his throat as he held his newfound daughter in his arms.

Stephanie wiped away a tear. "I'm sorry," she apologized. "I've been looking forward to this for so long; I didn't know what kind of reception I'd get."

"I'm glad you're here. I'm looking forward to us getting to know each other." Dan felt a bit of awkwardness still present. The woman was his daughter, yet she was a total stranger. He was seeing her for the first time and yet he felt like he had known her all his life. It left him with a very odd feeling.

* * *

Stephanie liked him immediately. Her anxiety was now dispelled; she looked forward to the evening ahead.

Over dinner, she told him about her life growing up and a little about her parents, but as she told him more about her husband and two children, she noticed a strange look in his eyes. "What is it?" she asked.

"I never really thought about it before, but I guess that makes me a grandfather."

Stephanie hadn't thought of Daniel in terms of her children's grandfather, but as he said the words, she realized that she liked the idea, too. Her adoptive parents had both passed away. Her husband's parents lived in England and weren't very involved in her kid's lives. She wondered what Daniel would think of meeting her kids one day.

They ate in silence for a moment. She noticed him looking at her a few times. Stephanie couldn't help stealing glances at him, as well. It was incredibly strange to think of this man as her father, but in other ways, being with him felt very comfortable and natural.

"You look like your mother."

At first, her mind associated his words with the only woman that she'd known as 'mother' all her life. She frowned as she wondered, for a split second, why he would say such a thing. Suddenly, she realized that he meant Valerie.

Laughing, she shook her head. "Sorry. I'm not used to thinking about her as my mother. We've become friends, though."

"How is she?"

"She's fine." Stephanie hesitated, wondering how much to say about the woman that she had recently come to know.

Deciding to be up front with Daniel, she replied, "I feel kind of strange. I'm not sure if it's my place to be telling you about Valerie or not. I have no idea how she'd feel about it. It's not something we've really talked about."

"I understand," he replied, graciously.

"I can tell you how I feel about her, though," Stephanie smiled. "It's been wonderful getting to know her. She's an amazing person. She's open and loving and has such a remarkable outlook on life. I feel blessed to have met her."

As Valerie came to mind, Stephanie felt a wave of appreciation for the birth mother that she'd come to know and love. Valerie really did have an amazing outlook on life. She had a quiet confidence about her that conveyed the message that she'd found what she was looking for.

Valerie's attitude had affected Stephanie in a way that she had never experienced before. Now Stephanie was beginning to ask questions.

She'd always been content in her life, but since meeting Valerie, Stephanie realized that there was so much more she wanted. Valerie believed that there was no limit to the things a person could reach for and attain in life. Stephanie truly wanted to believe that.

Looking at Daniel, she could tell that he wanted to ask more and Stephanie would have loved to share with him everything she'd come to know about Valerie—especially the fact that she was single, but she decided to tell Valerie about her meeting with Daniel and feel her out first.

The rest of the evening went well. They talked and laughed and shared their lives with each other. She was sorry when it had to end.

As she went back to her room, she began to feel tired again; it had been a long day. Her mind was full, however. The evening had gone better than she'd even dared to imagine.

Daniel had proven himself kind and generous. He seemed loving and compassionate, as well. She couldn't help thinking about the possibility of Dan and Valerie reuniting.

"Dan's a widower and Valerie's single. What would it be like," Stephanie wondered, *"to have my birth parents together and have a relationship with them both?"*

It wasn't her place to mention it and she knew that she probably shouldn't speculate, but she couldn't help but notice that the thought of it felt very good.

* * *

Notes

1. Jane Austin, *Sense and Sensibility*, published 1811
2. Esther and Jerry Hicks (The Teachings of Abraham), *Ask and it is Given: Learning to Manifest your Desires* (Carlsbad, CA: Hay House, 2004), p. 113.
3. Paraphrased words of Abraham (www.Abraham-Hicks.com)
4. Paraphrased words of Abraham (www.Abraham-Hicks.com)
5. Abraham, Excerpt from Abraham-Hicks workshop recording, San Antonio, TX 11/13/04.
6. William Shakespeare, *Hamlet, Prince of Denmark,* Act III, scene I
7. William Shakespeare, *Hamlet, Prince of Denmark,* Act I, scene V
8. Abraham, Excerpt from Abraham-Hicks workshop recording, Boston, MA 10/02/04.
9. Abraham, Excerpt from Abraham-Hicks workshop recording, Phoenix, AZ 2/24/01.
10. William Wordsworth, "*I Wandered Lonely as a Cloud*", 1804
11. Abraham, Excerpt from Abraham-Hicks workshop recording, Phoenix, AZ 2/24/01.
12. Esther and Jerry Hicks (The Teachings of Abraham), *Ask and it is Given: Learning to Manifest your Desires* (Carlsbad, CA: Hay House, 2004), p. 27.
13. Ernest Holmes, Willis H. Kinnear, *Thoughts are Things* (Deerfield Beach, FL: Health Communications, 1999), p. 59
14. Ernest Holmes, Willis H. Kinnear, *Thoughts are Things* (Deerfield Beach, FL: Health Communications, 1999), p. 85
15. Ernest Holmes, Willis H. Kinnear, *Thoughts are Things* (Deerfield Beach, FL: Health Communications, 1999), p. 15
16. Ernest Holmes, Willis H. Kinnear, *Thoughts are Things* (Deerfield Beach, FL: Health Communications, 1999), p. 55
17. Ernest Holmes, Willis H. Kinnear, *Thoughts are Things* (Deerfield Beach, FL: Health Communications, 1999), p. 45
18. Abraham, Excerpt from Abraham-Hicks workshop recording, Kansas City, KS 11/13/04.
19. Esther and Jerry Hicks (The Teachings of Abraham), *Ask and it is Given: Learning to Manifest your Desires* (Carlsbad, CA: Hay House, 2004), p. 128.
20. Esther and Jerry Hicks (The Teachings of Abraham), *Ask and it is Given: Learning to Manifest your Desires* (Carlsbad, CA: Hay House, 2004), p. 105.

Paulette Grant – Cover Artist

Paulette has been painting for more than 30 years in a variety of mediums and subjects. She is inspired by the beauty around her to create and her creativity extends to writing poetry as well. To see more of her work please visit:

www.autumnredstudioart.com

I met Paulette on an internet site called Beliefnet and we became fast friends. Our shared interests include a passion for writing as well as our spiritual beliefs. When I saw her artwork, I knew that I wanted to have her do a painting for the cover of my book. As I described the image that I had in my head, she was able to bring it to life and add depth and emotion, just as I had dreamed of. It is another perfect example of the Law of Attraction at work. Thank-you, Paulette.

Jeane Watier